MEET HARRY . . .

"I saw him," Charles told her and earned an astonished look as she turned back to stare full at him. "I saw Harry."

"Are you teasing me?" Jane asked.

"I am quite serious. I wasn't going to tell you. I tried to tell myself it was merely a dream. But I think—that is—did he wear very old-fashioned clothes, rather like tattered purple velvet?"

"Yes," she exclaimed, "and he looked as young as you!"

Charles stared at her. "I was afraid of that."

"I beg your pardon?"

"I was afraid it wasn't a dream," Charles replied.

"I must talk to him again," Jane told the Earl. "I must find out why he can't leave this building and how we can help him. He is so lonely. I was hoping to see him this morning."

Charles watched her. "I rather b_____ ____ be part of the attraction."

"I—do not understand."

She started to back ____ ____ and came up slowly to touch ____ ____ ere gown. His fingers trail ____ ____ precisely, but moving, delibera ____ ____ ood where she was, torn between her ____ ____ heart . . .

In *The Reluctant Gho__ ____ ___s the show . . . destined to become one of the genre's favorite ____ __s." (*Rave Reviews*)

In *The Meddlesome Ghost*, "Harry's lines are funny" (*Baton Rouge Magazine*) and in *The Helpful Ghost*, "only couples who are in love can see and hear Harry, and the result is hilarious." (*Rendezvous*)

And in *The Passionate Ghost*, "Sir Harry is guaranteed remembrance as Regency fiction's most engaging ghost." (*Romantic Times*)

LOOK FOR HARRY'S UPCOMING ADVENTURES AT YOUR FAVORITE BOOKSTORE!

The Reluctant Ghost

Sheila Rosalynd Allen

DIAMOND BOOKS, NEW YORK

THE RELUCTANT GHOST

A Diamond Book / published by arrangement with
Walker and Company, Inc.

PRINTING HISTORY
Walker and Company, Inc. edition published 1989
Diamond edition / October 1992

ISBN: 1-55773-803-3

Diamond Books are published by The Berkley Publishing Group,
200 Madison Avenue, New York, New York 10016.
The name "DIAMOND" and its logo are trademarks
belonging to Charter Communications, Inc.

PRINTED IN THE UNITED STATES OF AMERICA

10 9 8 7 6 5 4 3 2 1

- 1 -

NEW-FALLEN SNOW crunched beneath the mail coach's wooden wheels, the equipage lurching suddenly as the right-hand horse stumbled off the road into a deep drift. The coach boy jumped down and pulled the horse back from the edge. Leaning far forward into the chill winds, the driver pulled his muffler close around his neck as he shouted instructions. The boy hauled himself back up to the top seat as the driver used all his skill to keep the worn public conveyance upright on the icy road.

Inside the old coach, three passengers were huddled into cloaks and lap rugs. The youngest passenger looked eagerly through the small window, apparently unruffled by the wildly swaying coach.

"I shall be sick if they don't stop!" said the farmer's wife who sat across from the youngest passenger, hanging onto the worn squabs.

Beside the woman a middle-aged man tried to read *The London Times,* but his eyes kept straying back to the young passenger across from him. Jane Steadford's drab-coloured pelisse and old-fashioned round bonnet at first gave the impression of a plain enough young miss, but one glance at her large grey eyes had made him look closer.

She was young, not above one-and-twenty or so. Her features were even and delicate in a pale oval face which was at the moment perusing the view out beyond the coach's small windows with immense interest.

The man glanced at the snow falling outside and then looked back at the girl. Lost in her own thoughts, she was obviously Quality. With the practiced eye of a businessman, the estate agent took in the fact that her old-fashioned clothes were of the finest materials and cut.

"This be your first time from home, miss?" The man's voice startled the girl. He gave her a wide smile when her eyes turned towards him.

"Can you tell that just by looking?" Jane asked.

"Nothing to fret yourself over." The farmer's wife spoke in a kindly voice. "We'll soon be at the Four Corners Inn. I travel this road once a month. Nothing to fear or fret about."

"I hadn't planned on fretting," Jane told the woman. "Actually, I'm rather enjoying myself."

"You must like a bouncy ride," the woman said.

"It is rather an adventure for me," Jane replied.

"Adventure!" The farmer's wife laughed heartily, her full bosom stretching the bodice of her plain gown even tighter. Her homespun cloak slipped from her shoulders. "There's no adventure about being upset into a snowdrift in mid-February. You must be funning us."

The woman chuckled into her knitting, the estate agent still watching the girl's pretty face. "You're not running from home or such like?" he asked after a moment of silence.

"I would never be so shatter-brained!" Jane told the man hotly.

"I'm sorry. I didn't mean to upset you," he said quickly, looking rather like a scolded puppy.

"That's all right, then," Jane said magnanimously. "You don't know me so you couldn't realise I wasn't a shatter-brain unless I told you."

The farm woman looked up from her knitting. "You must admit it is passing strange, a young lady such as yourself being without a chaperone and travelling on a public conveyance."

"I'm not running away from home and that's flat. As it happens, I am running *to* my family, to *save* my home!"

"How thrilling," the estate agent said, Jane rewarding him with a gratified smile.

"Yes. I rather thought so," Jane told the man.

"How do you intend on doing that?" the estate agent asked. "If you don't mind my asking, it seems a rather tall order for a young person such as yourself—and all alone too—rescuing an entire family."

"Well, yes it is," Jane said warmly. Then, feeling duty-bound not to take too much credit, she continued, "Actually, it's rather a small family. That is to say, there's just my grandmama and myself—and Fannie, of course. She's our abigail. She's raised me since I was small."

"She sounds wonderful," the estate agent said, thoroughly smitten with the young beauty.

"Does she?" Jane thought about it. "She has been awfully good to us. You see, Grandmama and I live quite frugally," Jane added piously, thinking of her great-uncle and the arguments which might convince him to stop his mad plan before it was too late.

"Does your grandmother approve of you traipsing off alone all over the county?" the farmer's wife asked bluntly.

Jane hesitated. "You see, it's rather that she doesn't precisely know about it."

"She doesn't precisely know about it?" the smitten man asked. He had bushy dark brows which were now knit together over a rather hawkish nose.

"She rather thinks I'm still at the Abbey," Jane explained.

"And you said you weren't running away," the farmer's wife put in.

"I'm not. I am going to speak to my great-uncle. Then I shall go home to the Abbey and tell Grandmama that she no longer has anything to fear."

"The Abbey, did you say?" the estate man said. "You're from Steadford Abbey, then, young miss?"

Jane didn't see quite how she could deny it.

"So there's trouble then, at the Abbey?" the farmer's wife asked.

"Not if I reach my great-uncle in time. But time is of the essence and there was no one to come with me upon such short notice."

Jane's cheeks coloured a little with the untruth. She had given no notice at all to her grandmother and had left only a short note for Fannie, saying not to worry Grandmama. In fact, if she could manage it, Fannie was to arrange not even to tell Grandmama. Jane had promised to be back before dark. She didn't mention where she was going, just in case Fannie took it upon herself to try to come after her.

Jane turned away from her curious fellow passengers and looked out at the stormy morning. Feeling more than a little guilty about her hasty decision, she drew herself up straighter, pushing uncomfortable thoughts away. Nigel Steadford had left her no choice. Someone had to persuade the heartless man that he was doing wrong. Unfortunately Grandmama would rather cut her heart out than ask a favour of any man—even her very own brother. Jane had no such scruples. Their entire lives were at stake.

She felt the others still gazing at her. Turning resolutely, Jane looked into the estate agent's admiring eyes. "Have you been travelling far?" she asked him politely.

"From Kent," the man said. "That is, I came from Kent to buy some prime cattle for my master."

"You've had a very long ride," Jane said.

"Yes, and many miles to go," he replied. "Lit by your presence, I'm sure."

"How kind of you, sir."

Jane smiled a trifle coquettishly, thinking she fit rather well as a heroine. Mrs. Edgeworth had never written of a young woman who saved her family home for her dear grandmama. At least Jane did not think she had.

"I've only come from Stoneybridge, meself," the farmer's wife put in. The woman leaned to look outside and started to gather up her knitting. "Looks to be, we've reached the inn. Lord, it will feel good to get a nice hot cuppa."

"Are we there already?" Jane leaned to see out past the falling snow.

The estate agent sat back against the mail coach's worn squabs looking quite dejected. "Is this as far as you travel by coach, then, miss?" he asked.

"Yes." Jane clutched her reticule tightly, her heart beginning to hammer a bit as the reality of her task came forcibly to home.

The farm woman looked at Jane shrewdly. "You've never been this far from home before—not alone now—have you, miss?"

"No," Jane answered honestly. "If truth be known, I haven't travelled at all. Alone or otherwise."

"You'd best stay close to me, then, miss. You never know who's to be met at a public inn. It's not a place for decent girls alone."

The carriage came to a stop in the innyard, Jane allowing the older woman to help her out and down from the coach. "Pick up your skirts, now," the farmer's wife was telling her. "There's mud and slush all churned up from the horses and such. You don't want to catch cold."

The estate agent leaned out towards the driver. "Is there time for me to go inside?"

"Sorry, sir, we're just picking up the mail and changing horses. It doesn't take but two minutes." As the driver spoke, ostlers from the inn stables were already unharnessing the spent horses and leading two fresh ones near.

Jane looked back towards the estate agent. "Have a pleasant journey," she told him with a smile.

He looked out of the coach, staring longingly at her. "I've had the pleasantest part already, I fear."

She treated him to another lovely smile. "Thank you again, kind sir."

"Come along, now," the farmer's wife said dampingly. "There's no reason to stand in the cold."

An ostler stood near the coach step, putting it back up into place as the estate agent watched Jane disappear inside the inn. When he sat back on the worn seat the coach seemed much colder than before.

"I'm perfectly all right," Jane told the overly solicitous woman who was grabbing at her elbow. "I assure you."

Jane stepped carefully across the slushy yard, crossing near a pair of greys which were being put back into the harness of a high-sprung black carriage. The farmer's wife opened the door to the small inn, hovering over Jane as they stepped inside.

They entered a coffee room where a fire leapt cheerily in a large fireplace. Jane walked ahead of the farm woman into the warmth. The sound of men's voices came from a tap room beyond a rough-hewn door they passed.

The coffee-room ceiling was low-pitched above the white-washed walls, the heat from the fireplace reflecting back downward towards the drafts of cold air which rustled along the straw-strewn floor. One long wooden table, having seen much use, stood near the fireplace, which was flanked by two wooden settles and a quantity of chairs. A massive sideboard constituted the only other furnishing.

Lanterns were lit on the table and sideboard, the dark morning outside letting in little light. The unpleasant odor of tallow candles mixed with the welcome aroma of coffee from the kitchen beyond.

A window embrasure to the left of the fireplace was filled with a cushioned seat. Jane made her way to it, sinking down upon the cushion gratefully.

"Here, you let me put my satchel by you and I'll hunt up a nuncheon for us both," the farm wife offered generously. "Why, girl, haven't you any luggage?"

"I have no need of any," Jane told the woman. "I shall be returning on the afternoon coach."

She watched the farmer's wife walk towards a door where the kitchen must be, then leaned back against the wall, glad to be left alone for a while. She looked out at the wintry landscape beyond the small panes of glass. A gust of the outside chill came through, making Jane pull her dark woolen shawl closer about her pelisse.

"Pardon me, are you quite all right?"

The deep male voice startled Jane. She sat forward, staring towards the sound. A dark-headed man sat across the room, enveloped in a large chair near the fire. Before him a small table had been drawn up and upon it sat a pint of ale.

"I'm sorry," he said. "I seem to have frightened you."

"I—I didn't see you. . . ." Jane found her voice, swallowing the sudden lump in her throat.

All the stories she had ever been told about the dangers of women alone in the world came rushing back to her now. The man across the room saw what looked to be an extremely young girl, her expression frozen in fear, her eyes large with worry.

"I did not mean to intrude," he said smoothly. She was as green as spring. And twice as pretty from what he could see.

"I'm not alone!" she said quickly, her voice rising. "My companion has gone in search of refreshment."

At that point the innkeeper's wife bustled in, the farmer's wife beside her. The innkeeper's wife bobbed a curtsey to the man as the farmer's wife carried a tray of biscuits and cheese towards Jane.

"They're scaring up a pot of tea for us; that should help warm our bones a bit."

Jane moved to make room on the window seat for the woman, taking a biscuit from the tray but shaking her head no to what looked to be fly-blown cheese. "I'm really not hungry. I just need a bit of tea before I start out for my uncle's estate. It will be a cold walk." Jane spoke in a low tone, trying to keep her words from the large man's ears.

He stood up as the innkeeper walked through the outer door. The gentleman was even taller than he had looked while seated. He had the massive shoulders of an athlete or a farmer.

"Your Lordship, they'll be just about ready with your carriage. It twern't nothing more than a bent shaft."

His lordship towered over the rotund innkeeper, his muddied coat bespeaking the trouble he'd had on the road. His top boots were spattered with mud too, as were his buckskin breeches. "I'd best be going if I'm to make Eastborne before noon."

Jane gasped at the words, turning gentleman and innkeeper both towards her.

"Before noon!" Jane repeated, interrupting their conversation further.

"Is something wrong, girl?" the farmer's wife asked.

"No . . ." Jane swallowed. The two men were still looking at her, the tall man's gaze decidedly quizzical. "Excuse me, sir, but do I understand that you are headed for Sir Nigel Steadford's estate, Eastborne?"

"Yes," the man replied simply. "I have that intention."

Jane swallowed hard. "I wonder— that is —I too am making for Eastborne. But I had understood it was an easy walk from Four Corners Inn."

The innkeeper grinned at her. "Well, now, Miss and that's as may be. In summer, it's a fine brisk walk. But here and now, well, it's more than the likes of you are about to do. What with that great north wind and all, you'd be lucky to get there by dark."

"But I must be home before dark!" Jane stood abruptly, upending the biscuit and cheese tray in her agitation. She bent to help the farmer's wife retrieve their light repast. "I'm terribly sorry!"

As she reached for the fallen biscuits the tall young lord moved closer, leaning to reach for a biscuit which had rolled near the long table. Handing it over he bowed slightly.

"I am afraid my carriage is not meant to weather the harsher elements, but if you are in need of conveyance to Eastborne, I am making for there at this very moment. It won't be a cosy ride, I fear. But in any event, it should afford some little comfort more than walking would in this weather."

"She can't go riding off with strangers! She's Quality!" the farmer's wife said stoutly, overlooking the fact that she herself was a stranger to the girl.

"Permit me to introduce myself," the man said smoothly. "I am Charles Graham, Earl of Warwick." He sketched a slight bow, trying to keep the corners of his mouth from turning up at the sight of the girl's frightened eyes and the old woman's dismay.

"An earl, is it?" The farmer's wife could barely speak. To be talking to one of the nobility was something she'd never thought she'd live to see. The innkeeper's wife came near with a tray holding a pot of tea and a chipped milk jug, as well as a glass of sherry. "Bless me. I don't believe it. The likes of Millie Smoot talking to a nob!" The farmer's wife reached for the glass of sherry, taking a medicinal gulp to steady her nerves. Then she took another.

Jane, meanwhile, had been staring at the Earl. Being a practical girl, she decided she dared not refuse his invitation unless she wished to be frozen solid on the narrow country road—or worse yet—home after dark. She could scarcely imagine what her grandmother would do were that to happen, and Jane knew she didn't want to find out.

"I would very much appreciate your help, Your Lordship," Jane said finally, "and I shall be eternally grateful to you, as shall my entire household."

Her words brought a brief smile from the Earl. "Eternity might be a touch excessive, since it is a very short drive." He glanced at the girl's travelling companion. "Are you both ready to leave?"

"Who, me?" The farmer's wife stared at the nobleman.

"We're not exactly together," Jane stammered, her cheeks reddening. "That is, we were merely on the mail coach together."

"My mistake," Charles said smoothly. "I had thought something was mentioned about travelling companions."

Jane's cheeks burned redder at the thought of the bouncer she'd told him. "I only had meant aboard the mail coach."

"Of course. How stupid of me." Charles turned towards the innkeeper. "Has my man settled with you?"

"Yes, Your Lordship. He awaits you outside."

Charles Edward Graham, Ninth Earl of Warwick, moved towards the door and then stopped, looking back at Jane. She hesitated and then walked towards him, gripping her reticule tightly.

"This way, Your Lordship . . . miss . . ." the innkeeper added politely, unsure what this highly unusual situation was all about.

Outside the wind still blew chill, snow swirling in the cold air, drifting off the thatched roof of the inn and the branches of desolate-looking trees.

The Earl of Warwick handed the girl up into his carriage, winking at his man Tom's look of consternation.

"Your Lordship," Tom blurted out.

"Yes?" Lord Charles replied.

"But, Your Lordship, it's a closed carriage!" Shock filled Tom's honest eyes.

"Yes, well, it had better be in this weather, don't you think?"

With that, the young lord climbed inside the coach, closing the door and settling onto the seat across from Jane. She avoided his eyes, every line of her body tensed.

"I don't believe we've been introduced properly," Lord Charles said as they felt Tom jump up to his seat and reach for the reins.

"What?" Jane stared at him again.

It was a frank, open look full of dread. Not accustomed to beautiful young women staring him straight in the eye, Charles was quite intrigued.

"Oh, I'm sorry! I'm Jane Steadford. Nigel Steadford is my great-uncle."

"I see. Or rather I do not see. Could he not send one of his carriages to convey you hence? After all, no matter how necessary your accepting my invitation in this weather, it is still totally improper."

"Why?" she asked.

He looked astounded. "Young ladies of good character do not travel alone with a gentleman in a closed carriage."

"I am counting on your gentlemanly behaviour," Jane told the Earl.

"Thank you. You need have no fear on that head. However, wagging tongues are never quite so trusting. I'm afraid your reputation may be quite ruined if any find out about this."

"Do you have a bad reputation, then?" Jane asked, her eyes rounding in awe.

"Devilish bad," Charles told the chit, watching the play of emotions across her expressive face. "In London they say I am the scourge of honest mothers."

"They don't!" Jane looked at him with renewed interest. "You certainly couldn't tell it by looking at you."

"I beg your pardon?"

"I mean you hardly look the part," Jane said.

Eyes as cold as the green of the North Sea's waters met her own. "Don't make the mistake of trying my civility too high, Miss Steadford." An edge of steel had crept beneath his words. "I may be two-and-thirty, but I am hardly past consideration, I would hope," he ended stiffly.

"Have I offended you?" Jane asked ingenuously. "I only meant that in the stories I've read all the romantic heroes are quite fair and slim, with the features of a Greek god."

"I hardly fit that description," he said dryly.

"Well, you are a great deal too tall, you know. And your eyes are a very strange sort of greeny blue, aren't they? So dark and quite cold at times. And your face is all angles and planes, not softly curved in the least."

"Surely there must be more to this inventory of my faults."

"Oh, it's not that they're faults. It's just, well, you're not even wearing a proper wig. And your hair is rather unruly, wouldn't you say? Couldn't you powder it so it wouldn't be so very dark?"

"I would say I stand before you, a sorry excuse for the male of the species. Or rather, I sit before you."

The corners of his mouth curved at her expression of sincere interest as she perused him from head to toe. She seemed to have no idea how forward she was being.

"You're big enough to be a farmer," she told him.

"Is that a compliment?" he asked.

"Well, it's rather better than being a city fop and the scourge of poor mamas, isn't it?" Jane asked back.

"Have you any acquaintance at all with good manners, Miss Steadford?" Lord Charles asked the girl.

"Not much," she answered cheerfully. "My abigail tells me I've been raised a heathen."

"Your abigail seems to be someone with sense," the Earl murmured. "And who else is there in your establishment? Surely your father or mother must have some words on the subject of your lack of education in the finer graces." He stopped. "What is it?" he asked, seeing the sadness that crept into her large grey eyes.

"My mother died when I was born," Jane told the nobleman. "My father soon after, fighting the French."

Charles felt suddenly sorry for the girl. "Forgive my bringing up painful memories."

Jane looked out at the passing countryside. "It's quite all right," she said softly. "I have my grandmother, and I have Fannie."

"So it is your grandmother that is to be thanked for your lack of social graces?" Charles returned to his bantering tone.

Jane turned her head, smiling impishly. "She hates men, you see. She'll have nothing to do with them. I've been trained to follow her example."

"You've certainly been very well trained for that," Charles said.

"Truly?" She looked at him hopefully.

"I dare say, there isn't a gentleman of my acquaintance who would pay court to you."

Jane's brow furrowed. She bit her lip a little, watching him thoughtfully. "I think some might."

"For all the wrong reasons, possibly."

"Such as?" she asked, earning a startled look.

"Such as assuming you are not a lady, young lady. And their view would be rewarded by seeing you alone in a stranger's carriage this day. Why didn't your relative send his carriage for you?"

"He doesn't quite know I'm coming," Jane replied.

A frown creased the Earl's forehead. "Doesn't *quite* know? Either he does or he doesn't," the Earl said in a practical tone.

"He doesn't," she said. "But it's all right," Jane added hastily. "Truly. He won't be upset or anything. At least with you. For bringing me, I mean."

"This is not then, a pleasant interview you're undertaking?"

"Pleasant?" Jane's gaze turned pensive. "If you can imagine confronting a monster who is supposedly your blood relation but who is capable of selling your very home out from under you, then you will recognise how decidedly unpleasant this interview will be."

It took Charles a moment to digest her words. When he had done so his dark green eyes glinted strangely. He leaned back against the soft, red velvet squabs.

"This is going to be most interesting," he said. "Most interesting, indeed."

He said no more, watching her expression grow more and more agitated as they neared their objective. She stared anxiously out the windowed door.

Lost in her own thoughts, Jane Steadford began to bite her bottom lip, worrying it back and forth as the Earl's carriage bowled forwards up the snowbound drive.

NIGEL STEADFORD HAD been informed that not only had the Earl of Warwick arrived, but it seems he'd had an accident and somehow collected Nigel's great-niece Jane along the way. Nigel's irritation erupted in his bedroom, forcing his long-suffering valet Jarvis to listen to his master's harangue on the subject of women in general and his sister Agatha in particular. If Nigel could have foreseen the immediate results of his brief missive to his sister Agatha, he would have put off posting the blasted thing, he informed the imperturbable Jarvis.

Jarvis listened in silence to his master's colourful description of where he would like to send the chit of a girl who had somehow gotten herself into the Earl of Warwick's carriage. Nigel's narrow face held a knowing look when he spoke of girls who were no better than they ought to be, and of the harm that would surely come to them. He knew whereof he spoke, he informed his valet.

"Where is the little baggage now?" Nigel asked suddenly.

"I believe her to be in the small parlour, sir. You were quite insistent she should not be left in the large parlour since the Earl will repair there as soon as he's changed."

"Damm right, she's not to be in the large parlour! And how, by Jupiter, did she *get* into his carriage in the first place?" Nigel asked peevishly.

"I believe she said she rode the mail coach to Four Corners, sir."

Nigel made a strangled sound deep in his skinny throat. His hand went to the top of his balding head. "Where is my wig? Mark my words, Agatha put her up to this! Somehow she knew he was coming, and she planned all this to throw a spoke in my plans."

Jarvis fitted his master's wig to his head, dusting a bit more powder onto the tight sausage curls. "It would seem, however, that neither the Earl nor Miss Steadford are aware of the other's mission here today."

"As far as we know," Nigel replied darkly as he turned before the mirror, inspecting himself. "I will not brook interference. And I will not have guests of mine accosted on the roads."

"Yes, sir," Jarvis replied calmly.

"I don't suppose there is any way of avoiding this interview." The leader of the Steadford family's tone was still fretful as his valet finished arranging the elaborate wig. "By Jupiter! I'll not ask her to stay the night!"

"She is, after all, family, sir," Jarvis pointed out.

Nigel waved the man away, his pale hand fluttering in the air between them. "My sister's grandchild, yes, yes. The most vexatious creature alive!"

"Young Jane, sir?"

"No, my sister Agatha!" Nigel sighed. "I suppose I shall have to suffer through this interview. But I shall rid myself of her before I deal with the Earl," he said. And sighed again. "I know all this will quite put me off my dinner. You know how argufying females quite deplete me."

With the fatalistic air of a doomed man, Nigel Steadford drew himself up to his full five-foot-seven-inch height and squared his narrow shoulders. "I want a coach arranged for her immediately. She must be off before she gets another chance to fill the Earl's ear with nonsense."

"Yes, sir. I shall see to it."

"Be sure that you do." Nigel allowed his valet to open the hall door for him. "If I have not rung for you in twenty minutes, interrupt me with an urgent message."

"What urgent message, sir?"

"Damn and blast, *any* urgent message!" With the air of a man much put upon, Nigel Steadford proceeded out into his upper hall and prepared himself to face his grand-niece.

The object of his agitation sat alone in the parlour below, her own brow far from calm. In her entire twenty years Jane had never done anything in the slightest way adventurous. She had never been farther from Steadford Abbey and her grandmother than the village of Wooster, and even those journeys had never been alone.

She had quite enjoyed the beginning of her adventure today. Everything had been new and exciting then, but now her heart pounded when she realised she was soon to confront the ogre in person in his own parlour. She jumped when the door opened.

A young maid entered, cleaning rags in hand. "Oh!" The girl stopped, gaping at the strange young woman who occupied the suite. "I'm sorry, miss." The girl lost all words. She stared at Jane as if she had never seen a woman in these rooms.

"It's all right," Jane told the maid.

"What's all right?" Her great-uncle spoke petulantly from the doorway.

The maid, certain his glowering look was on her behalf, scurried out, her apologetic words lost as the heavy oak door closed.

Nigel was short and frail-looking. But his eyes were ferociously angry as he walked towards Jane. He saw the letter crumpled in her hand and veered away, reaching for the bellpull next to the cold fireplace. "I suppose you'll have to be given something to eat and drink," he said ungraciously, his back to Jane as he spoke. "Sorry about the cold but you'll have to endure it since you weren't expected. I only keep a fire going in one room downstairs."

"Sir." Jane's voice trembled but came out stronger than either of them expected. "How could you possibly?"

"You may think me old-fashioned but there's no need for waste, I always say."

"I couldn't care less if there were a hundred fires or none," Jane burst out.

"That's easy enough to say when you don't pay for them," the elderly man replied darkly.

"How can you *do* this to your own sister? Have you no heart? No shame?"

Jane had risen to her feet, her small hands clasped around his letter and each other. She was shaking, anger and fear churning within her breast until she could feel her heart trip-hammer against her ribcage.

"Keep your voice down. Do you want the whole county hearing your complaints?" Nigel glanced nervously towards the wall that separated the two parlours.

"Why shouldn't they hear? They shall soon know. *All* shall soon know how heartless and cruel you are." Jane's voice rose and fell with her laboured breath.

"What a horrid girl you are," Nigel Steadford told the chit. "I don't scruple to say, I can see my sister's fine hand in your upbringing."

"And whose else?" Jane demanded. "I owe my life to Grandmama."

"Yes, well, go back and tell her that I am not impressed. My decision stands. Steadford Abbey is to be sold and that's that. This fine trick of hers won't work."

"Grandmama is not a trickster," Jane blurted out.

Her great-uncle finally looked her square in the eye. Then his gaze slid away, unable to stare down the girl's outraged grey eyes which filled with unbidden tears as he spoke.

"Your rattle-pated adventure here is doing more harm than good." Upset beyond endurance by mortal man, he barked the words at her.

"How can you turn your own sister out of the only home she's ever known?" Jane asked.

Nigel was now convinced she had been raised with a complete lack of manners and finer feeling. "She's welcome to the Dower House here on my estate, as I've already told her. I don't know what more you both can expect of me." He cursed under his breath and grabbed the bellpull again, nearly yanking it off the wall.

A tap at the hall door was soon followed by the appearance of the butler. "You rang, sir?"

"What more can be expected?" Jane continued. "A bit of compassion, the merest hint of a tender feeling for your only sister!"

"Do be quiet!" Nigel's voice squeaked with his pique. He glared at the impassive face of his butler. "Sherry, please."

"I wish no sherry!" Jane said ringingly.

"Well, I do," Nigel snapped.

As the butler bowed slightly and withdrew, Nigel clasped his hands together behind his back and tried to look dignified. The thought of the tales which would soon be spreading throughout the servants' quarters hardened his heart still further against his sister's plea.

"I must insist you keep that flapping aperture some might call a mouth under control in front of my servants. I had no idea what fripperies my sister was teaching you, but I now know she has surely omitted the simplest decencies from your education. There is such a thing as keeping one's tongue in front of the servants. I am appalled she could send you here to beg for her."

"She doesn't know I'm here," Jane put in quickly, stopping Nigel's lecture in midflow. He looked startled, his frown deepening. "And Grandmama would *never* beg," Jane added defiantly.

"She doesn't know you're here? Good grief, are you telling me you've run away again?"

"Again?" Jane stared at the man as if he were demented.

"If you're planning on making a regular habit of this, I don't know what's to be done with you. Mind you, I won't put up with this nonsense once you've moved here."

"Sir, are you demented?" Jane demanded. "I've never run away in my life."

"You've just told me you have this very day," Nigel retorted. "And I well remember the time Agatha had the entire county searching you out."

"I didn't run away. I was five years old and got lost in the spinney. And I haven't run away now. I've come to make you see reason," Jane told the old man flatly.

They were interrupted by the butler with the sherry tray. Jane was hard pressed keeping herself from continuing their argument in front of her great-uncle's servant—or servants—as another liveried manservant appeared in the doorway, telling Nigel there was urgent business awaiting him. Even to Jane's unpracticed ears, the man's words sounded false.

Nigel Steadford turned towards his great-niece, pasting an insincere smile on his narrow lips. "It seems I'm needed elsewhere, but I've arranged for you to be transported back to the Abbey. My coach awaits." Nigel turned towards his valet. "At least, I believe it does."

"Yes, sir." Jarvis spoke without inflection, not allowing himself to look towards the young personage who was so obviously upsetting the master of the house.

"Good," Nigel said. "In any event, you shall arrive home with a proper escort and perhaps we can keep the entire county from spreading word of your misadventure today."

Nigel turned to walk out.

"Sir!"

Jane Steadford's ringing tones stopped him just short of the doorway. He gazed longingly out into the hall but turned back to face the young woman, his expression a study in mixed feelings. He waited for his butler and valet to march past him, telling the latter pointedly he would be out momentarily.

"Well?" Nigel asked none too politely once he and his great-niece were alone again in the large, cold parlour.

"I have not yet received the kindness of a reply," Jane told him stiffly.

Nigel stared at her. "I scarcely know what to reply, Jane."

A tiny bit of hope flared within her. She smiled tremulously. "Oh, sir, it is so very little we ask, merely to be allowed to keep our home. Surely when you have all this—you need not sell off the Abbey just because you hold title. If Grandfather had not gambled all his monies away to you the Abbey would still be Grandmama's."

The young woman came forward towards her great-uncle, who backed away at her approach. "A coach is waiting" he told her. She hesitated. "Is that your final reply?"

"There is nothing else to be said," Nigel Steadford told her stiffly.

Thoughts of murder flitted across her agitated mind, but she wasn't quite sure how to go about the deed—nor that the deed would necessarily allow her grandmother to continue on at the Abbey.

At her silence, Nigel visibly brightened. Before Jane could find voice for further complaints her great-uncle was out the door and into the hallway, calling for Jarvis to lead the young person to the waiting carriage and for the butler to clear the small parlour and for the housekeeper to ready dinner as he would soon be dining with the Earl of Warwick.

Jane found herself in the middle of the great hall, two man-servants watching her with impassive eyes and waiting for her to move forwards. She was suddenly very aware of her shabby cloak and dowdy gown. Although the house was ill-used and bleak, its every furnishing bespoke great wealth. The main hall itself was floored with marble and lined with oak. Two complete suits of armour flanked the huge iron-banded front door.

Jane drew herself to her full five-foot-six, her head held high as she marched past the servants, through the open front door, and out onto the terraced porch.

A sedate black carriage stood waiting. Beyond it the Earl's high-sprung carriage was being unharnessed. Jane looked towards it, then back at the large, bleak mansion.

As she stood there the Earl of Warwick crossed the hall inside, glancing towards the still-open front door. His man Tom was beside him, carrying a pile of muddied clothes. The Earl hesitated, slowing, looking out towards the girl. He said something to his man, then came forward alone towards the butler and Jane.

"I say, are you leaving already?" Lord Charles asked.

She stared up at him. He had changed into spotless fawn-coloured pantaloons and a navy-blue coat. Even his boots had been cleaned, regaining most of their lustrous black polish. As she looked up at him, tears began to sparkle within her grey eyes, making them seem deep wintry pools filled with pain.

"Are you quite all right?" he asked, his deep voice filling with concern at her expression.

She had removed her old-fashioned bonnet when she arrived and had not replaced it. She now held it in her hands, her pale blond curls sadly crushed. She obviously had not bothered to consider her appearance in a mirror from the moment of arrival until now.

"Your Lordship?" Jarvis came through the doorway, his smooth voice interceding between Jane and the Earl. "Sir Nigel awaits you."

"Are you the usurper?" Jane asked the man, her voice quavering over the words.

The Earl looked down at the young woman. He watched her for a long moment before replying, "I'm very afraid I might well be."

"You are to buy Steadford Abbey," Jane said flatly.

"That is the arrangement," the Earl of Warwick told her. "Although I take it the matter does not meet with your approval."

"Why should it?" she replied. "You have no need of my approval simply because I and my aged grandmother are to be thrown out in the cold. After all, what can that matter to you? Perish the thought that any consideration other than greed should enter into the transaction."

With that, she swept past the tall Earl and down the steps.

Charles, Earl of Warwick, watched as she raised a regal hand to the groom and was assisted into the waiting carriage. The Earl was still watching as the sedate black coach rolled down the wide drive past his own carriage.

The valet was bowing low. "This way, Your Lordship."

"Is she always like that?" the Earl asked, bemused.

"I couldn't say, Your Lordship. She is, after all, merely a young relation. This way, please. . . ."

The Earl of Warwick followed Jarvis into the house but stopped in the doorway, looking back towards the coach as it negotiated a turn down the long drive, disappearing from view.

"Bloody hell," the Earl of Warwick said.

"Quite so, Your Lordship," Jarvis agreed and led the tall nobleman towards the main parlour, where Nigel Steadford stood waiting before a blazing fire.

- 3 -

THE SKY WAS a wintry grey, dark clouds drifting high above the Dorset hills as Jane's carriage found its way back along the snow-covered roads. January storms had left the English countryside bleak, stripping all the trees of their leaves, and covering the ground with ice and snow.

Jane leaned against the dark blue squabs of her great-uncle's coach, tears falling unheeded down her cheeks. She had gone a great distance, had chanced her grandmother's wrath, and it had all been for naught. The Earl was as heartless as was her great-uncle himself; as were all men according to her grandmother.

Sniffling, Jane rubbed her nose with her handkerchief and leaned against the swaying side of the coach, sighing prodigiously. Looking down at the bonnet still in her lap, she picked it up and clapped it back upon her head with another heart-rending sigh.

Nonetheless, her youthful optimism soon made itself felt. She began mulling over and discarding, one by one, plans to circumvent her great-uncle.

Steadford Abbey came into view as she worried over what to do next. In the waning afternoon light, the Abbey's three-story stone walls looked bleak amidst the wintry world of white, grey, and black which encompassed the countryside all around. The long driveway to the top of the Abbey hill was edged by bare-branched oaks and copper beeches in this deep winter's month. Nigel's coach clattered under the great stone archway abutting the gatehouse, then passed beneath the gate clock, and continued towards the entrance court.

Large oriel windows supported by sturdy stone corbels were set to each side of the Abbey's entrance. Within the ancient Abbey, panelled ceilings of Spanish chestnut looked down upon the family portraits which marched one past the other along the length of the Long Gallery. Tall, square, mullioned windows lined the walls, letting in slender fingers of pale wintry light which stabbed down across four generations of portraits towards the stone floors of the front hall far below.

The Abbey was silent as death in the wintry afternoon. Alabaster busts of long-dead Steadfords gazed blindly out towards the center of the empty main hall and the beautiful linenfold panelling which surrounded them. The rustle of a young maid's skirts disturbed the empty vistas. A green baise door banged shut behind her, the sound carrying through the empty, silent halls.

"Yes?" An old woman's voice, querulous in pitch, peevish and petulant, sounded unnaturally loud in the silence. "Jane, is that you, then?"

There was no answer.

The old woman sat within her suite of rooms at the front of the upper floor, one floor above the grand parlours and empty ballrooms and lounges which made Steadford Abbey the greatest house ever built in this tiny backwater of Regency England.

Agatha Steadford-Smyth had celebrated her sixtieth birthday in the November just past. The year 1804 had brought her into a new decade of life and, as it ended, the news arrived that her home would soon be taken from her. Neither event had sweetened her disposition.

"Jane?" Agatha's voice rose again. "Have you died then?"

"And what is it you want with Jane?" Fannie Burns asked her employer with the familiarity of long, honest service.

The nicely rounded abigail had spent twenty-five of her forty-three years of life tending to the elderly woman who sat by the fire, her cap askew from her afternoon nap. Fannie bustled across the room, her arms laden with linens.

"It's no one's business but mine and Jane's," Agatha told the serving woman. "Where is she?"

"She's somewhere about," Fannie replied, rather ambiguously, then proceeded to put away the linens she had brought up from the washrooms far below.

"I swear, I don't know what's to become of the girl. I've tried to raise her proper. I've tried to do my best by her, but after all said and done, I've made a pure confusion of it."

"Don't go giving yourself airs and graces," Fannie said, pouring ice on her aging mistress's fast-rising pique.

Agatha Steadford-Smyth, at sixty, still held much of the beauty of face and figure which had led her astray long years ago—and which had saved her reputation in the end, when Homer Smyth asked for her hand and saved her position in Society. Granted, both her lover before and Smyth thereafter had turned her forever against the male of the species. Still, she had been rescued the fate worse than death and had lived on to see her daughter grown, married, and full with child.

Evelyn's child Jane had been born twenty years ago last November, here at the Abbey, a week before Agatha's own birthday. A lusty child whose wild cries promised to ring in new life within the ancient stone walls, while in reality those selfsame cries were sounding the death knell for the weakened woman who was her mother and had given birth after three solid days of labour pains.

Agatha closed her eyes as if to close her mind against Evelyn's travail. Jane was a wonderful child—a respectful, practical, dutiful grandchild—and at least Agatha had the comfort of that in her old age. Her mind turned unbidden to her only and long lost son Daniel, but she pushed away the thoughts of the boy and of his childhood here at the Steadford family home where Smyth's gambling losses had sent them within the first fortnight of marriage.

Daniel had run away at fourteen, in 1777, and in 1778 he was reported killed along with many other English heroes on the HMS *Victory* under Admiral Keppel. His mother had never quite recovered from the message she received. Agatha might deny it to her deathbed, but Daniel's death had broken the last of her resolve and ensured the fury of her antipathy against the male of the species.

There were no males to be trusted, young or old. Living or dead. Life had taught Agatha this from her earliest days, and she intended to impart the wisdom of those sixty years to her granddaughter Jane.

Fannie finished putting away the freshly laundered linens and closed the huge mahogany clothespress. "I suppose you're ready for your tea," she said.

"Where has that girl gotten to?" Agatha asked crossly.

"I hope she's in the spinney," Fannie replied.

Agatha stared at her serving woman. "Why on earth would you hope that?"

"Because the girl is too housebound and too dutiful by half. I told her while you napped she should take a walk in the fresh air, get some colour in her cheeks."

"She's more likely to catch cold," Agatha replied tartly.

"Yes, well, that's not the worst could happen to a young gel asked to live with us old doddering ones about her and nary a chance at a normal life."

"Normal life?" Agatha nearly spit out the words. "You still believe in those romance books you sneak in to Jane, Fannie Burns, and don't you deny it."

"And if I do?" Fannie asked with some asperity.

"Hmmmph." Agatha showed her derision in her tone of voice. "Some of us never do grow up."

"And perhaps some grow up too quickly," Fannie cast back. "Or think we do."

"Where is Jane?" Agatha asked again, more petulantly.

Fannie moved towards the door. "I'll go find her, shall I?"

"It's about time," Agatha said and watched Fannie let herself out of the bedroom, wondering at her distracted expression. "Are you quite yourself today?" Agatha asked and was rewarded by a furtive look from her abigail before Fannie covered her discomfort with a false smile.

"I'm fine, Your Ladyship. Just fine."

Fannie closed the hallway door between them, leaving Agatha to her own thoughts and speeding quickly down the upper hall to the main staircase. The huge grandfather clock at the foot of the stairs began tolling the hour. Fannie squeezed her eyes shut, praying Jane would arrive back soon, before it became necessary to tell Lady Agatha the truth.

The sedate black coach was releasing its lone passenger onto the Abbey porch as Fannie descended from her mistress's rooms, taking out her worry on the downstairs maid who had the misfortune of coming upon the aging abigail unawares.

"Is the fire properly set in the blue parlour?" Fannie demanded.

"Why, yes, Fannie, it is." The girl had never heard such an angry tone from Fannie in all the years she had worked at the Abbey. "Is something wrong?" the young maid asked faintly.

"If it is, it's no business of yours," Fannie replied with asperity.

"No . . . it isn't."

The girl slid past the older woman and ran back towards the green baise door to the kitchens. Fannie watched the maid go, upset with herself until sounds out front banished all other thoughts. Fannie rushed to the door and thrust it open to find a coach stopped at the bottom of the wide, shallow steps. Jane was thanking the young groom who had just helped her down. She turned towards Fannie's voice as Fannie came forward, calling out for Jane to hurry.

The young groom glanced towards the older woman, then jumped back up on the top seat, taking his place beside the driver who began to pull away even before the boy was properly settled.

"We should have asked them to tea," Jane said, looking after the coach.

"And what would we have told her ladyship? Just how would you explain their presence? And what did you think you were doing, running off like that this morning?"

"I didn't run off," Jane said tartly. "I went on an errand."

"A fool's errand," Fannie said.

Jane turned to face the abigail who had helped raise her for as far back as she could remember. "A fool's errand, yes. And you knew that when I left?"

"Of course I did. Any addlepate could have told you so."

"Why didn't you tell me then?" Jane asked.

"I did."

Jane drooped with tiredness. "I suppose you're right," she said in a meek tone. "I wasn't listening."

Fannie hesitated. "Jane, there are times when it's better not to hurt your heart by pining for things that can't be and that won't change."

"No one is going to force Grandmama to leave here." Jane spoke slowly and distinctly. "I shan't let them."

"How do you propose to stop them, then?" Fannie asked practically.

"I don't know, but I shall. And that's a fact. No one is going to take the Abbey away from Grandma."

Fannie watched her young charge. "Or away from you?"

Jane bit her lip, sudden tears rising unbidden in her large eyes. She tried to hold them back. Then she tried to pretend they weren't there. "I'm thinking of Grandmama."

"Sometimes things have to change," Fannie said more kindly. "That's the way of the world." And then: "She's been asking for you for over an hour. Ever since she woke from her afternoon nap."

"Is she all right?" Jane anxiously searched the abigail's face.

"She still looks a little tired, and she's been upset by another letter which arrived this noon. She wants you to come up."

Jane followed Fannie up the stairs to her grandmother's bedroom. Hesitating at the closed door, she removed her hat and pelisse, handing them to Fannie before tapping, then stepping quietly inside.

Agatha was dozing in her rocking chair near the windows, tea tray beside her, cap askew. Her crocheted shawl had slipped from her lap to the floor beside the wooden rocker. Jane moved forward to retrieve it, Agatha's dark eyes opening as Jane bent near.

"So, they've finally found you."

Startled, Jane settled the shawl back onto her grandmother's lap. "I was out, Grandmama."

"That much is obvious," Agatha replied. "I've received another letter from that unmentionable brother of mine," she informed her granddaughter.

"What does he say?" Jane asked faintly.

Agatha reached for her tea tray and pulled a piece of parchment towards her. She handed it to Jane, who took it without hesitation, reading quickly down the short page of script.

"Dear Sister," it began, "I shall arrive within the week. I shall be bringing the prospective new owner and will expect all to be readied at the Abbey so that this transaction can be completed in good order."

Agatha watched Jane's expression as the young woman read the short missive. "He's offered us the Dower House on his estate," Agatha told Jane.

"He's positively odious!" Jane replied.

"He says the Abbey is a drain on the family resources."

"He's dicked in the nob."

"Jane!" Agatha looked aghast. "Where did you learn such language?"

"In the stables with Homer and Jake," Jane answered truthfully. "And it's true. He must be crazy or he'd never think to throw us out on the parish."

"As bad as it is, it's hardly that. He's promised us a roof over our heads, even though it will have to be with him and at his beck and call. And you still have your little competence from your father."

"He can't do this to us," Jane cried out.

Agatha knew better. "You've had little experience with men, my girl. Men are capable of any kind of crime. Nor do they ever feel remorse about any of their evil deeds. He will eat his dinner happily and be as complacent as ever, never thinking what he's done to someone else. That's how men are."

Something crashed to the floor, startling them both. The sound reverberated in the silent house. Jane turned towards where Agatha was looking. Across the room, an ivory casket had fallen from the dressing table to the floor below. It was a music box filled with Agatha's pins and necklaces, its jewelled contents now spilled out onto the dark Turkey carpet.

Jane moved to pick up the fallen jewels, Agatha watching her. "It must have been too near the edge," Agatha said.

"I can't imagine how such a heavy thing could just jump off the table," Jane replied, scooping up the pearls and the jet and garnet jewels.

"It must have been a draft from the hall," Agatha said.

Jane looked towards the open hall door. "This is much too heavy for a draft to dislodge."

As she spoke something chilled her to the bone. Shivering, she stood up and replaced the casket.

"Are you all right?" her grandmother asked.

"Yes. I'm fine." Jane shivered still. "Perhaps there's more of a draft than I realised."

"Come help me up. If we're to lose the Abbey, I want to enjoy it while I still can."

"Oh, Gram, don't even say it, please. It breaks my heart to hear you talk so."

Agatha allowed Jane to help her to her feet. "There's no use skirting about the truth. We females are at the mercy of the male of the species from birth to death. Lord knows, I've tried to shield you from the worst of their excesses . . . so far," Agatha added darkly. "When I'm gone, I don't know what's to become of you."

"You're not going anywhere without me," Jane told the older woman stoutly. "I won't have it. I need you too much here."

Agatha's expression softened at Jane's words. "Child, I wish I could protect you forever." Then, in a more bracing tone, she said, "Let's see what they've done for our dinner."

Jane walked beside her grandmother towards the hall and the main rooms below. Jane's arm was crooked within Agatha's as they approached the stairs.

"We'll fight the lot of them," Jane said.

Agatha sighed. "You'll have to fight them, my dear. I've no heart left for it."

"Well, I have enough for both of us," Jane said stoutly.

"You really think there's anything we can do?"

"There's always something to be done," Jane said. "You taught me that yourself."

"Did I?" Agatha sounded wistful. "It must have been a very long time ago." She pulled herself together, reaching for the banister. "I hope Cook hasn't made mutton again tonight."

"You like mutton, Grandmama."

"I did until we had it all week long," Agatha replied acerbically. "At this point, I'd prefer gruel."

They walked down the last of the steps and into the dining room off the main hall. A footman held Lady Agatha's chair at the head of the long, mahogany table, helping Jane hand her into it before moving to pull back Jane's own chair at the side. A maid came in with the soup tureen and ladled out a mutton stew. Agatha screwed up her nose at it as the butler put her bowl before her.

"At least it's not the main course," Jane said softly, a giggle lightening her tone.

Agatha took up her soup spoon with a resigned sigh and reached for one of the thick slices of fresh-baked bread which sat on a hand-painted plate before her.

"Well?" Agatha demanded of her granddaughter after a moment. "Where have you been all day?"

Jane swallowed. "I've been off figuring out what can be done to save the Abbey."

Agatha looked across the table at her. Branches of candles on the cherry-wood sideboard haloed Jane's pale blond hair, making her look angelic. "And did you come to any conclusion?" Agatha asked.

"Not yet, but I shall think of a way!"

"You'd be better served by beginning to pack," Agatha replied.

"They shall remove me from these grounds over my dead body," Jane pronounced dramatically.

"I sincerely hope that does not become necessary," Agatha retorted. "For either of us."

- 4 -

THE ARRIVAL OF Nigel Steadford and the Earl of Warwick was accomplished much sooner than Nigel had originally planned. The Earl, after his interviews with Jane, had been most anxious to see exactly what was going on at Steadford Abbey and would not take delay for an answer.

Thus, the Abbey household was caught unawares the following Friday afternoon by carriage wheels rumbling up the drive. Two large coaches came to a stop at the Abbey's great stone steps, and Jarvis stepped down from beside the first driver to open the coach door.

Within the hour Agatha was to find out about her grand-daughter's adventure across half the county. The handsome young Earl who was presented to Agatha bowed low and asked—by the way—where was Jane? A strangled objection from Nigel Steadford did not stop Agatha from calling for Jane and demanding an immediate explanation of how this strange man was on such familiar terms with her only grandchild.

"What has been going on behind my back?" the old woman demanded even before Jane was fully into the room. Fannie hovered in the hallway beyond, looking worried. "Fannie? Did you know about this?" Agatha asked, but the abigail had disappeared out beyond the blue parlour.

Jane gave a pointed look to the Earl. "It doesn't seem diplomacy is your strong suit either, Your Lordship," she told him with some asperity.

"Jane!" Nigel protested vehemently, then admonished his sister, "Surely you can stop this child's tongue." Nigel turned towards the Earl. "Please accept our apologies, Your Lordship, for my young relative's waspish tongue."

Jane paid no attention to Nigel. "You told me yourself you were the scourge of London mamas," Jane continued to Charles. "You steal people's houses and haven't even the sense to be a bit tactful when you arrive to do so."

"He tactful?" Nigel burst out. "Agatha, get this girl out of my sight before I strangle her on the spot!"

Nigel stood across the room, shaking with rage from the tip of his powdered wig to the soles of his polished Hessians. He fumbled for his ornate snuffbox, pulling on his scented hand-kerchief—fobs, seals, and a quizzing glass all displayed on his canary-yellow waistcoat. The wadded shoulders and wasp-waist cut of his clothing bespoke his having been a very tulip of fashion in his prime. Beside him the Earl of Warwick stood tall and plain, wearing butter-soft leather country breeches and a black coat of severe military cut.

Watching her great-uncle, Jane decided side-whiskers were decidedly repugnant. Nigel took a delicate pinch of snuff, Jane's nose twitching at the sight. When she turned, she found not only her grandmother, but the Earl as well, contemplating her. Jane did her best to look demure.

"Don't go trying to bamm me," her grandmother said sharply. "I want to know what's been going on behind my back."

"Your ward," Nigel spoke quickly, "took it upon herself to barge off across the county, travelling alone, mind you, by public coach and putting down unattended at Four Corners Inn. From there she engaged to speak to a complete stranger, begging your pardon, Your Lordship, and demanded to be taken up in his *closed* carriage and brought to my home. After having gone beyond the pale with such actions as no lady would ever think of taking, she proceeded to berate me in my own house and in front of my own servants. *And then*," his voice rang out, "she accosted and maligned the Earl of Warwick in front of servants." Nigel stopped for breath. "I tell you, Agatha, she needs to be well-hauled over the coals."

Jane jumped up. "Just try to spank me. Just you try, you ogre! I shall take my father's pistols and give you what for!"

Nigel's horrified expression told all. He sank to a wing chair by the fire, shaking his head and once again raising his snuffbox to his nose.

Jane found her grandmother's gaze unwavering. "You wouldn't have let me go," she said after a silence.

Charles had to work his jaw to keep a smile from forming. Agatha's gaze swung toward him, and he tried to look appropri-ately put upon.

"I take it the gist of what my brother said is true?" she asked.

"The gist!" Nigel objected. "Well, I never!"

Charles bowed slightly. "Unfortunately, that complexion can be put on her movements, Lady Agatha."

"Sit down, I can't stand people hovering over me," Agatha told the Earl.

He sat.

To Jane her grandmother said, "I hope you've learned a lesson from all this." Then she looked towards her brother. "How long do we have before we're thrown out?"

"Agatha!" Nigel looked pained.

"I trust," Lord Charles put in, "that you will allow me the honour of having you stay on for as long as you like here at the Abbey."

"Tell her that and you'll never be rid of them," Nigel said darkly.

Agatha stiffened. "I have never stayed anywhere I was not welcome."

"You are most welcome, Lady Agatha," Charles replied. "In fact it would be a very great help to me if you were here to assist in the . . . transition."

"Transition?" Jane said tragically. "It is not an accomplished fact."

"Oh, yes it is," Nigel assured her with a tight little smile.

"I have, however," Charles continued smoothly, "thought of a solution to both our problems."

"Both?" Lady Agatha stared at him.

"My need of help for an orderly transition and your need to reconcile your granddaughter to the idea. Would you consider the gatehouse as a temporary abode?"

"No!" Jane cried out.

"Not immediately, as I said. But at your convenience," Charles repeated.

Nigel stared at the Earl. "That's demmed civil of you, Your Lordship, I must say. After all this girl's done to put you off."

"She won't do it," Jane said hotly.

"Jane." Her grandmother quelled the girl with one scathing look. "No one speaks for me." Agatha regarded the man before her. "I shall consider what you say."

"On both heads," Charles said meaningfully.

Agatha nodded, distrustful of why this strange Earl should be thinking of young Jane's feelings about the move in any event, let alone why he should attempt to make the transition easier for the girl.

"I shan't be needed then," Nigel was saying, Agatha finally attending to his words. "If all seems to be settled, I shall depart at first light. After all, I have my own estate to run."

"Can you send on my valet when he arrives?" Charles asked Nigel. "He's expecting to find me at Eastborne. He can bring the small carriage," Charles added as an afterthought. He looked reflectively at the young woman who sat silently staring into the fire.

"Of course, of course." Nigel's narrow face was wreathed with smiles, his side-whiskers curving outwards. "By Jove, it's good to deal with a man who knows his mind."

"I daresay," Charles replied rather enigmatically, earning a questioning look from Nigel and a searching one from his sister.

"I don't suppose there's any refreshment about?" Charles asked into the quiet.

"By Jove, Agatha, where are your manners?" Nigel demanded. He turned back towards the Earl. "They have so few visitors, I'm sure the household staff will be in a complete tizzy, knowing the new master has arrived." Nigel moved closer to his sister. "Agatha," he said meaningfully, "shall I ring for something?"

"Do so if you wish," Agatha told her brother. "I'm not thirsty."

At this Jane stood up. "Please pardon us." She spoke to the Earl. "We may be poor, but we have not yet lost all sense of hospitality. I shall see to some sherry and then to some proper tea."

Nigel stared after the girl as she swept out of the room, her slim back ramrod straight. "Now what has gotten into her?"

"Perhaps she's hungry," was all Agatha offered in answer. She caught Charles's amused expression.

"Perhaps so," Charles agreed charitably. "I can see you will be a great deal of help, Lady Agatha . . . in the transition," he added.

She thought she heard echoes of irony in his tone, but his face and demeanour were the picture of seriousness. She watched him, her dark eyes assessing the nobleman. Finally she spoke. "We'll see," was all she said. She stood up. Charles reached to help her, but she refused his proffered hand, steadying herself with her cane. "I shall retire to change for dinner. The butler will show you to your rooms."

"Will Jane—Miss Steadford," Charles corrected himself, "be joining us for dinner?"

Agatha gave him a hard look. "Why are you so interested in my granddaughter?"

"He's not interested," Nigel put in. "He's politely asking you to have her eat elsewhere and I, for one, second the idea. She will quite put me off my feed."

"Oh, no," the Earl of Warwick told them both. "Quite the

contrary. I look forward to her company." At Nigel's shocked expression, the Earl smiled blandly. "I have never met anyone quite like her."

"One should hope not," Nigel said.

"My granddaughter is too young and too inexperienced to have attention paid to her by an experienced man of the world," Lady Agatha told the Earl coldly.

"Really, Agatha, this is the outside of enough," Nigel protested.

Lord Charles's expression was unreadable. "I assume you feel me to be an experienced man of the world."

"Extremely so, I should assume," Agatha said.

"Now, really, Agatha, you can't possibly be serious. Lord Charles, she's merely funning, I assure you." Nigel spoke quickly, looking from one to the other, wishing himself far away, and even more fervently that the papers were signed and sealed and the estate properly transferred so he could put the county between himself and Steadford Abbey.

"I assure you, I have no ulterior motives, Lady Agatha," the Earl of Warwick told Agatha Steadford-Smyth. He looked and sounded totally sincere.

"And I assure you, Agatha, that the Earl of Warwick is quite the most eligible catch in London and can have his pick of any girl in the realm. If you could possibly think he would be interested in dallying with the likes of that hoyden you've raised, you are totally mistaken."

"Am I?" Agatha asked the Earl pointedly.

Lord Charles hesitated. "I'm afraid I do have that reputation."

"Then I have your word you will not put ideas into Jane's head?" Agatha asked.

"My dear Lady Agatha, I rather doubt that anyone could," Charles replied.

"That's not an answer," he was told.

Nigel threw up his hands. "I must apologise, it seems, for my entire family, Lord Charles."

"Not at all," Charles replied calmly. He looked towards Lady Agatha. "I assure you, I have not yet, nor shall I ever, take any liberties with your granddaughter."

Nigel glared at his sister. "Can we now retire to change for supper, or do you intend to grill the entire House of Lords, Agatha?"

"As long as it's settled," his sister replied. But when she turned away her dark eyes were still filled with disquiet.

"Lord Charles?" Nigel was waiting for the Earl to precede him out the parlour door.

After a moment's hesitation, the Earl walked past Nigel, into the hall where Fannie greeted them.

"If you'll follow me, Your Lordship, Sir Nigel." She led them up the wide oak stairwell to their apartments.

They walked down the drafty corridor, Nigel hoping Charles would notice neither the carpet of worn drugget nor the winter winds seeping through the window cracks. The daylight faded around them, a sliver of moon climbing high in the evening sky out beyond the windows.

Nigel stood with the abigail as she showed Charles into a large front suite of rooms beside Agatha's own. The fire was already laid in the large sitting room.

"This used to be the master's suite, Your Lordship. If there's anything you need, the bellpull's here. Oh, and your man said he was seeing to the horses if you should send for him. Dinner will be at seven-thirty."

"Thank you," the Earl said.

"See you at dinner, then," Nigel was saying as the door closed between them.

Agatha's brother followed the maid to the guest suite across the hall, leaving Charles to himself.

Later that night Charles Edward Graham, Ninth Earl of Warwick, had his first encounter with The Ghost.

- 5 -

THE CHAMBERS THE Earl of Warwick had been given consisted of two huge rooms and three smaller ones. Of the former, one was a sitting-room which faced the wide front lawns sloping towards the gatehouse and the ancient stone walls which surrounded the Abbey lands. The other was a bedroom with a view of the west lawns, the stand of ancient oaks, and the glimmer of the River Stour beyond. Both rooms were wainscotted with oak and papered in a dark blue design flecked with tiny golden crescents. The three smaller rooms were a valet's bedroom, a dressing room, and a private bath installed by the last owner, Sir Ambrose Steadford, father to both Agatha and Nigel.

It was a richly appointed, masculine apartment in which the Earl of Warwick stood before a pier-glass in the bedroom struggling with his cravat. Managing a gentleman's proper attire without a valet in attendance was a trial Charles had never before been forced to endure. The knock on the hall door came in the midst of his struggles.

"Yes?" he called out rather irritably.

The door opened slowly, Jane appearing around it, a tea tray in her hands. "I thought—that is, you had said you wished some refreshment and then you left the parlour before it was brought."

Charles looked down at the silver tray laden with hot tea, old cognac, and brandysnap cookies. Uncomfortably aware of his cravat and dishevelled appearance, he spoke curtly. "Thank you."

Jane regarded him with a steady gaze. "Where would you like your tea?"

He looked around at the unfamiliar room, truly seeing it for the first time. "Oh, sorry—"

Jane moved towards a cherry-wood table near the fireplace. "Would this be all right? The tray is a bit heavy."

"I'm sorry." Charles apologised yet again, hurrying to reach the table ahead of Jane.

He removed the oil lamp, then picked up the framed portraits from the tapestry cloth and set them on the black marble fireplace mantel.

The Earl stood watching as Jane busied herself with the teapot, not daring to look up. "I understand from Great-Uncle Nigel you have not yet signed the purchase papers for the Abbey."

"That formality will be accomplished tomorrow morning," he replied repressively.

"I assure you, you will find it a poor purchase. I'll wager he hasn't even told you about the roof. It has to be completely redone." The words came rushing towards him, tumbling over one another. "And the windows, the casings have warped terribly, there's ever so many drafts!"

"The drafts can hardly be overlooked," he told her. "However, well-brought-up young ladies do not wager."

Quick anger flashed towards him before she dropped her eyes to the tray, puttering with the cookies and plates. "There is just everything wrong with the old place." Her gaze darted up to meet his, trying to gauge his reactions to her words, and then angled away again. "At night the wind positively howls through the halls."

"You have made your point, Miss Steadford. The Abbey is about to crumble to the ground."

"You will spend every penny you own just fixing it over."

"I rather doubt that," he said sardonically.

"Sugar?" she asked.

"You do not need to bother to serve me yourself, Miss Steadford." When she simply looked up at him, waiting, he replied, "Yes, please. And milk."

"Even if you spend your fortune on the repairs, the cost of running the Abbey will still be a constant drain on your pocket."

He took the Bristol porcelain cup and saucer of scalding hot tea from her, blowing on the liquid lightly. "I have found matters of finance to be beyond the area of intelligent conversation for young ladies."

He sounded so placidly superior. Angry words came to the tip of her tongue, but she bit them back, speaking through tight lips. "I am sorry to hear you have been surrounded by shatter-brained females." She was rewarded by a startled glance. "I, however, have been well schooled in the arts of estate management and know whereof I speak. I myself handle the account books."

"How bizarre," he drawled. "However, it is my decision, since it is, after all, my fortune. I should think, as a Steadford, you would applaud the possibility of someone refurbishing the Abbey."

"Why should I applaud it?" Jane asked bitterly. "It will no longer be *Steadford* Abbey. It will be *Warwick* Abbey!"

"I have no intention of changing the name of the house. I don't even intend to spend that much time in it as I have a London establishment and my family to consider."

Jane was shocked. "But surely you will bring your wife and family here. You can't buy it and then just abandon it."

He stirred his tea, taking a sip and considering Jane over the rim of his cup. She stood before him, defiant, her delicate fingers making little fists at her sides. Her face was pinched and pale with anger, except for twin splotches of angry blush at her cheeks. She looked adorable.

"I doubt that I would bring a wife here—assuming I had one— which I do not. As for my family, I rather expect the Duke would think I had lost all sense, asking him to close his London establishment and home in Kent and remove to the wilds of Dorset. Even if he were to be so minded as to allow his son to convince him, I assure you my mother would never leave the London Season, not for all the Abbeys in the world."

"Why then are you buying it?"

"You are the most bad-mannered, school-girlish young woman I have ever met. I don't know why I bother to answer you."

"You haven't answered me," Jane pointed out.

Exasperated, he drained the teacup and set it on the silver tray. "I have a notion to do something constructive with the time I am forced to spend in the country."

"Why are you forced to stay in the country?" she asked baldly.

He was shocked at her forwardness. "It is a long story and none of your business, Miss Steadford. I intend to enjoy myself renovating the Abbey. If I have the time," he amended.

Jane started to protest, then thought about his last words. "You said if you have the time?" she questioned.

Charles was becoming impatient. "My father has holdings in the New World, in the Americas, which may call me away. Now, I would appreciate your allowing me to continue my toilet in private."

"If you have all these other places, you don't need the Abbey," she blurted out. "You won't even be living here."

She looked so upset he found his anger dissolving. She really was a most appealing little creature. "It is, after all, an historic property," he told her. "I understand Queen Elizabeth herself stayed overnight on her annual progressions." He spoke blandly, repeating Nigel's sales speech.

"You don't care a fig about that and we both know it," Jane protested.

"I hardly see how you could know what I do or do not care about," Charles said, nettled back into irritation.

"You don't need the Abbey. You don't even plan on staying here, so what difference can any of that historical mishmash make to you in the New World?" Jane cried out. "This place is my grandmother's and she'll be forced onto her brother's largesse if you buy it. The Abbey means nothing to you, and it means her *life* to Gram!"

"Young lady, the Abbey is the property of Nigel Steadford, not of your grandmother."

"It was stolen from her."

"Not by me. May I point out, Miss Steadford, that your great-uncle is determined to sell the Abbey? If I do not buy it, someone else will. Besides, I may not have to leave England. If I am here, I will enjoy owning the Abbey and restoring it to its full glory. If I am not, I'm sure it win fetch a good price on the market again, especially with all that history behind it."

"A good price on the market!" Jane was incensed at his insensitivity. With a great deal of effort, she controlled her spleen. "Great-Uncle Nigel overstates the case. The truth is—the truth is—" she said and stopped.

Charles waited. "Yes?" he prompted politely as she simply stared at him.

Her eyes had grown even larger and darker with her concern, the flush of her cheeks a soft shell pink against skin the colour of ivory porcelain.

She wore a plain grey dress, high-collared and long-sleeved, her only ornament a small cameo brooch. Yet she was more appealing than any London debutante in expensive finery. He wondered idly why this was so.

She took a deep breath. "You must not buy the Abbey."

"I was already rather aware you are against the idea," the Earl of Warwick said as he turned his back on her. "If you have not the social grace to remove yourself, I shall have to continue to dress in your presence or dinner will be delayed unnecessarily."

"It's over an hour 'til dinnertime," Jane corrected impatiently.

His look was sardonic. "As I said, hardly enough time." He turned towards the pier-glass and pulled his half-knotted cravat apart, beginning to fold it again.

Jane's voice rose with her passion. "I tell you, you must not buy the Abbey, not if you value your life!"

Her words confounded him. He stared at her in the glass, then turned to face her. "Are you by any chance threatening me?" he asked.

"Of course not," she said indignantly.

Charles allowed himself a wry smile before turning back to the mirror. "I'm so glad. For a moment, I thought you might be threatening to murder me in my bed."

"I could do no such thing," she scoffed, "but the Ghost well could."

It took Charles a moment to reply. He finished tucking in his cravat, surveyed it with a dissatisfied glance, then looked at her in the glass, his expression dancing with humour. "That is really the outside of enough, Miss Steadford."

Jane saw derision in his eyes. "I do not jest," she declared.

"You can hardly be serious. A ghost? Is there more tea?" he asked.

She thought about throwing the teapot at him. Instead she bit her lip, her eyes blazing as she reached for his cup. "You'll learn to take him seriously," she predicted.

"A male ghost, is it?" He could not keep himself from smiling.

She trembled with anger and frustration. "Yes, it is."

"Too bad."

"I beg your pardon?" Her tone was frigid.

"I rather fancied owning a female ghost."

"Owning a ghost?" She stared at him.

"Why, yes. Miss Steadford, I must congratulate you. You've made the prospect of owning the Abbey totally irresistible. I must have it now. I shall own a ghost."

"I assure you none of this is a laughing matter. You are in danger."

"From ghosts, or from your talking my ear off?" He saw his shot hit the mark, her anger rising and darkening the colour of her cheeks. He smiled blandly. "I promise I shall be on my guard against any and all ghosts, and in particular your Ghost."

Jane still held his teacup. She thought of hurling it at him, or of turning her back on him and walking out of his rooms. She thought of the pleasure she would derive from slapping his insufferable face. Instead, she put milk and sugar into his tea and handed it to him. "If you need anything before dinner, please ring," she said in a voice of ice.

"I can't imagine that I should—unless your Ghost puts in an appearance—in which case I shall immediately call upon your help, I assure you," he said, smiling.

"You do not take my warnings seriously. I have done what I can," Jane said coldly. "If you need anything, please ring for one of the household help."

She swept out of the room, wounded pride holding her head high. Charles watched her leave, an amused expression still lighting his eyes. He took a deep swallow of the tea she had given him and gagged as a mouthful of salt met his palate. His surprise turned to anger and then to action. Two long strides brought him to the hallway door.

"Miss Steadford!" he thundered.

Jane was almost to the end of the hall. She looked back, her expression frozen. "Yes, Your Lordship?"

"I must tell you that putting salt in my tea is neither funny nor inducive to gaining either my sympathy or my support."

"I had no idea you had sympathy or support to give. As for your tea, I don't know what you can mean," she said as she came back towards him. "You are shouting loudly enough to be heard in the next county."

"I shall shout as I please."

The door to Nigel's rooms opened, Jarvis looking out towards Jane and the Earl.

"My master asked if there is something I can do for you, Your Lordship," Jarvis said, ignoring Jane.

The Earl of Warwick prepared a biting reply, then thought better of it. "No," he said, nearly strangling on the word. "Thank you, Jarvis."

"I am, of course, at your disposal until your man arrives, Your Lordship."

"Yes." Charles summoned all his willpower to answer the man politely. "Thank you." Charles glared at Jane but did not speak until Jarvis closed the door across the hall. "I have no doubt you would also shout your head off with a mouthful of salt in your tea," Charles told her.

"I don't know what you mean," Jane said.

"You very well know. You gave me tea with salt in it." His words were heated, but he kept his voice low.

"I gave you two cups of tea with sugar. You didn't complain about the first."

He glared at her. "I don't pretend to know how you did it, but you put salt in the sugar bowl. Come with me and I'll prove it."

He turned on his heel, marching back inside the suite.

Jane followed, standing in the doorway while he retrieved the sugar bowl and held it out towards her. She came forwards, taking it from him and sampling it with one finger. "Sugar," she told him.

Charles nearly grabbed the bowl from her, reaching his fingers in to taste it himself. The sweetness cloyed his tongue. "How did you do it?" he asked.

"Are you sure there's salt in your tea?" she asked.

"Of course I'm sure. Would you care to taste it?" he challenged.

"I take your word," she told him.

"Then how do you explain it?" he demanded.

Jane allowed herself a small smile. "It must be the Ghost."

He was ready to strike her, but used all the willpower he could muster to regain his self-control. "The Ghost indeed."

"Unless you need something else, Your Lordship, my grandmother is expecting me to attend her."

"By all means," he replied through gritted teeth.

Jane turned away, a small smile tugging at the corners of her mouth. Behind her she left a highly incensed and very dissatisfied-looking nobleman.

Dinner was served at seven-thirty prompt, Nigel, for once, congratulating his sister as the first courses of soup and relish removes were served. The burgundy was of the best, perfectly complementing the standing rib roast which was surrounded by potatoes, onions, and carrots. The winter meal was both appealing to the eye and delicious to the tastebuds.

Nigel even managed a smile in her general direction. "I must give you credit, Agatha. You have set a tolerably good table. I hope his lordship agrees."

"Most excellent," Charles replied in a perfunctory manner, his thoughts obviously elsewhere. His fork moved food about his plate, searching for signs of tampering.

The young footman, Timmy, stood silent beside the buffet, waiting to be motioned forwards by Lady Agatha to replenish plates or pour more wine.

"How on earth did you manage all this, Agatha?" Nigel asked suspiciously. His small eyes narrowed. "I trust you haven't been using any of the tenant rents," he said.

Agatha's eyes flashed. "Hardly," she said in clipped tones as she looked across the table at the Earl's plate. "Aren't you hungry,

Your Lordship? Would you care for something else?"

"No, thank you, Lady Agatha. I am quite content," he replied. Jane watched him test a tiny piece of the roast and then a vegetable.

"Are you sure we can't get you anything else? Perhaps something more to your liking?" Jane asked, looking the soul of innocence.

"Not yet," Charles said cryptically.

"Are you always such a cautious eater?" Jane asked him.

"Jane," her grandmother interrupted, "that is an impolite question."

Charles looked across the table at Lady Agatha. "You have no idea how impolite," he said dryly.

Agatha spoke slowly. "I take it you are definitely buying the Abbey, Your Lordship."

"He hasn't signed the papers yet," Jane told her grandmother.

Nigel swallowed his food. "Just a minute, there, miss. There is no reason to assume his lordship will not sign them." Nigel glared at Jane. "Is there? I heard some commotion earlier in the hall—"

"What are you both talking about?" Agatha asked.

"Perhaps you should ask your granddaughter," Nigel said. "If she has done anything to interfere with our business transaction, I shall hold you accountable, Agatha."

"There is nothing to discuss," Charles said quickly. "I have made no change in my plans."

"Therefore," Agatha said, "you will be staying on when my brother leaves?"

"I shall be making my home here for the immediate future," the Earl of Warwick told Agatha Steadford-Smyth.

Agatha studied the Earl's expression. "Then I can tell you I have decided to make use of your kind interim offer and have made arrangements for my granddaughter and myself to remove to the gatehouse in the morning."

"The morning?" Jane's consternation was writ large across her features.

Charles frowned. "There is no need for you to uproot yourself so quickly—"

"It's a demmed good idea," Nigel said. "Soonest done, soonest over."

"Tomorrow morning?" Jane stared at her grandmother. "*Why?*"

"We are a household of women, Your Lordship." Agatha ignored her brother and her granddaughter. "I have my young

granddaughter in my charge and her reputation to consider. My
brother proposes to leave immediately for his own property—"

"Demmed straight!" he put in. Seeing the Earl's surprise, Nigel
continued in an unctuous tone. "I have pressing business which
needs my personal attention."

Agatha began again. "Without my brother in the house, it would
not be proper for either of us to remain under the same roof with
an unmarried bachelor."

The thought of Jane and Agatha both having to protect their
virtue from the handsome young Earl made the two men stare
across the table at each other in a brief moment of communion,
the reasoning of women well beyond their comprehension. Nigel
scowled at Agatha, afraid the Earl would take affront at the
implication behind her words. He was still couching a biting
reply when the Earl of Warwick himself replied.

"All bachelors are unmarried, Lady Agatha."

Agatha responded in a very definite tone, "Nevertheless, I want
to ensure all the proprieties."

Nigel made a snorting sound. His sister cast him such a look, a
more sensitive man would have cringed. Agatha glanced towards
her granddaughter and saw a very rebellious young woman staring back.

Jane's attention turned towards the Earl, her glare apparently
unnoticed by the titled nobleman across the table. "Are we then
to be cast out upon the parish in the morning?"

Agatha intervened before Nigel could. "Jane, don't be so melodramatic."

Nigel added, "The Abbey's gatehouse is hardly . . . Good Lord,"
he said, his nose wrinkling. "What is that smell?"

The others reacted as smoke and a terrible stench began to fill
the room.

"We're on fire!" Nigel cried.

Agatha was gagging. Charles swallowed hard and helped the
old woman from the table as Jane held her nose and went to
Agatha's other side. "I've got her," Jane insisted, but Charles
paid no attention as they hurried the older woman out into the
hall.

Nigel was ahead of them, calling for the entire staff at the top
of his lungs and ordering them to put out the fire.

The Earl tried to gain Nigel's attention, but Nigel was beside
himself, dashing back and forth, wringing his hands, seeing his
profit going up in smoke before his very eyes. Men came running,
buckets in hand, as Charles and Jane helped Agatha, sagging and

coughing, to the blue parlour. Nigel came behind, a scented handkerchief to his nose.

"This isn't by chance. This is sabotage—downright sabotage. I assure you, Your Lordship, there is nothing wrong with this house. A few minor repairs and all will be well. I wouldn't want you to think this had anything to do with the house itself, or that it should affect the sale. This building has withstood *wars*. It will withstand a minor inconvenience such as this mad prank!"

"No doubt," Charles replied, glancing towards Jane.

Fannie ran into the parlour. "My God, Aggie, are you all right?"

Realising others were present, she stopped in her tracks, at a loss for words as the Earl and Agatha's brother Nigel stared, disbelieving the abigail's familiar tone.

Agatha did not deign to notice either their consternation or Fannie's. "I'm fine. Would you see to some food and drinks for our guests, please, Fannie? I'm afraid our dinner was completely ruined."

Fannie left, passing Jarvis who came to report to Nigel on the status of the fire. "There is none, sir."

"None?" Nigel was near hysteria. "None what?"

"No fire, sir."

"No fire? Then what was all that smoke and stench?" Nigel demanded.

"It seems to have come from the candles."

"Devils in hell," Nigel said, "what are you talking about?"

"The candles? That's not possible," Agatha said. "We've never had anything like this with our candles. We make them ourselves, and there's nothing in them that could cause something like this. I've never heard of such a thing." She looked around the room from one person to another. "How could that be possible?"

"They seem to be tallow candles which have been tampered with," Jarvis told her. "Dipped in some—ah—farm wastes."

"Wastes?" Agatha stared at Nigel's valet, trying to make sense of his words.

Nigel walked towards Jane, trying with his paltry inch of additional height to loom over her. His expression was very nearly demented. "How dare you?" he demanded.

"How dare *you* accuse me!" Jane shot back. Her grandmother looked towards Nigel, while Charles never took his eyes away from Jane.

"Well, we both know I certainly wouldn't be doing something to upset the household—let alone waste all that food. Why, there was a small fortune wasted in there tonight!"

"I didn't do anything," Jane insisted. "It must have been the Ghost."

"*What* ghost?" Nigel demanded.

"Jane, don't be a ninny," her grandmother put in.

Jane moved towards her grandmother. "It's no use pretending anymore, Gram. We must tell them the truth." Before her grandmother could speak, Jane hurried on, "He's been seen for years !"

"Good grief, child, what utter nonsense."

"At last," Charles said, "someone who is showing some simple common sense."

"Ghosts!" Agatha said disparagingly. "One silly maid who was a liar, and a thief to boot, got scared into confessing her theft because of her guilty conscience and a drapery which moved in the shadows. I never thought I'd hear my own granddaughter spouting such nonsense. You've always been such a practical girl, Jane."

"I rather think Jane is a little less convinced of ghostly sightings than she lets on," Charles told Agatha.

"I don't understand." Agatha gave the Earl a hard look.

"I think Jane only believes in enough ghost stories to scare me off purchasing this property," Charles said.

Agatha stared at him. "That is dishonest." She looked closely at her granddaughter. "Tell the Earl this is not true. Tell him you have not been underhanded, Jane."

Jane started to speak and then couldn't. Having never in her life lied to her grandmother, she subsided into moody silence.

Nigel glared at Jane. "You, miss, are incorrigible!"

Jane smiled as sweetly as she could. "Dear Great-Uncle Nigel, your wig is askew."

Nigel reached towards his wig, scowling. "Well I, for one, have had quite enough for one evening. I intend to retire to the peace and quiet of my bedroom."

Fannie opened the door, carrying a tray of food. Nigel swept past her, then turned back to take a dish of meat and bread with him.

Agatha stared at the food on the tray. "Mutton," she muttered under her breath.

Remembering his manners, Nigel turned to bow towards the Earl. "If you have no objection, Your Lordship, I shall retire to my chambers."

"As you wish," the Earl said. "I shall follow suit, I think. It has been a rather tiring day."

Nigel walked out of the room as Agatha apologised again for the interruption of dinner and for Jane's extraordinary behaviour. Jarvis was closing the dining room door. Nigel grimaced. "Waste. Nothing but waste." Jarvis took the plate from Nigel and followed him up the stairs. "I was right to sell this place."

"Yes, sir."

"And as usual, I've been much too generous with my relatives."

"Yes, sir." Jarvis opened the bedroom door for his master. "Would you care for something to drink, sir?"

"Bring up some brandy. You can undress me later."

"Certainly, sir."

Jarvis left as Nigel reached for his food, still grumbling as the door closed between them.

- *6* -

HARSH NORTH WINDS rolled across the Dorset hills as the gate-house clock tolled midnight. The moon was high above and far away in the black night sky. Winds gathered force from the hills and travelled down the moors, whistling around the Abbey's stone corners and rattling the windows. Cold air seeped through chinks in the Long Gallery window frames to rustle the heavy draperies.

The inhabitants of the household were long since abed and deep in dreams. In the guest suite, Nigel Steadford slept soundly, his nightcap pushed askew over one ear, his sleeping brain counting over and over the money the purchase of the Abbey would bring him.

Within the master suite, the Earl of Warwick had finally drifted off to an uneasy sleep, the strange bed and strange sounds of the unknown house having kept him wakeful far longer than the others. His long frame stretched out on the intricately carved walnut bed, comforters piled high against the night's chill.

Only the whine of the wind crept through the huge house, met by an occasional snore in the servants' quarters and elsewhere—until a resounding crash startled Charles into groggy wakefulness, so loud it set his heart thudding against his ribcage. The crash had come from beside his bed, and his every muscle was readied for danger as his mind slowly cleared.

"What the blue blazes—"

He bounded off the bed and reached for the lamp, but it wasn't there. He felt in vain for it on the night table, the room pitch-black and alien.

He peered towards the windows but could see nothing save utter darkness. Groping his way with his hands, Charles started towards the far wall of windows, barking his shins on a table and then a chair which seemed to have been deliberately placed in his path. Swearing aloud, he reached for the drapes and pulled them wide open. The moon cast an angle of pale-white light across his angry face and the room behind him.

He felt for the window latch in the shadows. Finding it locked, he shoved the drapes back out of the way, thus letting in enough light to see his way to the sitting-room door and then across to the hallway.

"Jarvis," he shouted at the top of his lungs, his booming voice reverberating in the empty hall. After a moment, the door to Nigel's chambers opened and Jarvis peered out, an oil lamp in his hand.

"Did you ring, Your Lordship?"

"No, I did not ring. I shouted! Someone's in my rooms," Charles accused as he continued to block the doorway. "Come help me catch them."

Jarvis shuffled across the hall, yawning. The commotion from the hallway ushered Nigel out after him a moment later, tying his robe about him.

"What is it now?" Nigel asked rather peevishly as he came into Charles's sitting-room.

"Stay where you are," Charles barked at Nigel. "Guard that doorway with your life!"

"My—life?" Nigel said weakly.

"Someone was in here and I'm going to catch her," the Earl told them both.

"Her?" Jarvis repeated, blinking rapidly as Charles used the valet's lamp to find his own and light it.

The table lamp blazed into brilliance, and Charles looked around the sitting-room. Nothing seemed amiss.

"Stay by that door," the Earl commanded Nigel while the Earl himself headed back into the bedroom beyond. Jarvis slowly followed, gazing about in every direction.

"I knew this was moved," Charles said grimly as he found and lit the bedside lamp which was on the floor beside the bed.

"And look where that chair is."

"Perhaps you placed it there when you went to bed," Nigel said.

"I told you to stay at the outer door, Steadford. I don't want her to get away with this." Charles held the lamp high, turning slowly in a circle to examine all four corners of the bedroom.

"They said there is a ghost," Jarvis put in hesitantly, still gazing about, nervously expecting something to jump out at them.

"Bah! I would as lief believe in fairies," Charles snapped.

Meanwhile, Nigel was complaining from the hallway door in the next room, demanding to know what was going on.

"I see nothing," Charles said, looking grim.

"Perhaps a mouse—" Jarvis began on a hopeful note, only to be cut off in midsentence by the Earl's growl.

"Mouse, my eye. It would have had to be an elephant to make such noise, not to mention the moving of the chairs and lamps!" As he spoke, Charles prowled the room, stopping finally at a small doorway. He turned the knob. It was locked. "Ah ha! Where does this lead?"

"I don't know, Your Lordship," Jarvis responded.

"Steadford," Charles roared, "get in here."

Nigel Steadford came quickly, already lamenting the sale of the Abbey slipping away from him. "Certainly, Your Lordship. I was merely doing as you bid me."

"Never mind that. Where does this door lead?"

"To my sister's suite, the companion of this one." As Nigel spoke, his manservant Jarvis came nearer Charles, peering at the door in question.

"Then that's how she did it," Charles pronounced triumphantly.

"She?" Nigel stared at the Earl. "Are you saying my sister came into your room in the middle of the night? She has always been a trial, but I never knew her to sleepwalk."

"Not your sister—your niece—Jane!" Charles roared her name.

Nigel would put nothing past Jane. Even so, he was a little confused. Before he could collect his thoughts, Jarvis spoke. "I rather think it impossible that anyone left by this door, Your Lordship."

"Oh, yes?" Charles glared at the man. "Why?"

"Because, Your Lordship, it's locked."

"And so?" Charles bellowed.

"The key is on this side," Jarvis answered as quietly as he could get the words out.

Charles looked down to the keyhole and saw the brass key neatly fitted into its slot. "She was here and I'm going to prove it," he insisted, unlocking the door and yanking it open.

A darkened dressing room met his eyes. He heard movement and hurried forward towards the door on the other side of the dressing room. In the next room someone was stirring. Charles pounced in as if expecting to slay a dragon, his lamp held aloft. He was, in fact, ready to do battle or to box her ears if necessary.

What he found was a sleepy-eyed Fannie. She sat up in her bed in the abigail's room, rubbing her eyes and staring at him as if he were the devil himself. He was behind the light. All she could see was a giant coming towards her across the shadowy room.

"Come one step nearer and I'll scream," she told him hoarsely.

"Scream away," Charles said grimly.

Fannie opened her mouth to call for help as the Earl placed the lamp on a table and raised its wick, then began prowling around her room. Fannie realised it was the Earl in the same moment that Jarvis and Nigel came through the door, moving slowly, looking every which way as they crept forwards behind Charles.

"Good Lord Above, have you all gone mad, scaring defenceless women out of their wits in the middle of the night?"

"Who came through here?" Charles demanded of her.

"What are you talking about?" Fannie demanded back. "No one's awake but you lunatics."

Nigel approached her. "My dear woman, keep a civil tongue in your head. This is a Peer of the Realm you are addressing."

Fannie sniffed. "In my day Peers of the Realm didn't come into ladies' bedrooms uninvited."

"And I suppose you didn't hear any noise from my rooms a few minutes ago," Charles said grimly.

"I've heard plenty and it's all coming from the three of you," Fannie retorted, grabbing her bedclothes tightly against her ample bosom.

"And I suppose your mistress is still sound asleep with all this noise in her outer chamber," Charles shot back at her.

"My mistress is hard of hearing, and I never knew till now how much I could envy her that," Fannie told him crisply. "Once she's asleep she wouldn't hear Gabriel's trumpet calling her."

"And is Jane deaf, too?" Charles shouted.

"No, she's not and neither am I," Fannie snapped. "So there's no reason to raise your voice to me."

"Keep a civil tongue I said, woman," Nigel demanded.

"You're not my mistress and the day you are, I'll quit my position," Fannie told Nigel.

"Where is she?" the Earl demanded.

"My mistress is in her bed, as are all Christian people!"

"I mean Jane," Charles roared.

"I assume she's in her bed as well," Fannie replied in very nearly the same tone.

"We shall see about that." The Earl turned on his heel and marched towards the hallway door.

"Where does he think he is going?" Fannie asked Nigel. "You can't let him barge into Jane's bedroom in the middle of the night!

She's a gently reared girl, she's your grandniece. She needs your protection!"

"She's as gently reared as a viper, and if anyone needs protection it's the Earl." Nigel walked out of Fannie's bedroom, calling Jarvis to follow.

Charles was striding down the long hall, wrenching doors open and glaring inside the rooms, his lamp raised high to reveal one empty room after another.

He finally found Jane, sitting up in bed and rubbing her eyes.

"What is it?" she asked, yawning.

The Ninth Earl of Warwick made a valiant effort to contain his anger. He spoke through clenched teeth. "I am trying to find out who has ruined my night's sleep."

She blinked at him, the light bright in his hand. "Well, I don't have to look far to see who has ruined mine."

"You are, without a doubt, the most vexatious creature it has ever been my misfortune to encounter."

"It's not my fault you wouldn't listen to me."

"Is that a veiled threat, Miss Steadford?"

"Of course not," Jane said rather crossly. "I am speaking of the Ghost."

"There's no ghost!" Charles Edward Graham roared at the girl.

"Your Lordship." Nigel appeared in the doorway, wringing his hands. "What has she done *now*?" He glared at the young woman sitting in her bed. "What have you done now?"

"I don't know what you're talking about."

"No? And I suppose you're dressed for bed under all those covers." He took two long strides to her bedside and yanked the covers off the girl.

"What are you doing?" she cried.

She wore only a thin white nightgown, high-necked and long-sleeved. Jane grabbed the covers from his hands and glared up at the Earl. Charles towered over her, ready to slap her silly and unable to do anything but glare back at eyes which despised him.

"If you're through bullying me, will you please leave, or am I to be subjected to more of your unforgivable excesses?"

"*My excesses?*" Charles roared, totally frustrated.

Jane placed her fingers delicately in front of her mouth and yawned. "If you are through yelling, please close the door on your way out."

Charles ground his teeth. "I can assure you, Miss Steadford, no matter how provoking you attempt to be, my mind is made up and nothing you can possibly do will change it. Steadford Abbey is mine."

"Your robe is open," Jane said.

Charles glanced down at his white cotton nightshirt, belting his satin robe tighter about him before looking back up, his face a frozen mask. Without another word, he stalked out of Jane's bedroom and slammed the door with a vengeance. In the hall Jarvis was already moving back towards Nigel's rooms while Nigel waited for Charles, positively beaming. "I am so glad you are firm in your resolve, Your Lordship."

"So I see," snapped the irritated nobleman.

"If there is anything I can do—"

"You can go to bed," Charles said ungraciously. Nigel followed him down the hall, but Charles slammed his door in the older man's face.

Inside the master suite, Charles set down the lamp he was carrying and retrieved the sitting-room lamp. Then, thinking better of it, he took both lamps with him into the master bedroom, placing them on his night table and glaring about him at the furniture.

As the others sought out their beds, the Ninth Earl of Warwick prowled the master bedroom, tapping the wall panels, feeling for seams, trying to find the secret access to the room. There had to be one. He knew someone had been in his room, someone who had not got out past him. He had awakened immediately at the sound of the crash, and no doors had opened or closed until he called for Jarvis.

In her own room, Jane lay very still, listening to the house quiet down around her. In the pitch-black darkness she reached to take off her slippers and put them on the floor beside her bed.

She lay back, a small smile forming at the memory of his irritation. Then, she remembered his words: Steadford Abbey is mine. A single large tear slipped down her cheek. Steadford Abbey belonged to Gram no matter what all the solicitors and paperwork said.

Her eyes closed upon the darkness all around her. She did not see the thick velvet drapes move at her window, and if she *had* seen, she would not have been concerned. She would have assumed it was only the hilltop winds drafting through chinks in the window casement.

THE ABBEY HOUSEHOLD was thrown into disarray at first light Saturday morning, with packing boxes all over Agatha's rooms and the upstairs halls. Fannie supervised two young maids and Timmy the footman as they began the job of packing up a lifetime.

Jane did as her grandmother bid, helping the others and organising her own few possessions. Her disapproval was silent but visible in the speaking glances she gave her grandmother when they passed in the halls.

Agatha handed Fannie an armful of patched linens after Jane had gone downstairs to see what kitchen equipment they would need for their temporary quarters in the long-unused gatehouse.

"I'm worried about Jane," Agatha confided to Fannie. "She's taking this very hard."

"She's not some vapourish little miss. She'll be all right," was Fannie's opinion.

But Agatha's concern went deeper. She smoothed the linens she was folding, a pensive expression furrowing her pale brow. "I don't understand why the Earl is being so accommodating to us, allowing us to stay on as long as we wish in the gatehouse. He has no reason to do us any favours. I'll warrant Nigel has given him an earful of all our worst traits."

"The Earl seems to be a gentleman," Fannie said.

Agatha's look spoke volumes. "Men may *seem* to be gentlemen, but never believe it for an instant. They are all alike. They are selfish to the core."

"Perhaps he's taken a fancy to our Jane."

"Nonsense," Agatha answered with asperity. "He barely knows her."

"I can just feature it," Fannie said, her eyes taking on a dreamy quality. "She could move us all back here where we belong. Think of it—our Jane a countess just like in a fairy tale." Fannie's eyes looked inwards, picturing a rich and happy future for the girl she'd helped raise.

"You are beginning to sound like those trashy romance novels you read," Agatha said. "Act your age and get on with your work."

"He would be such a handsome husband and quite the catch of the Season," Fannie replied.

"I don't trust him," Agatha said.

"Whyever not?"

"He reminds me of someone," the old woman replied.

"Who?" Fannie asked.

"At the rate you're working, we'll be at this one pile all day." Agatha's words turned testy as she backed away from the topic she herself had brought up. She was not about to discuss her youth with Fannie.

"Gram." Jane came towards where they stood. "Have you seen the inside of the gatehouse? It's a mess."

"A little dusty, that's all."

"Dusty? The place is full of cobwebs," Jane declared.

"Don't exaggerate so, Jane. I am firmly committed to moving to the gatehouse this very day," Agatha Steadford told granddaughter and servant alike. "I have never in my life pushed myself on another or stayed one moment where I was not welcome. And I will not have your name bandied about as village gossip by staying here one more night. If we have to leave this house today with only the clothes on our backs, I promise you we will leave it today."

She stared them both down, her dark eyes challenging, daring them to argue. "I want no more conversation on the topic," she told Fannie and then turned toward Jane. "And from you I have had quite enough of the sullens. I am as cross as I can be with you, Jane, for so jeopardising your reputation as to take unchaperoned carriage rides across the county, let alone an unchaperoned ride with a *bachelor*." She spit out the last word as if it were a piece of rotten fruit. "I am shocked and disappointed with both of you for going behind my back and asking my brother for anything. I will *not* be in this house by nightfall. Is that understood?"

"I'm sorry, Grandmother." Jane's eyes held tears, her grandmother softening a little at the sight of them.

"Jane," Agatha continued, "for the time that we are still on the Abbey property, before we remove to Eastborne with Nigel, I want you to stay away from the Earl. Do you understand? I do not want you to have anything to do with the man."

"What would I have to do with him?" Jane demanded. "I can't abide the insufferable, odious toad!"

Agatha looked pleased and a great deal relieved. Fannie, however, being wiser in the ways of human nature, was not so very sure Jane's vehemence meant what her grandmother thought—or even what Jane herself might think.

In the midst of the early-morning household confusion, a carriage arrived and deposited on the doorstep a tall thin man of indeterminate age and extremely aristocratic bearing.

"I am Pickering," the man told a young footman who was manhandling a trunk down the wide stone steps towards a waiting cart. The three words had the same inflection that might have accompanied the statement "I am King of England."

"Yes, sir?" The boy stared in awe at the impeccably dressed man. "Are you another lord, then, sir? We've never seen one before, let alone two." Timmy lapsed into silence, afraid he had overstepped the bounds of propriety from the imperious scowl which greeted his words.

Pickering's quizzing glass was planted firmly in his eye. "We can hardly be so far in the country as all that," Pickering said in his obviously city-bred voice, but he was secretly pleased for being taken as Aristocracy. His next words spoke of untold pride in his position. "*I* am the Earl of Warwick's gentleman's gentleman." The title sounded like a knighthood as it rolled off Pickering's extremely correct tongue.

"Oh, cor, ain't you the one!"

Pickering gave up on the boy, turning towards the open front door and escorting himself across the threshold.

"They all be upstairs," the boy called after the man's man.

Pickering found himself in the empty, echoing front hall, shaking his head at the ramshackle running of this establishment. He started up the stairwell, gingerly picking his way, looking for someone in authority to whom he could present himself. He found Jane, weighed down with a pile of bedding and staggering a little under the load.

"Girl," he spoke in an authoritarian tone, just the tone which was needed to bring these servants slap up to the mark. "Where is your mistress or master?"

Jane peered over the bedding. "I don't have a mistress or a master. Who are you?"

"I am Pickering, gentleman's gentleman to the Earl of Warwick."

"Lord, how many of you is he bringing?" Jane asked.

Pickering almost lost his eyeglass. "I beg your pardon?"

"You've no need to apologise. It's not your fault. His precious lordship is in there." Jane nodded her head towards the door to the master suite sitting-room, then swept past the bemused valet before he had a chance to recover his voice.

Pickering tapped gently on the door the young woman had indicated. Opening it carefully, he peered into an empty sitting-room and across to the bedroom beyond. The valet put his personal valise down and walked to the doorway. In the shadowy room his employer's long frame was stretched from one end of the bed to the other, tangled bedclothes bunched all around him.

"Your Lordship?" Pickering moved across the room to open the drapes. "Your Lordship, it's past your normal waking hour."

Charles rolled over, tangling the bedclothes further. He strained against them, coming awake and feeling as if he were being held down. "Confound it, if this doesn't stop—" His eyes opened as Pickering reached to help the Earl extricate himself from the sheets and blankets.

The groggy Earl scowled upwards. "Pickering?"

"Yes, Your Lordship, I have arrived." The valet looked from the Earl's tousled hair to his growing beard and clucked over the young nobleman. "And it would seem, I have arrived none too soon."

"By God, that's the plain truth. You will not believe what has been going on in this establishment."

Pickering thought back to his arrival just past. "Your Lordship, I would believe anything of these people."

"Confound that confounded girl and her confounded stubbornness!"

"I beg your pardon, sir?"

"It's about time somebody did!" was the Earl's only reply.

Pickering took the Earl's aggravation in stride. After all, the poor man had been roughing it without Pickering's peerless help for over a week. In those circumstances, any man would lose his good humour.

Jane insisted Agatha take time to eat at least a little breakfast. They arrived in the dining room to find Nigel already tucking into eggs, kippers, toast, and tea.

He glowered at them, receiving a fulminating look from Jane, who was ready to do battle at the first opportunity with the author of their distress.

"Good morning, Nigel," Agatha said without a smile. "I understand you had some trouble during the night."

"*I* had no trouble, Agatha, but the Earl was inconvenienced beyond endurance." He reached for a quizzing glass hung from a black ribbon around his neck and scowled at Jane. "If anything happens to dissuade his purchase of this property, God is my witness, I shall put it on the public auction block the very next minute. And I assure you I shall not be so full of largesse as to allow you to stay on in the gatehouse."

Jane took toast and tea from the buffet and plunked herself down on the chair directly across from her great-uncle. "And I assure *you*, Uncle Nigel, the thought that you would show any largesse whatsoever never entered my mind."

"Jane—" Agatha spoke repressively. "Ladies sit down properly. They don't bounce into their chairs."

Nigel gave his sister a look. "If you think there is any hope of ever training this hoyden into anything resembling a lady, I fear you are the most optimistic person I have ever met in my life. And, furthermore, if she so much as—"

His words trailed off as the Earl of Warwick entered the dining room, dressed for riding. Nigel Steadford waited anxiously as the Earl walked towards the foot of the table.

Agatha stood up from her usual chair at the head of the table. "Your Lordship, I'm sorry. This is your place now." She moved to a chair next to Jane as the Earl spoke.

"Nonsense, please, it is not important."

"It is to me," the old woman said firmly.

Charles hesitated, feeling Jane's unwelcoming gaze upon him. He walked to the head of the table. The moment he sat down, Pickering appeared, as if by magic, from the pantry doorway, hurrying to fill a china plate from the buffet.

"Good morning," the Earl of Warwick said politely to Nigel as Pickering placed his food before his master and withdrew.

"Good morning," Nigel answered as heartily as he knew how. "Wonderful morning, isn't it? Weather's quite fairing up. How did you sl—" Nigel clamped his mouth shut.

The Earl looked directly at Jane. She was wearing a white mobcap from which strands of flaxen hair escaped to curl around her brow and the nape of her neck. A serviceable white cotton apron covered most of her old grey workdress.

"Good morning, Miss Steadford."

"Is it?" she inquired of him, her eyes moody.

He spoke pleasantly. "I think I shall send for a horse. I feel like riding my new estate and getting to know the property."

"Did you rest well, Your Lordship?" Jane asked, Nigel nearly choking on the tea he was swallowing. "Or did you have more visitations?" she continued.

Charles smiled blandly. "I'm sure you, above all, would already know if I had."

His attitude irritated her almost past endurance. "I'm sure we all would," she said tartly, "since you are in the habit of rousing the entire household with your least inconvenience."

"Jane Steadford!" Her great-uncle spoke sharply.

"Not quite the entire household," Charles answered pleasantly.

Agatha was staring at him, her dark eyes gauging the man. She did not look as if she liked what she saw. "Jane," she spoke more bluntly than she intended, "are you through with your food? We have work to do."

"I saw the packing crates when I came down this morning, Lady Agatha. Before you leave," Charles began, as Agatha's penetrating gaze returned to rake his eyes, "I would appreciate a few moments of your time."

"Of course," she said. "Jane."

Jane pushed back her plate and followed her grandmother from the room.

After they had left, Nigel flashed the Earl his most ingratiating smile. "If you're ready to conclude our business, Your Lordship, I should like to depart at the earliest opportunity."

"I don't blame you," Charles said sourly, Nigel losing his smile instantly.

He spoke quickly. "I assure you, you will be very glad you have bought the Abbey."

Charles stared at the man. "Has that girl always been like this?" he asked.

"Oh, always, Your Lordship." Nigel sighed prodigiously and to rather good effect, or so he thought. "You see, she's not quite right." He tapped his forehead. "In the attic, don't you know."

"What in blue blazes are you implying?" Charles asked, his brow furrowing.

"No inference, my dear Earl. Simple fact. She's quite daft. Comes by it honestly, though. Can't really blame the twig for the rot in the tree trunk, can we?" Nigel leaned forwards. "My sister is, as you can see, quite the eccentric. Her daughter married a cousin. That's why Jane's a Steadford, worse luck. And you know what happens with intermarriage." He tapped his head again.

Charles stared at the man and then stood up. "Bring the papers you want signed and ask Jarvis to scare up the bailiff. I want to ride the land."

"Actually, I have the papers right here," Nigel began, but the Earl cut him off.

"Yes, well, find the bailiff first."

"Certainly." Nigel was quite spry for his age and nearly sprang to his feet. Charles left the room as Nigel smiled after him, rubbing his hands together. "Yes," Nigel said to the empty room. "I have carried it off."

Then, a dark thought crossed his mind. What if Agatha had talked against the sale to the bailiff? What if he was uncooperative, or too truthful about the state of the estate grounds and the upkeep needed?

Nigel Steadford marched as fast as his short legs would carry him out of the room, searching for Jarvis. He was determined to have a very private word with the bailiff before the Earl spoke with the man. Nigel would remind the man exactly who paid the bills and what would happen to his job if he did not encourage the sale.

While Nigel cornered the estate bailiff, Charles sent Pickering to find Lady Agatha. He found her with Jane in the topmost attic, staring helplessly at several lifetime's accumulations.

"I don't know what to do with it all," Agatha was saying as Jane heard footsteps behind them.

Pickering bowed his head slightly towards Lady Agatha. "His Lordship requires your presence in the library, Your Ladyship."

"Oh, he does, does he?" Jane began, but her grandmother cut her off with a wave of her hand.

"I shall be down directly." The old woman looked towards Jane. "I find I shall have to ask him the favour of leaving some of our things behind until I can go through them."

Pickering stood where he was, watching the girl he had mistaken for a servant upon his arrival. He recovered his composure and favoured her with the tiniest fraction of a bow. "I must apologise for my behaviour earlier, Miss Steadford."

Jane looked at him quizzically. "Whatever for?" she asked, earning a shocked look.

"For my unforgivable forwardness upon my arrival."

"I don't know what you're talking about," Jane replied.

Pickering nearly gritted his teeth. Her manners were worse than deplorable. They were positively shocking. "I am speaking of my mistaking you for a serving girl," he was forced to explain. "I do wish you would accept my apologies."

She shrugged, earning even more distaste. Well-brought-up

young ladies did not shrug their shoulders like a common street merchant.

"Being a maid is an honest occupation," Jane was saying as she followed her grandmother down the attic stairwell.

"I must insist on your accepting my apology," he said stiffly.

"Oh, all right, if it means so very much to you," Jane replied ungraciously.

Pickering's eyes rolled skywards. Amazed at his own patience, he followed the heathen girl and her grandmother towards the lower floors. How the woman had endured raising this urchin was beyond imagining.

Agatha sent Jane with Fannie to oversee the cleaning of the gatehouse, then continued downstairs to the library and the waiting Earl. In the library Nigel held a sheaf of papers in his hands and was beaming at the Earl when Agatha walked into the room. He was so cheerful he was even disposed to be pleasant to his sister.

"Well, Aggie, the deed is done."

"I could have guessed as much," she replied quietly, then turned towards the Earl and the bailiff. "You wished to speak to me?"

"Yes." Charles dismissed the bailiff and glanced at Nigel, who did not seem ready to leave. "Is there anything else?" Charles asked pointedly.

"What? Oh, no, old chap—oh, sorry."

Nigel thought about arguing. One of his sister's most besetting faults was a penchant for total honesty. However, the signed sale papers were already in his hands. Nigel Steadford gave a stiff little bow and left his sister with the new owner of Steadford Abbey.

There followed a moment of silence which Agatha finally broke. "I'm afraid I must ask you a favour."

"Anything which is in my power, I shall gladly grant," Charles said formally.

"I find I must leave quite a few belongings behind at least a short time. There is no way to move them all today."

"There is no need to move them all today. There is no need for you, yourself, to leave today, for that matter," Charles told her.

"Yes. There is." Agatha did not explain again.

Charles came around the desk, bringing a large parchment with him and handing it over. "I do not agree, but I respect your decision. I wanted to see you to give you this."

"What is it?" Agatha asked.

"This is your copy of the deed of sale," he said.

She looked surprised. "I don't understand. I have no ownership in the property. It belonged to my father and afterwards to my husband, who lost it to my brother." There was bitterness in her tone.

"Gambling debts, I believe, were responsible." Charles studied her.

Her face closed over, her eyes expressionless. "That was a long time ago," was all she said. "However, the point is I am not involved in the transaction."

"You are now," Charles told her.

"I beg your pardon?"

"If you look at the paper I gave you, you'll see the gatehouse has been deeded to you and your granddaughter."

Agatha looked stunned. "I—I beg your pardon?" For once in her life she was at a complete loss for words. "I don't understand. Nigel said nothing about including me."

"Nevertheless, the gatehouse is deeded to yourself and to your granddaughter for as long as either of you shall live."

The old woman sat down. She looked at the paper she held, reading it slowly, trying to digest what had just happened.

"You will not have to remove to your brother's estates," Charles explained. "You will be able to stay on here, in the county that so admires you from what I hear."

"I can't imagine who would admire me," Agatha said faintly. "Or where you heard such nonsense." She stood up. "If you'll excuse me, I must speak to my brother."

"As you wish." Charles watched the old woman leave. Her carriage was regal, her figure still trim and straight as she walked away.

It wasn't until Agatha entered the guest bedroom and tried to thank her brother that she found out this arrangement was not Nigel's idea.

"Are you saying it wasn't you who suggested we stay on in the gatehouse?" Agatha wasn't sure she had heard him correctly. She watched her brother, trying to comprehend what was going on.

"I mean exactly what I said," Nigel answered waspishly. Agatha was his older sister and she had always irritated him past endurance. He directed Jarvis in the packing of his inexpressibles and unmentionables as he answered his sister, "The Earl insisted the clause giving you the gatehouse for lifetime use be part of the sale or he would not sign. I have no idea why he should want to be so magnanimous to strangers, especially since your protégée Jane has been bound and determined to interfere with his comfort and convenience at every turn."

Nigel felt better after he relieved himself of the words. He looked rather pompous as he stood before her, one hand placed in a Napoleonic position within his vest. "I can't even imagine why he should bother," Nigel ended.

"I can," Agatha Steadford-Smyth said grimly.

She turned on her heel and left the room, determined to have Jane out of the Abbey immediately. There was only one possible explanation for this unexpected largesse, and it confirmed her worst suspicions about men in general and this man in particular.

He had barely arrived and he already had designs on Jane's virtue.

Agatha squared her shoulders. Jane might be young and inexperienced, but her grandmother was not. She would protect Jane at all costs. Her sweet, innocent, and naïve granddaughter was not to become some rich man's toy.

- 8 -

NIGEL'S CARRIAGE WAS waiting at the front door when Jane arrived back at the Abbey to help supervise the removal of more trunks of clothing and linens and kitchen utensils and plates and silverware. The door to the study was open, Nigel's good-byes to the Earl audible as she passed.

"If there is the slightest problem, I am at your disposal, Your Lordship."

The Earl's reply was oblique as they walked into the wide echoing hallway. "I'm surprised the books are so well kept. I had rather thought they would have been neglected."

Jane, just past and behind them in the hall, stiffened. She resolutely headed up the stairs.

Nigel was in an expansive mood having accomplished his purpose. "Oh, no. Jane has handled the books, as I told you. She is, amongst other unhappy things, a bookworm. She's the one who's been keeping the accounts, a most unfeminine pursuit of course. She's probably fair on her way to being a blue-stocking."

"Quite a combination, hereditary insanity and book-learned intelligence," Charles said dryly.

He heard movement and glanced upwards. Jane was halfway up the broad front stairs.

"Poor girl." Nigel shook his head as if in true sadness. "I hope you can forgive all that ghost nonsense she was putting about."

Charles replied in a tone loud enough to carry up the stairwell. "My dear Steadford, it was the talk which convinced me I must buy the Abbey. After all, how many men have the chance to own their own ghost?"

His words were no more than out of his mouth before a resounding crash made both men jump. They wheeled around. A large vase had fallen, or been thrown, from the upstairs gallery and had smashed against the floor directly behind them, breaking into tiny shards which were still scattering across the entrance hall.

As they stared in open-mouthed stupefaction at what had so nearly hit them, a huge portrait came falling down from the Long Gallery overhead. Jumping back out of the way, Charles looked up to see Jane pressed against the wall at the top of the stairs, her eyes large with fright.

"What the devil do you think you're doing?" Charles thundered.

Nigel recovered from his shock to shake his fist at his grandniece in impotent rage. "I warn you, you'll be held responsible for every bit of damage, young lady. None of these things you're breaking belongs to you."

Jane was mute. She stared at the shambles on the floor below as Nigel reached to pick up the portrait. "Someone should give that girl a proper melting! Look at this. It's my father's portrait."

Charles *was* looking at it, then up to where the slim young woman still stood at the top of the stairs. "How did you do it?" Charles asked her. There was no answer from above.

Nigel inspected the elaborately carved and painted frame. "A piece right here has been broken, but at least the canvas wasn't torn."

"How?" the Earl of Warwick asked.

"I beg your pardon?"

"How did she do it? We're twenty feet below and at least thirty feet beyond her." Charles hefted the portrait. "And this weighs at least thirty pounds, maybe more. I'm not sure even I could throw it that far."

Nigel looked up at the tall, formidable-looking Earl, his face pinched into peevish lines, his side-whiskers quivering with annoyance. "How should I know how she did it? How should I know how she does anything?"

Charles looked back towards Jane, who was still staring at the portrait, wide-eyed. Her gaze rose to meet his, and then she turned away. Finally galvanised into action, she ran away from them, disappearing from view upstairs.

"That girl looked positively frightened," Charles said, more to himself than to Nigel.

"She should look frightened after what I just said to her," was Nigel's response.

While vases and portraits crashed down inside, Jarvis stood with Pickering in the chill air of the wide portico, commiserating about the lot of the latter, having to stay on in such a disreputably managed household.

"If I were you," Jarvis recommended, "I'd weed out the staff straightaway and bring in people who understand discipline and the respect due a gentleman's gentleman and his master." He paused to lend weight to his words. "I've found it's always best to begin as you intend to go on."

Pickering agreed wholeheartedly. The idea of a household without a proper butler, with only two footmen, and such excessive informality between master and servant would have been unthinkable in London. He was waxing eloquent upon the subject when the two were interrupted by their masters' arrivals on the porch.

Two burly farmhands trailed along behind Nigel and the Earl, carrying a double-sized brass-bound trunk between them.

"Excuse us, sirs," one of the men said as they neared the doorway, his thick country accent colouring the words.

Charles stepped out of the way. Nigel glanced at them and then proceeded at his own pace towards his own carriage. The farmhands struggled through the doorway, slowed by Nigel's deliberate obstruction of their progress. A farm cart loaded high with boxes, cases, and trunks waited to one side of the wide stone steps with Nigel's serviceable black carriage in front of it.

"I'd best say my good-byes to you, Your Lordship." Nigel spotted his sister and great-niece behind the farm men, each carrying a personal valise. "And to you, Agatha," he added unwillingly, ignoring Jane.

"Good riddance," Jane said.

"Well, really!" Nigel replied.

"Yes, really," Jane told him and cast a baleful eye in the Earl's direction as she passed him. He merely smiled politely.

"Lady Agatha." Fannie came bustling behind them. "I've got one more little thing to fetch. I'll be with you directly. Oh, excuse me, Your Worships," she said to the Earl and Nigel. "I didn't mean to interrupt."

Agatha had reached the step where her brother stood. She looked him in the eye. "Good-bye, Nigel."

"I hope you'll soon be entirely settled in the gatehouse," Nigel replied.

She gave him a thin-lipped smile. "On *that* point, Nigel, we agree." She looked at the overpiled cart. "Jane, we shall walk."

"Nonsense," Charles came down the last steps, "Your brother is leaving, and there is more than enough room in his carriage for the two of you."

Nigel, who had not intended to have anything further to do

with either his disliked sister or her perfectly odious charge, nonetheless did not want to look less than a gentleman in the Earl's eye. "Of course," he said. "I was about to suggest the very same arrangement."

"How kind." Jane's voice dripped with sarcasm.

Nigel stiffened. Agatha glanced at the distant gatehouse, then gave Jane a little push towards the carriage. "We thank you," Agatha told her brother.

Charles watched as the ladies were handed up, and the carriage departed down the winding drive towards the distant gatehouse. The farm cart, top-heavy with crates and trunks, followed with the horse's hot breath creating little vapours of steam in the wintry air.

Fannie came out of the house, fastening her cloak, and stopped beside the Earl, staring after the carriage. "Oh my, I must have taken too long."

"I'll stop them for you."

"Oh, no, sir!" Fannie said quickly. "There's no need."

The Earl observed the woman's empty hands. "Did you find what you sought?"

"What? Oh, yes, Your Lordship. I was just—checking to make sure Lady Agatha had—remembered her, her jewel box." Fannie tried to look innocent.

"And had she?" he asked.

"Yes, Your Lordship," Fannie replied. She watched the Earl turn to reenter the Abbey. "It's truly a shame, such a big house and you alone and all, Your Lordship."

He looked at her quizzically. "I beg your pardon?"

"And you shouldn't go taking our Jane's attitude to heart, either. She's a little upset right now, but you'll soon see her in a different light. She's a good girl and a beauty as can plainly be seen. She doesn't mean any harm."

Charles stared at the servant. "Are you positive of that?" he asked dryly.

"Oh yes, Your Worthiness. Our Jane will make a good and proper wife one day."

Charles wasn't sure how to answer this non sequitur, finally replying, "I rather doubt it."

Fannie smiled. "I'm not saying she might not need a husband with a firm hand, of course."

Charles Edward Graham, Ninth Earl of Warwick, thought he saw the serving woman wink at him before she turned away. He stared after her in total amazement.

* * *

At the gatehouse Agatha and Jane were supervising two stable-men, a footman, and a young maid when Fannie arrived. They were still unloading crates and trunks from the farm cart and hauling them inside the gatehouse, a comfortable three-bedroom establishment with sitting room, dining room, large kitchen with a pantry, and stillroom. Behind the kitchen were two small servants' bedrooms with their own bath. An attic was on a level with the large archway which stood above the drive and housed the gate clock. On the other side of the archway were the stables and the stablemen's rooms above.

"It's cosy, that's what it is," Fannie said, looking around herself. "We'll be all right here."

"It's cleaning up well," Agatha added on a positive note. Both women looked towards Jane, Fannie smiling and Agatha watching her grandchild pensively. "Have you finished putting your things away, Jane?" Agatha asked.

"No, Gram."

"You'd best see to it, you'll want a place to sleep tonight," Fannie said practically. She was already rolling up her sleeves, preparing to do battle with the unused kitchen.

"It's so unfair!" Jane burst out.

"It's done and there's a fact," Fannie said. "Now it's our business to make the best of it."

"It could be worse, child," her grandmother told her. "At least we're not left on Nigel's mercy, nor needful of moving in with him."

"How long can we stay here?" Jane asked. She saw her grandmother's hesitation.

"It seems this house has been deeded to us," Agatha finally replied.

Jane's eyes widened. "You mean we won't have to move in with Uncle Nigel?"

"Isn't that grand news?" Fannie put in.

"I don't understand," Jane said slowly. "Why would he be so generous to us?"

"Perhaps he felt badly about what he'd done," Fannie said.

Jane stared at her in disbelief "Uncle Nigel? He has no feelings, only avarice and greed. How can this accommodate him?"

"I don't know," her grandmother said testily. "And furthermore I don't care. You should be putting things away and not nattering on about nothing."

Agatha was obviously upset and Jane departed up the stairs to the room she had chosen, worried that this move would affect her grandmother much more than she wanted to admit.

While Jane's door closed upstairs, Fannie watched Agatha closely, her eyes narrowing. "What's happened I don't know about?" she asked.

"Nothing's happened," Agatha replied in a cross tone, earning another appraising look from her servant.

Upstairs Jane stood looking around herself at her new bedroom. Across the room, beyond a pair of dimity curtains and wide casement windows, the Abbey rose in the distance up the gently rising drive. Jane had picked the room, she told herself, so that her grandmother would be spared waking every morning to the sight of what she had lost. Across the hall her grandmother's room looked out towards the countryside beyond the gate, a vista of rolling hillocks and huge winter-barren oaks. Fannie's bedroom, the smallest, was wedged between Jane's and the archway. The large room-sized bathroom completed the upstairs floor.

Jane drifted towards the windows, her thoughts a jumble of worries and doubts with an angry edge of defiance to them. She gazed towards the house which had been her home since birth— her grandmother's home until today. Movement up the hill caught her eye, and she shielded her eyes to see.

Charles was riding down the drive astride one of his matched greys. The Abbey's bailiff rode beside him on a brown mare. Halfway down they veered off the drive, striking out across the wintry grounds.

"The work won't get done if you waste time daydreaming instead of getting to work," her grandmother told her from the doorway.

"I may be wasting time, but he certainly isn't," Jane said hotly as she turned away from the window. "He's already off to gloat over his new purchase."

Agatha watched her granddaughter reach to unclasp her cloak. Throwing it aside, Jane bent to pull clothing from a trunk which squatted on the floor beside the wooden bedstead.

"He has the right," Agatha said mildly.

Jane was lighting into her work with a fierce determination. Agatha looked towards the window where Jane had been standing. All she could see was the Abbey in the distance at the top of the hill. A twinge of bittersweet longing showed in her dark eyes.

"You mustn't let this overcome you, Jane."

Jane sighed. "I know, Gram." She tried to smile. "If you can manage, I'm sure I will."

"We must take what life offers us the best way we know how. The Good Lord's ways are mysterious."

"They certainly are," Jane said with a great deal of asperity. "Letting the likes of Uncle Nigel take your house away from you because of Grandfather's debts is most mysterious. Your father left the Abbey to you, not your husband and *not* Uncle Nigel."

Inwardly Agatha agreed wholeheartedly, but she did not want Jane pining for things which could not be. "The law gives a wife's dowry to her husband to do with as he pleases."

"Men's laws are designed so they can gamble away anything and everything, and when they've done and naught is left, then they can steal what belongs to another just because she's a woman and foolish enough to be a wife. I shall *never* marry!"

"I've raised you to be self-sufficient, Jane. Nigel and others may not approve, but with a little frugality you can live quietly and comfortably for the rest of your life on what I've managed to save away. You need never suffer the ignominies I've suffered, nor shall you have to call any man master."

"Nor do I intend to," Jane said stoutly.

Agatha Steadford-Smyth wondered for one brief moment if she had been right to raise Jane to be so self-sufficient. Agatha dismissed the thought, telling herself it was the best of the limited alternatives Jane could have had. Jane would never be at the mercy of a gambling fool, nor endure the fate of the unloved wife. And, thanks to the unexpected and probably self-serving generosity of the new owner of the Abbey, Jane would be assured a roof over her head until her dying day.

Agatha looked towards the windows and the Abbey beyond. All she could wish for now was that the roof over Jane's head was a great deal farther away from the man who would be living at the top of the hill. He reminded her of days long gone, of a man she had thought she'd forgotten. No good would come to Jane if she were foolish enough to come under the Earl's sway. Agatha knew the terrible things which could happen to an unsuspecting girl.

Before she turned away and headed across the hall, she took one last look up towards the Abbey. It stood foursquare and solid against the wintry sky, a study in shades of grey—grey sky, grey stone walls, grey-black and barren trees, ready for the next onslaught of snow, patiently waiting for the warmth and greenery of the distant spring.

No harm would come to Jane, Agatha vowed to herself again,

not as long as she was here to prevent it. Men were not to be trusted, and this was a man's world—a cold place for a female unless she fortified herself against it.

Jane would be so fortified.

- 9 -

NIGHT BROUGHT SNOW falling gently outside the Abbey's thick stone walls. Lights from the gatehouse windows could barely be seen in the distance down the drive. Charles paced the Abbey study as snow blotted out the view beyond the tall, mullioned windows. He clutched a letter from his father's New World holdings, his brow furrowed in concentration. A tap at the door announced Pickering carrying a cut-glass decanter of brandy and matching snifter on a silver tray.

Charles looked towards his valet. "I see you've unpacked a thing or two of our own."

"Yes, Your Lordship. I'll have this household whipped into shape before the week is out." Pickering poured the brandy and then went to the windows, drawing the dark-red damask drapes closed.

"Leave the drapes on the far window open," the Earl said.

Pickering did as the Earl bid, then tidied the carved desk as the Earl continued to pace.

Charles stopped his pacing at the table nearest the fireplace and a wine leather wing chair. He reached for the brandy and swirled it, staring into the crackling fire within the grate.

"Disturbing news, Your Lordship?" Pickering asked politely.

Charles glanced down at the letter he still held. "I'm not sure. There's an offer to sell off my father's estate in the Americas."

"Is it a good one? The offer, I mean?"

"Not particularly. Which surprises me. I had thought the land to be worth much more. It's in a place called the Territory of Orleans."

"I've never heard of it, Your Lordship." Pickering's tone implied that it was not worth mention if he had never heard of it.

"Be that as it may, my father asks if I will ferret out the facts for him."

"That would seem a difficult thing to do from such a distance."

"Yes," Charles agreed. "It would."

"Does His Majesty's Royal Mail go there, Your Lordship?"

The Earl of Warwick threw himself into the wing chair. "His Majesty's mail goes everywhere, Pickering."

"Ah, yes, Your Lordship. Of course. Will that be all, Your Lordship?"

"Yes, thank you."

"Have you noticed that there is a quite unnatural chill to these rooms, Your Lordship?"

"I have tonight," Charles replied moodily.

"I'm told by the cook it's the drafts down the long hallways."

"At least she didn't blame the Ghost," Charles said darkly.

Pickering stared at his master. "What ghost, Your Lordship?"

"Precisely," Charles replied sharply.

Noting his master's very obvious irritation, Pickering felt it was wisest not to pursue the subject further. "Shall I ready your bedchamber, Your Lordship?"

"What?" Charles stared at the fire and then heaved a sigh. "I suppose you might as well. I'll be up directly. Thanks to that chit of a girl, I got precious little sleep last night."

"At least you shall have a good quiet night tonight, sir."

"I had better," Charles said darkly.

He took a long swig of his brandy, draining the glass as Pickering left the room. Repouring, the Earl stared at the fire's reflections in the cut glass, thinking about the New World holdings.

Restlessness brought him up out of the chair, to pace the room again. He threw the letter on the desk and roamed to the open window. Staring down the drive, he took another sip of his brandy, moodily watching the landscape as he finished his second glass.

Finally he decided to turn in. He was more tired than he had realised from his interrupted sleep the night before. He kindled a candlewick from the fireplace before venturing into the wide, cold hallway.

The ancient house was silent around him. He thought about the early days of the Abbey, when monks had filled these halls and tilled the grounds. The winds outside hissed through cracks in the walls and chinks in the window casements, rustling in the darkness around his candle like a hundred whispered conversations.

The candle flickered in the drafty hall. Charles cupped his hand around the flame to protect it as he mounted the stairs towards the master suite. Halfway up a powerful rush of cold air hurtled past him, dousing the candle's flame and leaving him completely in the dark.

"What the deuce!"

He reached for the banister and continued to climb, the chill air swirling around him as if he had stepped suddenly outside into a raging gale. Groping his way, he reached the top of the steps and turned towards his rooms, where Pickering looked up from stoking the fire.

"Are we ready for bed, Your Lordship?"

"Yes. And first thing in the morning remind me to have all the windows and doors checked. There is no possible way the draft I just passed through could have come from some little chink in a window or a wall."

"Very good, Your Lordship." As Pickering moved to help the Earl undress and ready himself for bed, the valet could not resist a question. "Was there some particular reason you decided to buy this property instead of the others we had been considering, Your Lordship?"

"What?"

"It's just that the Abbey does seem to be in rather ramshackle condition, Your Lordship. And it is farther from London and our usual haunts than I would have thought you would wish to be."

Charles grimaced. "Or *I* thought I would wish to be for that matter. Actually, it was my father's idea that I should find a country retreat for a season or so. He seemed to feel London wasn't agreeing with me."

Pickering kept a wise silence. Charles's father, the Duke, had bailed his son out of mounting debts at White's and Crockford's gambling clubs, not to mention a few far less reputable gaming hells. It was not to be wondered that he had insisted his heir repair to the country and mend his ways for a bit. As a matter of actual fact, the Duke had taken it upon himself to inform Pickering of his desire to have the Earl out of his sight and out of temptation's way until the Earl developed a more serious nature.

In Pickering's opinion that could take quite some time. And, in Pickering's opinion, the missive about the land in the New World was another of his father's attempts to put even more distance between his eligible and rather reckless son and the designing mothers and wayward ways of the nation's capital.

"Would you care for anything more before I retire, Your Lordship?"

"No, I'm turning in myself. And if I were you I wouldn't brave those halls again until morning. It's a wonder Lady Agatha and her foul-tempered granddaughter didn't freeze their noses off in this house."

"It's a wonder that you bought it, sir," Pickering told his employer, "as opposed to so many other choices we had."

Charles looked at the man grumpily. "Yes. It is, isn't it? I wish I knew why I decided on doing so."

Pickering left as Charles got into the large bed, lowering the wick on the bedside lamp. He noticed the extra lamp, a reminder of last night's interrupted sleep, and grimaced as he lowered its wick.

Alone in the semidarkness of the master bedroom, Charles's eyes closed, the whole long length of him luxuriating in the softness of the mattress and the warmth of the blankets. Lulled into slumber, he began to drift towards a dreamless sleep.

Then footsteps sounded beside his bed.

He sat bolt upright, his heart pumping hard, and strained to see who was in the shadowy room with him. He reached for the bedside lamp, but a clammy coldness startled him, making him withdraw his hand.

Blaspheming to himself he reached towards the lamp once more, ignoring the icy cold, and turned the wick up, illuminating the large bedroom.

Charles could see no one. His eyes searched out the corners of the room and then he stood up, shrugging into his brocaded maroon robe. He leaned down and looked under the bed. Nothing.

He went to the windows and checked their locks. The snow was still falling against the panes and building up on the stone sill outside. No tracks nor foot- nor hand-prints marred its surface.

Charles moved to the connecting door, checked that it was locked, and pocketed the key before walking to the sitting-room and the outer door. He collected that key as well, then gave the room yet another thorough search—behind the horsehair settee, around the chairs and tables, even looking up the fireplace flue.

Charles returned to the bedroom, closing the door between bed and sitting rooms and placing a chair under the doorknob, to prevent the door from opening. Finally he returned to bed and lowered the lamp wick until the tiniest flicker of light glowed on the night table. The rest of the room was in darkness.

The minute his head hit the pillows the footsteps began again. He turned the lamp up, and the footsteps stopped. "Who's there?" he called out. "I know you're here. If you're not a coward, show yourself this instant!"

There was no response.

He debated with himself, then lowered the wick to plunge the room into darkness once more. This time, however, he kept his fingers on the wick knob, ready to rekindle the lamp into blazing light on an instant's notice.

This time footsteps advanced all the way to the edge of his bed. He turned up the wick and pounced towards the sound. He landed on his feet, on the floor, with nothing in sight but chairs and tables and the huge walnut clothespress.

"Ah ha!" he said, and sprang towards the press.

He wrenched the door open to expose the insides. One wall held shelves of his own belongings, most of them neatly stacked there this very day by Pickering. Against the other wall hung the rest of the Earl's wardrobe. He plunged his hand amidst the jackets and pantaloons, cloaks and greatcoats, searching for a human form as he held the lamp high and peered within.

He found nothing.

The Earl considered his options. Anger overrode all else. He was not going to let some little country wench make him look the fool. He made his decision and carried the lamp to a table across from the bed. The table was flanked by two easy chairs. He sat down in one, pulling the other forwards. Putting his feet upon it, he placed the lamp on the table, daring his nocturnal visitor to come forwards.

Sunday morning Charles awoke with a crick in his neck, an ache in his backside, and a temper which would brook no more nonsense from any quarter whatsoever.

Pickering kept wise silence as he helped the irritable Earl dress for the day, then went downstairs to inform the cook all had best be exactly right this morning or woe betide the entire staff, such as it was. The cook informed the maids and footmen, and word travelled all the way to the stablemen that the new owner had not only ousted Lady Agatha and young Jane, but now he was intent on firing the lot of them.

The Ninth Earl of Warwick ate a lonely and silent breakfast served only by Pickering. The Earl ate little of the food placed before him, informing his man he would interview each of the staff in the study directly after breakfast.

The cook was first. She stood, stolid and unblinking, on flat broad feet, eyeing the nobleman distrustfully.

"I understand you have worked for Lady Agatha for a great many years."

"Since I was a young'un," the woman told him.

"Do you think it is possible you will be able to work for me?" he asked.

"I don't know," she answered honestly.

Charles watched her with tired eyes red from lack of sleep. "I will understand if your loyalty makes you want to move on to Lady Agatha's new establishment."

"Is she going somewhere?"

"I meant to the gatehouse."

"Lady Agatha informed us she would need none but the under-maid. Fannie will take care of the meals."

"Then, I take it, you do wish to stay on here?" Charles asked.

The woman stared right straight back. "If you're going to fire us all, why don't you just get on with it?"

Charles stared at her. "What are you talking about?"

"Mr. Nigel's man told us that Mr. Pickering would be bringing in a new staff. People more to a city person's liking."

"Mr. Nigel's man had no business saying any such thing," Charles sputtered. "Nor have I requested it."

The cook squared her shoulders. "Mr. Pickering himself said we weren't to his liking, and he would bring in a proper butler to run things."

"Enough." Charles held up his hand. "I shall speak to Pickering." He watched the woman start towards the door. "One more thing. Have you ever heard mention of a ghost?"

She looked back. "I've heard mention of lots of ghosts."

"I mean a so-called Abbey ghost."

The woman took her time. "I've heard a silly maid or two try to slumguzzle Fannie into letting them off their work because they had the vapours over some nonsense."

"So you don't believe it?" Charles asked.

"I don't believe anything I don't see with my own eyes, and only half of that," the cook replied.

"Then you've never seen any ghost."

"I'd like to see the ghost dared show himself to me."

The Earl looked at the large, sturdily built woman and found himself agreeing. He asked her to send in the head maid next.

The head maid had never seen a ghost, although she had seen strange happenings, she confided. Pictures popping off walls, things crashing to the floor, things not where they should be and then turning up where they shouldn't.

All easily explained, the Earl said, dampening her enthusiasm for the subject.

He questioned the other maids and the two footmen and even finally the stablemen, informing them each in turn they were secure in their jobs when and if a new butler arrived, assuming they did their work well. As for the Ghost, none of them were able to do more than repeat stories of odd things happening which could be explained without resorting to supernatural connexions.

Charles saw Pickering last, telling him to have the bailiff bring in plans of the Abbey.

"Plans, Your Lordship?"

"Architectural plans. We are going to renovate this structure so that these ridiculous drafts are done away with, and I also intend to find out how my nocturnal visitor is getting into my rooms."

A quarter of an hour later, the Earl was stymied by the bailiff's apologetic response. The plans were missing.

"I knew it," Charles said.

He actually looked pleased, which confused the poor bailiff so much he was tempted to question the Earl's mental stability.

Charles paid no attention. "Have a carriage hitched up," he told the man on his way out.

- 10 -

AT THE GATEHOUSE Agatha, Jane, and Fannie were just leaving to walk to Sunday service, dark cloaks wrapped over their warmest woolen dresses and pelisse overcoats. Woolen shawls, scarves, mittens, mufflers, and leather boots completed their harsh-weather garb as they started down the snowy path towards the village.

The sound of horses turned the ladies round to observe the large covered estate-carriage coming down the drive and pulling up beside them.

"Ma'am—" Homer, one of the stablemen, leaned down from his driver's perch and tipped his cap to Agatha. "The Earl says as how you're to ride with him to church, Lady Agatha."

Agatha shook her head. "I need no charity, Homer."

The carriage door opened, and the Earl looked out towards the two women.

"If you will not accept charity, is it possible you will lend some?" the Earl of Warwick asked.

Surprised at the request, Agatha peered up at the handsome nobleman. "I do not scruple to tell you I am at a loss. What do you mean?" she asked.

"I am asking you to do me a simple kindness and accompany me to church. I have spent the morning trying to win over the staff. They are very loyal to you, by the way."

Agatha regarded him with a mocking look in her dark eyes. "Loyalty from your staff is something you will have to build yourself, something which always takes time. However, what that has to do with accompanying you to church is quite beyond me."

"You may not be able to help with my problem with the servants, but you can help me with the villagers," he told her. "They will have undoubtedly heard stories from the Abbey staff about me. As I have yet to meet any of them, if they see the new owner of the Abbey arrive to church services in the Abbey carriage, quite alone, while you arrive having had to walk through the snow, they are bound to dislike me upon first sight."

"They, also, will soon learn to judge you on your own merits, whatever those may or may not be," the old woman replied to the Earl.

"I am at your mercy," Charles said. "It would be a great kindness if you would not make me appear to be an uncaring interloper before they have a chance to form their own opinions of me."

Fannie smiled up at him encouragingly. "I think his lordship's right."

Agatha Steadford-Smyth gave her abigail a quelling glance and was prepared to say no. She had no reason to help the man who had taken her home, no matter it was not his fault, but her own brother's. However, he'd had the graciousness to deed the gatehouse to herself and Jane. Grudgingly, Agatha acquiesced to his wishes.

"Gram," Jane protested as her grandmother agreed. "You're not going to ride with him, are you?"

"It will be for the best," Agatha said.

Jane watched Homer step down from the driver's seat and help her grandmother into the carriage which had been their very own just last Sunday. Not their very own, Jane corrected herself. They only had the use of it. It was Great-Uncle Nigel's to do with as he pleased—and he had.

"Jane?" Her grandmother called to her. "We're waiting for you."

"I, for one, shall walk," Jane told them.

"Don't be ridiculous." Agatha's small store of patience snapped, but Jane's determination was plain on her face.

"I'm sorry, Grandmother. You must do as you think best," Jane said. "But so must I!"

Agatha looked towards Fannie, who sighed.

"I know, I know . . ." Fannie said philosophically. "I'll walk with Jane."

"You don't have to," Jane told the serving woman.

Fannie made a face at her. "Your walking alone won't fadge with your grandmother and you know it."

Agatha did not remonstrate further with Jane, deciding it might be just as well not to have Jane and the Earl riding in the same carriage. The Earl watched the young woman and her abigail start off down the road.

"It will be a very cold walk," Charles said.

"They'll survive it," Agatha told him.

Charles gave the order for the carriage to continue, whereupon Homer quickly overtook and passed Jane and Fannie.

"I understand the Abbey has been in your family for a very long time," the Earl said, making conversation as they rode towards the village.

"Since Henry the Eighth secularized the old Roman church lands," Agatha replied and added no more.

To each of the Earl's attempts to make conversation, she replied politely, giving him an exact answer, but not expanding upon it.

He glanced out the small window at the slowly passing country-side. It was snowing again. He thought of Fannie and Jane trudging along behind them. "I understand from Nigel that Jane is an orphan," Charles said.

"Jane's history is no concern of yours, Your Lordship," Agatha said. And then, goaded by Nigel's description, she added, "She is most definitely not an orphan. I am her grandmother."

Charles continued mildly. "Your daughter, I understand, married another Steadford?"

Agatha looked at the young man who sat across from her. His many-caped coat of dark green superfine was obviously well cut, his chiselled features patrician, his manners of the most charming variety. She could imagine the string of broken hearts he already had to his credit amongst London debutantes, and she was determined Jane's name would not be added to the list of his conquests.

"Nigel seems to have kept very busy talking about our family history," she said in a cool tone.

"He mentioned a few things."

"I don't understand why it should interest you."

"It does, however, interest me," Charles replied easily, as if noticing nothing untoward in her manner. "Especially the parts about an Abbey ghost."

The old woman's eyes widened. "Surely you don't believe that nonsense."

"I hardly would believe a bouncer such as that," the Earl replied.

"Jane doesn't tell lies," Agatha replied curtly. "She merely has a vivid imagination."

"I would say her imagination is more than merely vivid. It is also convenient," Charles said, smiling politely.

Agatha grudgingly agreed. "At times my granddaughter has a tendency to get a bit carried away by her emotions."

"Her loyalty to you and her attempt to protect her family home do her credit. However, I hope you can persuade your granddaughter that I am not an enemy." He looked into the old woman's penetrating eyes. "I hope I will be able to persuade you I am not an enemy of either hers or yours."

"Why?"

"For one thing I should like her harassments to end," the Earl replied honestly. "I need a good night's sleep."

Agatha chose her words carefully. "Fannie told me about your nocturnal disturbances. I am sure Jane had nothing to do with them. However, the question is academic since she is no longer at the Abbey."

"It certainly did not seem merely academic to me last night," he told Lady Agatha.

Agatha's brows knitted together. "What happened last night?"

"My nocturnal visitor again found a hidden way into my rooms."

"You can't possibly be accusing Jane of that sort of behaviour." Agatha's voice rose with indignation. "Of coming to a man's rooms alone at night?"

"I assure you there was nothing carnal about her intentions. She merely continues her effort to drive me away from the Abbey," the Earl replied.

"You are insane. Stop this carriage at once!" Agatha's voice rang out. "I will not have my granddaughter accused of crime."

Charles spoke quickly. "Lady Agatha, I apologise for putting it so baldly and so badly. But as we agree there can be no ghost, the only logical source of my problems is your granddaughter. If she has not done the deeds herself, she has put someone else up to it."

Agatha spoke in freezing accents. "It is one thing to accuse her of having a servant invade your rooms. It is quite another to say that she did so—unchaperoned—herself."

"She could hardly be chaperoned if she were carrying out secret missions," he pointed out.

"Precisely," Agatha snapped. "You ask the favour of my company and then you accuse my granddaughter of unspeakable behaviour—and all without one shred of proof!"

Charles watched the old woman carefully. "Are you certain there is no proof?"

"Quite certain. She has done no such thing, therefore you have no proof." Agatha was going to continue by reminding him he was questioning everyone about a ghost, which he would not be doing if he had proof against Jane or any other. She bit back the words, unwilling to have further speech with the man.

"At least we agree there is no ghost," the Earl said pleasantly.

Agatha glared at the odious man who was rich enough to buy the Abbey out from under them. "She was merely funning with you. I've lived here for over sixty years. If there were a ghost I surely would have seen it in that time."

"It would seem unavoidable," he agreed.

"Well, I never have," she snapped, "because there is no such thing as ghosts, let alone an Abbey ghost."

He smiled. "I couldn't agree with you more."

"Then why do you keep bringing the subject up?"

The carriage stopped in the midst of other carriages and gigs in front of the village church as she repeated her query.

"I wanted to ensure that we agree there is no such thing, and, therefore, someone very human is causing my sleepless nights. I hope to gain your help with your granddaughter so that she, or whoever, will not resort to any more of these silly escapades."

Agatha's voice was filled with contempt. "Will you be so kind as to allow me to descend? I find the air in here unbearable."

Meanwhile, the entire village of Wooster was perishing of curiosity about the nobleman who had come to live in the Abbey. The servants had long since told all they knew, and that was much too little to satisfy the people who suddenly had a Peer of the Realm in residence at the Abbey.

The other Church of England parishioners watched as the Earl helped Lady Agatha out of the carriage. They walked through the snow, bundled in their warmest apparel and ignoring the stares.

"Shall I send the carriage back for your granddaughter?" Charles asked quietly. "She may not mind the carriage ride now that she has been walking all this time in the snow, especially since it is without me."

Agatha was acutely aware of the interest all around them as she started forward towards the small chapel, its moss-covered stones dusted with new-fallen snow.

"They are no concern of yours," she told him and turned away, greeting someone close by in an attempt to rid herself of his presence, but as each person she greeted stopped and very obviously looked from her to the Earl, Agatha was left with no alternative other than introductions.

"Where is Jane?" Molly Beecher, the wife of the village butcher, asked after she had diffidently acknowledged the Earl's polite greeting.

"She'll be along shortly," Jane's grandmother replied.

"Is she ill then?" the plump, plain butcher's wife asked.

"No." In an attempt to end the discussion, Agatha turned reluctantly towards the Earl as they walked down the center aisle of the small church, surrounded by oaken pews and the smell of damp woolens. "This is our family pew," Agatha told him, "or rather the Abbey's pew," she corrected herself. It was the first pew on the right hand side of the aisle.

"It will, of course, remain your family pew," the Earl told her. "I will be honoured to share it."

"Agatha, dear—"

Leticia Merriweather came near—all rounded curves and wrinkles, her round, lined face wreathed in smiles as she greeted Agatha and then smiled coquettishly upwards at the Earl of Warwick. Agatha introduced the widow coolly, though considering that they had never been close, Agatha saw no reason for the polite small talk in which Leticia was indulging.

Before Agatha could form a scathing enough rebuke, Margaret and Charlotte Summerville also approached, going on about the inclement weather and their hope for an early spring. Agatha was reminded of why she had never bothered to engage in social visits with her neighbours. She kept a tight-lipped smile upon her face and said very little. If the Earl was so pining for London and polite society he was willing to suffer such interminable chatter, he could do so. She saw no reason to encourage an intimacy she had resisted for over forty years.

Blasts of cold air accompanied the openings and closings of the outer doors as more parishioners arrived. The entry of the Reverend Whipple finally relieved Lady Agatha and the Earl of the Summervilles and the widow Merriweather as they went to their own pews, all wearing properly pious expressions.

The thin, frail-looking minister and his youthful altar boy began the services as the door opened again, sending a blast of cold air through the small chapel. People turned in their seats to see the late arrivals and so were treated to the sight of a very bedraggled-looking Jane Steadford and her long-suffering abigail. Fannie had been telling Jane the whole way how they were going to catch their deaths from their wet clothes. Her last words died on her lips as all eyes turned towards them.

Jane stalked down the aisle and started into the front pew, then realised she would be beside the Earl and stepped back as if stung. Fannie hurried up beside her. Jane could feel the eyes of all as the reverend stopped in midsentence, waiting for her to be seated. She shoved Fannie into the pew, the poor woman almost bumping into the Earl as she sat down hard. Meanwhile,

Jane slipped onto the bench between Fannie and the hard wooden aisle-side arm.

It wasn't until Reverend Whipple had begun his sermon on the Good Samaritan that Jane began to sneeze. The villagers looked questioningly from Jane to the new Earl. What was going on at the Abbey, and why had Jane walked to church in the snow?

After the services, the Reverend Whipple came to greet Agatha and Jane and Fannie. He was introduced to the Earl and offered any assistance he might be able to give to his newest parishioner. "Any at all," he ended, smiling up at the taller man.

"How good are you at exorcisms?" the Earl asked as they walked slowly towards the door, the other parishioners filing out ahead of them.

The eyes of the man of God widened. "I beg your pardon, Your Lordship?" he asked as they reached the door.

"I believe that is some kind of London humour," Agatha told the reverend sourly as she shook hands and stepped outside into the cold.

Beside the minister, the Earl held the door, catching Jane's attention as she passed. "Are you intending to walk back, or ride, Miss Steadford?"

She glared at the man who had disrupted their lives. "You'd like that, wouldn't you? You'd like me dead and in my grave, no doubt, just like the poor Ghost. If you did believe in him, you'd try to kill him by having him exorcised." She stood on the porch, facing the Earl.

"Ghosts are, by definition, already dead," the Earl reminded her.

"You know perfectly well what I mean," she snapped.

Charles was very much aware of the curious and unfriendly glances of the parishioners as Jane stood, shivering and sneezing between Fannie and her grandmother. "You did this on purpose, didn't you?" he asked as he found even the minister still watching them from the doorway. Charles put on a smile and a congenial tone. "I'm sure you've already heard quite a bit about me, Reverend Whipple."

The spindly-looking man of the cloth looked a little taken aback. "Ah, yes—a bit."

"From Miss Steadford, no doubt," the Earl said easily. "And, I am sure, all of it was to my credit." Charles spoke loudly enough for many around them to hear, smiling at Jane as he finished. "She is such a kindly young lady."

The minister agreed with the sentiment, waving at them as he closed the church door and retreated back to the warmth of the rectory.

Fannie had her wet shawl over her head as they stood in the foot-deep snow. "I don't know about the rest of you," Fannie said, "but I'm heading for the carriage and a lap robe."

"Fannie," Jane said quickly. She moved near the abigail, speaking low and urgently. "You can't ride back."

"I'll ride or someone will have to carry me," Fannie replied. "For I'm telling you now, there is nothing which will make me go back the way I came."

"But if you ride, I must."

"Yes, and that just might save your life." Fannie sneezed loudly. "You see? I told you we'd both catch our deaths."

Jane wanted to say more but found both her grandmother and the Earl obviously waiting for her and Fannie to walk forwards. Jane's dark expression was not lost on those they passed as she followed the Earl, allowing him to escort them back to the carriage. Homer came up from behind them to help them all inside and out of the gently falling snow.

The occupants of the Abbey carriage rode home through a world covered over with white. Even the bare black branches of the oaks were frosted over with snow. Charles tried to make conversation about the most immediate renovations he was planning, Agatha grudgingly admitting that many of them were things she would have loved to have been able to do. While they talked Fannie dozed beside Jane, who sat stiff and silent the entire way.

They passed under the stone archway, arriving at the gatehouse. Icicles were forming from the eaves, with drops of water dripping down and freezing as the icicle tips grew longer and longer.

"I'm afraid I have not made the best of first impressions upon the villagers," the Earl was saying as the carriage stopped. He looked towards Jane rather pointedly.

Agatha gave him an appraising look. "You are young. If you truly intend to make the Abbey your residence, you will have ample time to convince them otherwise," she told Charles before letting Homer assist her out of the carriage.

Jane said not one word, nor did she meet anyone's gaze as she waited to follow her grandmother. Fannie paused to thank his lordship for the ride, then followed the silent Jane as she hurried into the gatehouse. The Earl, meanwhile, ignored Agatha's protests and escorted her to the door of the cottage. Ahead,

Fannie and Jane shivered in their wet clothes as they disappeared inside.

"We're not used to change in this county. Or newcomers," Agatha told him.

"I've noticed," he replied dryly. "By the by, as you know, it was not my idea for you to have to leave the Abbey so precipitously. You are welcome to take your meals there and use it in whatever other ways you find convenient."

"Thank you, but we are content where we are," Agatha said. "The Abbey no longer belongs to us."

"Then will you help me with one more thing?" Charles asked her.

"What now?"

"A very immediate matter which has to do with the renovations you said you approve of. The plans of the Abbey are missing."

"Missing?"

"Yes, and, since you are a lifelong resident, I need your help in reconstructing them."

Agatha glanced towards the doorway through which Jane had disappeared. "I'll ask Jane about the plans. I don't understand how they could be lost or who would take them, but I promise I will let you know what I find out. And, of course, I will assist the Abbey renovations in any way I am able."

"Thank you." He bowed to her before returning to the carriage and heading on towards the huge house at the top of the drive. Agatha watched the carriage depart, her distrust of the man making her search for hidden reasons to all he did and said.

At the Abbey itself Pickering waited in the Earl's suite to help his master change.

"And how was your excursion to the village church, Your Lordship? Did it go well?"

"Yes," Charles told the valet, "I think it went even better than I had hoped."

11

IT WAS PAST midnight when an exhausted Charles was awakened for the third night in a row, having only just fallen into sleep. Footsteps echoing beside the bed brought him to startled wakefulness and then to frustrated anger.

"Of all the addlepated, misbegotten baggages ever born, you are worst," he called out in the darkness.

Something thudded to the floor.

Charles thrust the covers back, swinging his long legs off the bed and barking his shin against the night table. Blaspheming, he raised the wick on the oil lamp to flood the now-familiar landscape of the master bedroom with brighter light. Across the room a painting lay on the floor. He stared at it, his frown turning grimmer by the moment.

"This is the outside of enough," he shouted at the room.

In two great strides the Earl was at the clothespress, snatching it open to grab a dark-green wool greatcoat, which he pulled on over his nightdress as he headed out of the master suite and down the stairwell. Halfway down the stairs he heard the warning chink of metal against metal. Instincts at full alert, he paused in midstride and turned towards the sound.

Narrow shafts of light from the full moon drifted down the stairwell from the tall front windows high above. In the shadowy moonlight something gleamed in the air, hurtling towards Charles. He ducked. An ornamental halberd cut the air where his head would have been and hurtled onwards, crashing to the entrance hall below. The clatter of spear and battle-axe hitting the floor resounded in the sleeping house, waking Pickering from his dreamless slumber.

Charles stared at the instrument of destruction which had come so near to causing his death by decapitation.

"Pickering!" he bellowed at the top of his lungs, awakening straightaway the new under-maid two floors above. The rest of the household stirred with the unfamiliar night noises, coming more slowly to groggy wakefulness.

Pickering appeared at the top of the stairs in his nightshirt and cap. He held a lamp aloft and peered down towards Charles. "Your Lordship?"

"Wake the house. I want everyone here when I return. *Everyone*!" With that the Earl of Warwick stomped down the rest of the stairs and strode towards the front doors.

"But, Your Lordship . . ." Pickering called out as Charles pushed through the door and out into the cold night air, " . . .your feet are bare." But there was none to listen.

Outside, the fact of his bare feet quickly became painfully apparent to Charles but did not deter him. He forged across the snow-spattered grounds, his cold feet reinforcing his anger.

The full moon gleamed on the snow patches which covered the branches of the tall bare oaks, a sharp frost nipped the night air. The countryside looked unfamiliar in the moonlight, the undergrowth silent and black, while small rustling night noises carried on the still air.

Charles noticed none of it. By the time he reached the gatehouse at the end of the drive, his feet were blue with cold and nearly frozen through. The pain added to the weight of his pounding fist as he banged loudly enough on the door to wake the dead.

"Come out of there you lily-livered sneak, or I'll come in and drag you out by the hair on your head!"

Light appeared inside. Even Agatha was awakened by the bellowing male voice which accompanied the incessant and insistent pounding.

Fannie's voice quavered over her words. "If you don't leave this instant, we shall tell the new owner—"

"Damn and blast you, woman, I *am* the new owner. Open this door before I break it down!"

Fannie opened the door. Jane appeared behind her, and Agatha was calling out from the floor above to ask what on earth was wrong.

"Do you often have these emotional storms?" Jane inquired politely.

She stood before him in robe and completely dry slippers, looking for all the world as if she'd just risen from her bed. She must have flown across the same damp grounds he'd just traversed. It took all the self-control the Earl possessed to keep from strangling her on the spot.

"I have no idea how you managed to return so swiftly. I had every intention of bringing your grandmother and your woman up to the house to find and incarcerate you!"

Fannie took a step backwards, as if to protect Jane from the obviously demented man. Behind them Agatha descended the stairs slowly.

"What is the meaning of this?" she demanded of the Earl.

"The meaning, Lady Agatha, is that your deranged granddaughter has this night very nearly caused my demise."

It took Agatha a moment to register his words. When she had, she stared at him in transfixed horror. "Have you gone quite mad?"

"I? Mad?" he sputtered, his eyes blazing from Agatha to Jane and back again. "I was nearly decapitated!" As he spoke he saw Fannie's glance shift to Jane for one brief moment, then quickly away. Agatha also noted the byplay between her serving woman and her granddaughter.

"Jane?"

"Grandmother"—Jane looked the soul of innocence—"I don't know what the man is talking about."

"You have no knowledge of the sneaking footsteps in my rooms, I suppose," Charles said caustically.

A guilty expression flickered across Jane's face. "Footsteps don't kill people," she replied defensively.

"Ah ha! Then you admit you were once again in my room tonight."

"Jane!" Her grandmother's scandalised tone brought Jane around.

"Gram, I swear I have not been in his rooms this night." Prudently, she did not mention any other nights.

Lady Agatha looked the Earl in the eye. "I can assure Your Lordship, my granddaughter may do many foolish, even reckless things. Such as traipsing off alone to her great-uncle's establishment, but she does not visit men in the night and she has never lied to me in her entire life. Therefore your agitation is from some other cause, as I told you earlier."

"Then I shall have to fire the lot of them," he pronounced.

"What?" Jane whirled back to face the interloper.

"If it's not one or all of you that's determined to drive me round the bend, then it's one or all of the Abbey staff. I've got them up, and, if I don't get an answer this very night, I shall fire every last bleeding one of them! I want an end to this nonsense immediately."

"Your Lordship!" Agatha protested his foul language. "There is a gently bred young lady present, not to mention myself and my servant."

"Gently bred young ladies do not traipse off alone, interject themselves into others' conversations, voice unappealing sentiments, hold others up to censure, or throw halberds at a gentleman's head."

Having delivered himself of this pronouncement, the Earl of Warwick turned on his bare heels and marched back outside, slamming the door behind him.

"My stars," Fannie stared after him, "he's wearing no shoes."

"He's wearing no clothes," Jane said.

Agatha was truly mystified. "Do you suppose he drinks to excess?" she asked the other two women.

"I haven't a clue," Fannie said, giving Jane a warning look, "but I want you both back in bed before we all catch our deaths."

"If anyone's to catch their death this night, it will be that demented man," Agatha said as they climbed towards their bedrooms.

After she made sure Agatha was comfortable in her bed, Fannie tapped on Jane's bedroom door, speaking softly when she went inside. "Jane, this has to stop. You are creating such a coil you will endanger Hetty's job and all the others as well. Mark my words, he'll do it. He'll sack the lot of them, and where are they to go after that but straight to the poorhouse?"

"I?" Jane stared at the woman in the candlelight from the taper near her bed. "I was going to ask *you* why you didn't tell me you were going up there tonight," Jane replied.

"Me? Don't be daft." Fannie stared at Jane. "Are you saying it wasn't you?"

Jane's eyes widened. "Fannie, God is my witness, I swear to you, I wasn't out of my bed this night."

"I don't like this," Fannie said. "I don't like this one little bit. It means one of the servants is taking a leaf from your book and will get himself fired."

"Himself?" Jane repeated.

"It's got to be young Tim, the footman. None else would be so shatter-brained. I tell you true, I don't like this one little bit, Jane Steadford."

Neither, of course, did Charles. His feet ached with cold by the time he arrived back at the Abbey to find a sleepy-eyed throng standing in the entrance hall. Dressed in nightclothes, robes, and heavy woolen sweaters they looked mutinous, dragged out of their beds by an equally tired looking Pickering who had brooked no back talk.

Charles glared at each in turn as he stomped past. "I'm sure Pickering has told you what this is about. If he hasn't, he will now. Of course, one of you must already know. My final word on this subject is that there will be no more nonsense. The guilty party will confess or I'll fire the lot of you. You have until tomorrow to ferret out the culprit."

"But, Your Lordship—" Pickering began.

"Yes?" Charles growled.

The gentleman's gentleman spoke in a low tone, trying not to be overheard by the sullen gathering of household help. "I'm sorry, Your Lordship, but I don't know what this is about."

Grim-faced, Charles turned back to challenge them all. "I want to know who is coming to my rooms at night and how they are doing it. I want to know who threw that halberd at my head tonight and nearly decapitated me. I want the Abbey plans back, and I want a good night's *sleep*!"

Charles stomped, barefoot, up the wide oak stairwell, leaving behind a small group of round-eyed people who stared after him, then at Pickering, then at each other, in consternation. Even Pickering was surprised. One by one, their stares turned towards the huge, heavy, deadly-looking halberd.

"It would take a very large grown man to lift that thing, let alone throw it," Homer said to Pickering. "Look around yourself, man. There's none here who could do it."

"What does he mean, trying to decapitate him?" the cook asked the others. "What is he talking about?"

No one replied.

Upstairs, Charles pulled off the greatcoat and threw it down before beginning to prowl the room, knocking on every bit of wall and panelling, determined to discover a secret passage. But he found nothing. His feet pained sharply as the circulation of his blood began to warm them.

He was sitting on the edge of the bed, rubbing his blue-tinged toes when Pickering entered with a basin of hot water and cloths.

"I thought you might want to soak your feet, Your Lordship."

"Why did you let me walk out of here before I was properly shod?" Charles asked irritably.

"I tried to stop you, Your Lordship," Pickering reminded him, defending himself. "You were not even dressed, let alone shod."

Charles looked down at his white cotton nightdress and bare ankles and feet.

"Serves them right," he said, still fuming.

"Yes, Your Lordship. Serves who right, Your Lordship?"

"That damnable girl and her family," Charles replied.

Pickering kept a prudent silence. The Earl blasphemed when his cold feet hit the hot water, but soon he felt the tingling of restored circulation as Pickering rubbed his feet in the hot water.

"I'm afraid," the gentleman's gentleman ventured into the silence, "the scene below was not one which will win the staff's confidence in us or induce great loyalty."

"They had best earn *my* confidence first," Charles told him sourly. "And by God, I'll not have another sleepless night, if I have to fire the lot of them and tie that girl up to a tree."

Pickering insisted Charles change his nightdress for a fresh, warm one, then dried off the Earl's feet, making sure he was comfortably in bed before reaching to lower the lamps.

"Let them burn," Charles exclaimed. "Let them all burn, here and in the sitting-room. By Jupiter, nothing is going to keep me awake for what's left of this night."

"Yes, Your Lordship."

Pickering left a highly irritated and noticeably wakeful man behind as he made his way back to his own bed.

Jane arrived at the Abbey kitchen early the next morning to give the cook Lady Agatha's market list. Monday was village market day, and Hetty always shopped early to get the best buys. Over tea and toast, the cook regaled Jane with a stirring account of the Earl's middle-of-the-night harangue and ultimatum.

"Nobody knows what's going on, Miss Jane, I swear it. None of us have done anything to the Earl. If he sacks us, where will we go? How will we live? He'll tell others we're all under suspicion and then what will happen to us?"

Jane's dispirited expression saddened even further. "I'll talk to him," she promised quietly.

"I don't see what's to be said or what can help," the cook replied. She was gathering up her shopping bag and reaching for her hat. "He said he'll know the answers today or else. I might be out on my ear by the time I get back."

"Never!" Jane said with force. "If all else fails, you will all come live with us."

"Miss Jane, your heart does you proud, but it won't wash and you know it. There's not room for all of us in the gatehouse. There's no need for all of us either, and—truth to tell—there's no money to pay or even feed us without the Abbey income."

Jane stood up. "I promise you, you have nothing to worry about. I shall straighten this all out."

"How?" Hetty demanded. "What can you do the rest of us can't?"

"I can tell him the truth," Jane replied quietly.

Hetty stared after the young woman who walked resolutely out the kitchen door and into the back hall. Wondering what Miss Jane was up to now, Hetty let herself out the back and headed towards the waiting farm cart and Jake, who would help her carry her purchases back.

Jane walked towards the green baise door which separated the servants' halls from the main halls. Her steps dragged slower and slower. Dreading the coming confrontation, she hesitated before pushing through to the main hall and proceeding resolutely in search of the Earl.

She found him in the library. He looked up to see her in the doorway and scowled. "Yes?"

"If you will allow me, I'd like to talk about the servants," Jane said.

He closed the account book he had been studying. "I wondered to what I owed this singular honour. However, unless you are here to confess, there is no reason for any discussion between us."

"I am," Jane said quietly.

"You are what?" he asked and then stopped, his entire attention on her unhappy countenance. "You are?" he finally managed to ask.

"I am here to tell you I had hoped to deter you from buying the Abbey from Uncle Nigel by—by—" She took a deep breath. "By whatever means I could. I made up the Ghost," she rushed on, "from stories I'd heard from the servants. The bad tallow at dinner, the salt in your tea, even the crash in your room which woke you the first night you were here." She gulped. "I—I engineered them all."

His eyes were cold as glaciers. "What did you hope to gain by killing me?" he asked, his voice even colder than his expression. "It could do you no good, unless you have taken an active personal dislike of my person and wished to sever my head from my body. If anything happens to me, your great-uncle will only sell to another."

"But I didn't mean to harm you. I swear it! All I wanted was to frighten you away."

His words were hard, and separate as stones being hurled at her. "So you tried to frighten me away and when that failed you attempted to kill me. I ask again—Why? You can't possibly imagine that your great-uncle would give the Abbey back to your grandmother's use, no matter what nefarious end you propose for me."

"I never meant to harm you," Jane burst out.

"Then I suggest not throwing halberds at my head."

She stared at Charles. "I don't know what you're talking about."

"I'm talking about last night's dangerous little escapade."

"But I wasn't here last night," Jane told him.

"Then you may pass this information on to whichever of your accomplices did it in hopes of gaining your approbation."

"I have no accomplices," Jane insisted, tears born of anger and frustration coming to her eyes. "Please, you have to believe me, Your Lordship, none of the servants had anything to do with this."

"Then who threw the halberd at me?"

Jane stared at him. "I don't know. But it wasn't any of our servants. It couldn't have been."

Charles glowered at her. "You were not here, by your own word—if your word can be trusted. So how can you know it wasn't the servants who attacked me?"

"Because you haven't been here long enough to make any other enemies."

"Thank you," he said coldly.

"Please—" Jane came towards him. "I'll show you where the plans are. I hid them because they show the priest's stairs into your room. I'll show you everything, just please don't take my folly out on the servants. They'll have nowhere to go and no references and they've done nothing to deserve such treatment."

"Priest's stairs?" he repeated, staring at her.

"There were secret stairs built from the abbot's quarters to the outside in Henry the Eighth's time because of the antichurch riots. I'll show you," she offered.

Curiosity was getting the better of the Earl's anger. He hesitated, then followed her up the stairs to the master suite and the built-in clothespress that covered half the interior wall of the bedroom.

Jane opened the door to the large closet. She moved his clothing aside and pushed on the side of the press that was against the outer wall. The panel slid slowly open, revealing a dark cavern.

"A narrow stairway winds down to the ground. A walkway leads from there around the building. There's a door at the bottom of the stairwell and two more along the walkway."

Charles peered into the exposed hole, seeing the outline of narrow stone steps just beyond "I'll be damned."

"Your Lordship," Jane protested as Charles pulled his head out of the clothespress.

"If you're protesting my language, save your breath. You are far past any missish airs with me."

"None of the servants know about the hidden stairs, so none of them could have been responsible for the footsteps which woke you," Jane rushed on, determined to protect the household help. "And as to the sword—"

"Halberd!" he thundered.

"Whatever it is, there's no one in this household—except possibly yourself—who could even lift that old relic let alone hurl it across the long gallery at you. Besides, it's so old it's probably terribly dull."

"It wouldn't have to be sharp to sever my head from my neck when thrown directly at me," he told her nastily. He looked even angrier as he continued. "Are you still trying to convince me that a nonexistent ghost is responsible for last night?"

Jane glared up at the tall man. "I'm saying you probably had too much brandy and experienced a bad dream."

"How could I have a bad *dream*?" he demanded. "I haven't been able to sleep since I got here!"

"Nothing like this ever happened when we lived in the Abbey," she told him hotly.

"Fine. Splendid! Then come back and spend the night and see what happens. Maybe the two of us can catch the culprit who's taken over your campaign to rid the Abbey of my presence."

"All right, I will," she very nearly shouted at him. "I will, if you promise to keep all the servants on."

"I promise to keep them on until the culprit is found. Yes or no?"

"All right, yes," she told him again, just as loudly.

"Good," he shouted back.

Jane marched from the room, down the stairs, and out of the Abbey, leaving a frustrated Earl of Warwick behind her, in the middle of his bedroom.

An hour later Agatha's reaction was less than enthusiastic. She stared at Jane as if her granddaughter were demented. "What on earth are you saying? I absolutely forbid it. You will not spend the night in that house with the Earl."

"Gram, I have to."

"Don't be ridiculous."

"Don't you see?" Jane reasoned. "I've caused this problem for them and I have to save their jobs. Besides, I've already given my word."

"I agree you were a meddling fool," Agatha said, and was rewarded by Jane's drooping posture and expression, "but I will not have you spending the night alone with that man."

"We wouldn't be alone. There are servants everywhere."

"Yes, and by morning your reputation would be forever ruined."

"Oh, Gram, don't be so melodramatic."

"Don't you tell me about melodrama. People have long and evil memories."

"Gram, I have to do this. I shall never be able to live with myself if I've ruined Hetty's and Martha's and June's lives—let alone Homer and Jack and the rest. Besides, I want to ensure that he does not blame the wrong person. I have to make him admit he's been drinking too much and imagining things."

Agatha stared at her granddaughter, her expression bespeaking her adamant refusal of this plan. Then Fannie put in her own two pence. "I can stay with Jane."

Agatha frowned. "You are the worst romantic in the world and would probably encourage some sort of folly."

"I would not," Fannie retorted. "Jane's right. She's caused this problem for the others and she has to fix it."

"If she were to spend the night there, all three of us would have to spend the night there."

"Oh, thank you." Jane hugged her grandmother. "Thank you, Gram."

"I didn't say we would do it," Agatha sputtered.

"But we have to," Jane exclaimed. She kissed her grandmother on the cheek. "I knew you'd understand. I knew I could count on you."

"Jane Steadford, I will *not* be manoeuvred into a harebrained scheme!"

"Of course not," Jane agreed stoutly. "We shall do exactly as you say."

Agatha looked from her granddaughter's relieved and smiling face to Fannie's amused expression. Agatha's own expression was sour with her dislike of the entire plan.

12

MONDAY NIGHT SUPPER was very nearly the sort of silent meal the Abbey had known when it housed its monks centuries before. Invited to eat with Agatha, Jane, and Charles, Fannie tried to make polite conversation while a subdued footman served them chicken potpie and peas.

Unfortunately, the abigail's several valiant attempts each died in the hush around her. Monosyllables at best greeted her cheery references to the good food, the state of the weather now that the worst snows of winter seemed to be behind them, and the lovely little room she had at the gatehouse. Her polite comment on the amount of cleaning Pickering had been able to accomplish in only a day or two finally aroused the Earl.

"He's taking down all the blunt instruments from the walls," Charles told the woman.

"Maybe that's just as well," Jane put in, "until the culprit is found."

The Earl scowled at Jane.

"Quite," he said in a clipped tone.

"What culprit?" Agatha was finally provoked into joining the discussion.

"The one who makes noises through the night, allowing me no sleep. The one who throws portraits and halberds and Lord knows what all at defenceless humans."

"Maybe even jewel caskets," Jane said quietly, earning a quelling look from her grandmother.

"Jewel caskets, indeed." Agatha dismissed the idea.

"What's this about a jewel casket?" the Earl asked.

"You mean the ivory one? The heavy one you're so fond of?" Fannie asked innocently.

"Now look what you've started," Agatha reprimanded Jane. "Jane is having a slight fit of fancy, nothing else. Furthermore, I for one have yet to hear any noises, strange or otherwise." She concluded by glaring at the Earl.

"I suggest that you reserve judgement," he told her. "The night is young."

After dinner Charles informed the three women they would spend the balance of the evening together in the library, where they could play a rubber of whist if they liked.

"I hate whist," Agatha pronounced. "And I have no wish to spend the evening in the library."

Charles appeared implacable when he replied that they would all stay together.

"He wants to keep an eye on us all, Gram," Jane explained.

"My goodness," Fannie said into the aggrieved silence which met Jane's words.

Charles stood by the dining room doors, waiting to lead them to the library. Agatha swept past, then turned in the hall to glare back at him. "A handsome countenance and impeccable lineage do not excuse atrocious manners."

Charles smiled coldly. "On that we agree." He looked back towards Jane and Fannie. "Ladies—"

Jane followed her grandmother, Fannie lingering to look up into the Earl's dark green-blue eyes, which at the moment were stormy and cold.

"She'd never lift a finger to hurt you, Your Graciousness, I assure you."

"You do, do you?" he demanded.

"Oh, yes, indeed. I know the girl better than she knows herself. I've raised her since birth, I have."

He stared down at the woman from his over-six-foot vantage point. "I would not brag about that if I were you. I would not even admit to it."

He stalked after the Steadfords, Fannie trailing along behind, her thoughts lost in a romantic glow of how handsome he was when he was upset—and such a catch. Right out of one of her books, he was, and fate and the good Lord had plunked him down in their midst—just for Jane.

On that score there could be no doubt—at least as far as Fannie was concerned.

The fact that the two young people did not seem to suit at all didn't faze Fannie's plans one little bit. They'd come around, one way or another, with a little help.

Meanwhile, the idea of cards came to naught. Fannie was unschooled in the games the others knew, and Agatha was unwilling to play in any event. Fannie pulled out her knitting, which she had brought along from the gatehouse, and told them all she'd be happy as a bug in a rug seated all right and tight in the corner

Agatha barely spoke to the man who had forced this night upon her or to her granddaughter whose meddling had provoked an emergency for the entire Abbey staff. Thus, Charles and Jane were bored enough with the prospect of a long, dull, and silent evening ahead to finally call a limited truce. They sat across from each other at the chess table in front of the fire and began to play, Charles rather gallantly, he thought to himself, allowing the little baggage the first move.

When her black knight captured his white bishop, he was less pleased with himself and began to play in earnest.

One hour stretched into another, during which Pickering appeared with a pick-me-up of sherry and cakes for the women and a decanter of brandy for the Earl. The very thin, very proper city-bred man also put another log on the grate and prodded the flames into active pursuit of the new wood.

Pickering felt eyes upon his back and turned to see Fannie studying him from across the room. Agatha's serving woman was a nicely rounded woman in her early forties. Her features were even, her eyes an intelligent blue. Taken altogether she was not unattractive at all, he thought to himself as she returned to her knitting. He squared his thin shoulders a bit as he passed by her on his way out of the room.

"The fire feels good," Jane said.

Charles realised in that moment that he was warm. "By Jove, it's actually warm in here tonight."

"I beg your pardon?" Jane looked up from her perusal of his attempts to corner her queen.

He was watching her from across the small table which held the ivory and ebony chess set. "In fact the entire house is warmer tonight. With a hound or two by the fireside, it could actually be considered cosy."

"It's time to go up," Agatha said sharply from her chair. She looked displeased.

"They've not finished their game," Fannie pointed out to Agatha. Leaning closer she added softly, "They're just beginning to get along a bit."

"That's just what I'm afraid of," Agatha hissed.

Standing up, the old woman walked towards the chess table and hovered over them, her impatience palpable.

"Grandmother, it's very difficult to concentrate with you standing over us so," Jane said.

"It's only a game," Agatha replied.

"Check and mate," Charles said, looking rather pleased with himself.

Jane glared at the pieces, determined to wiggle her king out of his dilemma. There was no hope. "I almost had you beaten and you know it."

"Superior talent always works best at a disadvantage," he intoned, then relented a bit. "I will, however, admit, you play better than any female I've ever met."

"That, sir, is a lukewarm compliment at best." She stood up. "I shall accompany Grandmama, unless you are afraid we shall get up to some mischief once out of your sight."

"I know you'll get up to some mischief at your first opportunity," he told her flatly, "but I think I am capable of dealing with it. I have people positioned, waiting to find the culprit and save their jobs."

"How trusting of you." Jane's tone dripped sarcasm. At the door she let Fannie and Agatha precede her into the hall. "Be sure and wake me if there are any goblins about."

Charles smiled coldly. "I assure you, you will be the very first person I inform."

"Good."

The door to the hall closed, leaving the Earl of Warwick to finish his brandy alone. He sat back in the fireside chair, sipping at the brandy and shivering slightly. He straightened up, startled. The chill was back in the now-silent room.

"What the devil," he exclaimed, staring towards the fire.

Flames leapt in the grate as high as the moments before but gave off too little heat to combat the sudden icy chill which seemed to hover around the handsome Earl.

He finished his brandy and stood up, an uneasy feeling accompanying the cold. Perhaps Agatha was right; perhaps he was losing his grasp on reality. He purposely shoved the fleeting thought from his mind. He was as right as rain and tonight he would prove it, unless the culprit was a craven coward unwilling to chance discovery now that all were alerted. In any event, if his night's sleep was again interrupted, so too would be that of everyone else under this roof.

An extra bed had been brought into Agatha's suite and placed in Fannie's old room. Jane was to spend the night with Fannie, and Agatha would be in her own connecting room—all three locked in together. There was to be no chance of gossip about the innocent

Jane sleeping under an unmarried man's roof.

Once Agatha was to bed, Jane and Fannie undressed slowly, talking softly.

"I don't see why I couldn't sleep in my own room," Jane was saying.

"Your grandmother wants to protect your reputation," Fannie replied mildly.

"What on earth does she expect to happen?" Jane asked.

"She's had a hard life," Fannie replied without answering.

Jane slipped under the thick down-filled comforter, the flannel sheets warming as she lay between them. She watched Fannie dim the lamp to a tiny nub of light.

"I used to think Gram was too harsh in her feelings about men, but after dealing with Great-Uncle Nigel and now with this odious Earl, I'm beginning to realize she hasn't been harsh enough. I, for one, shall never be the chattel and property of some dreadful male tyrant."

"I should hope not, but all men are not dreadful tyrants," Fannie said from her bed.

"How do you know?" Jane asked.

"Go to sleep," Fannie told her.

"How do you know they aren't?" Jane persisted.

"Because for one thing all those writers could not write about such lovely heroes if they'd never encountered one."

"I wonder," Jane said. She yawned, stretching her arms out above her head and snuggling down into the covers. "I wonder . . ."

She did not know how long she slept. All she knew was that she awakened later, her eyes opening to look at the gloom which surrounded her. Lying very still, she felt a chill up her spine. Across from her, Fannie slept on, peacefully snoring. Jane assumed Fannie's snoring had brought her to wakefulness, then she heard someone walking in the next room. Jane stepped out of bed, opened the door to the adjoining dressing room and tiptoed towards the connecting entrance to the two suites. She could hear nothing.

She gently twisted the knob, but it was locked from the other side.

Jane went back into the bedroom, glancing towards the sitting-room door. The sound came again. This time it seemed to be from the sitting-room beyond. Someone else must be up and stirring. Jane walked softly to the sitting-room door, opening then closing it between herself and the sleeping servant. If the Earl was trying to concoct some funny business, Jane intended to expose it and get this entire mess sorted out.

The sitting-room ahead of her was pitch-black. She felt her way to her grandmother's door and listened for a few long moments. There was no movement. Then she heard the sound again. It seemed to come from the hallway beyond the sitting-room door.

Tiptoeing, Jane moved nearer, trying to listen. When she heard nothing moving, she cautiously opened the door. The wide upper hall was murky with shadows. She glanced towards the rear of the hall, then felt her way the short distance forwards, toward the front and the door to the master suite's sitting-room.

She tried the handle and then gasped, feeling something beside her. The Earl of Warwick stood in the darkness, staring down at her.

"All right, you've gotten a bit of your own back," Jane whispered.

"What are you talking about?" he asked softly.

"Getting me out of bed. I heard your noises and came to investigate. You have accomplished your purpose and disrupted my sleep," she told him.

"I? Are you telling me you were not walking in my rooms?" As he asked the question, he realised she could not have been. She could not have come past him and sneaked back into her grandmother's room without his seeing her. He had looked well at the plans earlier. There were no secret stairwells connecting the mistress of the house's rooms with any others save his own and for that door he had the key in his pocket.

The thought that she might have a duplicate key occurred to him. He grabbed her wrist, hearing her muffled sound of protest as he dragged her forwards into his sitting-room.

"What do you think you are doing?" she demanded.

"Checking the connecting door!" Charles replied as he half-dragged her with him across his lighted sitting-room and to the door of his bedroom.

In the lamplight the chair he had propped against the connecting door was still in place. There was no way she could have gone through that door and replaced the chair behind her. He slackened his grip as he realised she could not have been inside. As he did so, she wrenched away from him.

"I am not accustomed to being hauled into gentlemen's rooms in the middle of the night," she whispered sharply, afraid of waking Fannie.

He apologised grudgingly as he escorted her back to the hall door, where they both heard something beyond.

"Who's there?" he asked, coming out into the hall beside her.

Jane peered towards the front of the house, trying to make out the outlines of the long narrow gallery. "Is someone there?" she called out softly.

Something fell, making a thudding sound as it hit the thick Turkey carpet.

She turned towards the Earl. "You have Pickering pretending to be an intruder," she accused.

"How dare you?" he began to protest, but she was already heading towards the gallery to confront the Earl's man.

Charles followed her, both of them stopping as a light came up the stairs from below. Behind the light, Pickering's face could clearly be seen, along with the cup of warm milk he was carrying.

"How did you get down there?" she demanded.

"I beg your pardon?" Pickering gazed from the young woman in her thin white nightdress to the Earl in his.

Charles looked grim in the lamplight, the angles and planes of his chiselled face harsh in the stark illumination. "Obviously, Pickering is not the culprit who is throwing things around in the middle of the night."

"Me, sir?" Pickering looked offended. "Hardly, Your Lordship. Why on earth *would* I do that?"

"Miss Steadford seems to think we are conspirators in some dire plot. Unfortunately, her hypothesis does not hold water since I am the one who is being plagued."

Jane ventured farther into the dark gallery, which was lit only by Pickering's lamp at the top of the stairwell. The moon outside was hidden behind clouds and lost from view.

She was trying to make out what had fallen, then something else crashed directly beside her. Giving out a little scream, she jumped backwards, so frightened her breath caught in her throat.

Charles heard the second crash and the scream in the same moment and came hurtling forwards, while Pickering followed behind with the lamp.

Jane turned and found herself directly in the Earl's arms. "You didn't do that," she told him in breathless panic.

"I told you," he reminded her.

His arms had wrapped instinctively around her shaking form. Now he felt the warmth of her flesh pressing against his own. Only thin nightshirts separated them from each other.

Pickering had come close behind, peering beyond them. "By Jove, it's another portrait!"

Charles was acutely aware of Jane's body pressed close against his own. He stared down at her eyes in the lamplight, and she was looking up into his. The realisation that the Earl was holding her, the feel of his strong arms and hard chest overpowered her senses. She watched his eyes as he leaned the least bit forwards, his lips nearing hers.

Fannie, having awakened and found Jane gone, had roused Agatha. At the moment when Charles bent forwards and claimed Jane's lips, Fannie walked out into the hall with Agatha beside her, both in search of the source of the commotion they had just heard. They found the Earl of Warwick with Jane in his embrace, their lips joined and Jane's arms around the Earl's neck.

Agatha's sharp intake of breath spoke volumes, as did the horrified expression in her eyes. Pickering turned to see the two women standing behind him.

"Would you care for some warm milk?" he asked Agatha politely.

She finally recovered her voice. "Jane!" she cried.

Jane, confused by her own reactions, moved out of Charles's arms in a daze. "Yes, Grandmama?"

"What do you think you are doing?" Agatha glared from the bemused Jane to the Earl. "How dare you, sir?"

"We were looking for the cause of the noise," Charles defended himself.

"You picked a peculiar way of doing so," Jane's grandmother told him sharply.

With that, Agatha and Fannie shepherded Jane back into Agatha's rooms, leaving a distracted Charles behind them.

"Shall I stay up with you, sir?" Pickering asked fatalistically.

"What? Oh, no. Go to bed, Pickering."

Charles seemed hardly to notice the man who seized the opportunity of escape to his warm bed and departed, leaving his master alone in the hall.

Charles gazed back towards the fallen painting, his mind torn between thoughts of Jane and of how good she felt held firm in his arms, and an analysis of the noises they'd heard. Perhaps the nails were so old they were all falling out of the ancient walls, he rationalised. He'd have them checked in the morning.

As he stood there, gazing towards the hall, the moon came out from behind clouds to shine down through the windows high above. In the sudden moonlight the form of a dejected man shimmered near one of the windows. He seemed to be suspended in midair. The moonlight poured through him as he hung there, looking straight down at the women's closed door.

Charles gasped, shocked to the very core of his being. He took a step towards the apparition, which seemed to sense the movement and glanced toward him, then slowly faded—vanishing into the thin, empty air.

Charles shook his head, closing and opening his eyes. It was a trick of light. That was all it could have been. There were no such things as ghosts!

- *13* -

THE NEXT MORNING Agatha lost no time in removing Jane from the Abbey and temptation. Nor did she let her out of sight for days afterwards, watching the girl like a hawk, afraid her head had been turned by the handsome and obviously rakish nobleman.

Finally, a week later Jane escaped the constant scrutiny for a few moments. She donned her cloak to walk in the gatehouse gardens, kicking at the clumps of icy snow, which the wintry afternoon sun was doing little to melt. She was upset with her grandmother for her continuing suspicion that Jane had been affected by the Earl's kiss. She was even more upset with herself because, unfortunately, her grandmother's concern was warranted.

No matter how much Jane tried to thrust the thought of him away, her dreams at night were full of Charles and the feelings his touch had roused in her.

"Jane?" Fannie called out across the small garden. "Your grandmother is asking for you."

Jane made a face as she walked back inside the gatehouse kitchen. "She has been asking for me, or looking for me, or calling to me, all week long."

"She's worried about you."

"She watches me as if I were about to commit some heinous crime," Jane complained.

"You upset her with all this talk about the Abbey. She doesn't want you thinking about what is no longer yours."

"She says I must not go *near* the Abbey."

Fannie shrugged. "She worries about your head being turned by the Earl."

"The Earl has nothing to do with it. Something was going on there," Jane burst out.

Fannie grimaced. "She knows something was going on, she saw it with her own eyes, and that's why she doesn't want you anywhere near him."

"I don't mean *that*. I mean something was happening up there that night."

"That's what she's afraid of," Fannie told the young woman plainly.

"But Fannie, please, you have to help me." Jane took her abigail's hand, beseeching her. "Something was there in the long gallery behind me, and nothing could have been. I started all the talk about a ghost to get him to leave, but now it looks as though there may really be one."

"Jane Steadford, that is the most ridiculous thing I have ever heard you say and, believe me, you have said some very silly things in your time."

"The idea frightens you, doesn't it? But if there is a ghost do you want one of the servants blamed? Do you want the Earl firing Hetty or Jack or Homer or Martha? Do you want him firing the lot of them? You must help me prevent that happening."

"The last time I helped you, we both got in trouble," Fannie reminded Jane sourly.

"I must find out what's really going on. There's no one else to do so, and I'm the one responsible for it all," Jane argued.

"Your grandmother won't let you go near the Abbey," Fannie said.

"If you assist me, she will never know about it, and I will have solved the mystery so that none of the Abbey staff lose their positions. Fannie, please, you must help me," Jane pleaded. She saw Fannie's half-persuaded expression. "Just this once more."

Fannie's sense of duty to Lady Agatha was at war with her love of Jane. The girl had always been able to twist Fannie around her little finger and well they both knew it. The problem was Agatha knew it, too. Fannie knew Agatha was dead set against Jane going near the Earl. But Fannie also knew Agatha was dead set against men in general and that was unfair to Jane. Jane's life would be that of a spinster if Agatha had her way. It might be safe, but it would surely be as lonely and lacking as Fannie's own had been.

Fannie's weakness for romance, fed by Mrs. Edgeworth's *Tales of Fashionable Life* and all the other romantic novels in their marbled board covers, told her the Earl of Warwick might be the fated husband of their Jane. If one ghost, more or less, had helped to bring this about, was it fair to deny Jane what fate intended for her?

"I don't know," Fannie began doubtfully.

"You don't know what?" a voice asked from the dining room doorway, startling them.

Jane and Fannie both looked guilty as they turned to see Agatha watching them suspiciously. Jane recovered first. "Nothing, Gram, we were just talking about how long it would be before we could begin planting spring flowers."

"Flowers!" Agatha said. "Better to be thinking of cabbage and carrots. Come along, Jane."

Jane gave Fannie a look, and her request was in her eyes. Then she followed her grandmother towards the front parlour.

"I've been thinking," Agatha told her granddaughter as they walked. "There are trunks in the Abbey attics that belonged to your mother. Since there is no hope of storing everything in the attic here, there are many things which will have to be left behind or given away. Since you had no chance to know your parents, I think you should be the one to go through Evelyn's belongings and decide what you want to keep."

Jane thought about the years in her childhood when she had hidden in the attics, going through those very trunks, trying to find pictures and pieces of the lives which had been cut so short.

She had never really known either her mother or her father. Her mother had died at Jane's birth. Her father left Jane with Agatha and rejoined his regiment, soon thereafter to be killed on foreign soil.

"Yes, Gram," Jane said, then realised this meant she would be going to the Abbey. Her eyes lighted up. "Oh, Gram, yes."

Agatha noted the change in her granddaughter's expression. "We can start tomorrow."

"We?" Jane asked, her enthusiasm fading.

"Naturally." Agatha watched her granddaughter carefully. "Why would you want to go up to the Abbey alone?"

"I don't," Jane replied. "I just meant that I'd like to get started right away. Today."

Agatha regarded Jane. "Today?"

"Yes," Jane said eagerly, "could we?"

Agatha surveyed the gatehouse living room, taking in the boxes of belongings waiting to be unpacked. "I suppose," she said slowly, "there's no reason to put it off. The sooner all our things are sorted out and our removal from the Abbey complete, the better all round."

Jane took a deep breath, trying to keep her anticipation in check. She would be in the Abbey, where she might be able to find something. She would not admit to herself that she might possibly want to see the Earl as well. She had not seen him all week, since the night they kissed.

Of course, that was unimportant and did not faze her in the least. In fact, she had felt absolutely nothing but fear at the noise behind her. She had merely been surprised when he kissed her, nothing else. She had only dreamt about him because it was such an unusual occurrence. That was all there was to it.

"Jane, is something wrong?" her grandmother asked.

"No, nothing."

"You appeared to be lost in thought," Agatha told Jane.

"I'm just very anxious to go through the Abbey—the Abbey trunks, that is."

Agatha was concerned about taking Jane anywhere near the lecherous nobleman, but her concern was abated an hour later when, as they arrived at the Abbey, he was leaving.

The Earl gave both women the slightest sketch of a bow as they walked up the steps towards him. "I understand you wish to go through the attics. If you need anything Pickering will assist you."

He seemed very distant, never looking directly at Jane as he spoke. Agatha thanked him for his permission and he left, mounting his horse and riding off beside the waiting bailiff. Jane found herself feeling strangely disappointed that he had not at least acknowledged her instead of riding off without even a backwards glance.

"Jane, stop dawdling. You're the one who wanted to get started."

"Yes. Grandmama."

For the next two hours the two women rummaged through trunk after trunk of past possessions, mementos, letters and clothing, the aroma of camphor from the opened trunks mingling with the musty smells of long-unused cloth and books.

Jane opened yet another trunk, pulling back yet more of the silver paper which lined the insides, and puttered through the contents. She added a diary, a painted fan, and several squares of silk to the pile of bits and pieces she was accumulating.

"Do you want—" Jane began and then stopped as she saw the pinched and weary expression on her grandmother's face. "Gram, what is it? What's wrong?"

"Nothing." Agatha's voice was weak. She suddenly looked much older and very tired.

"You look strange. Are you sure you're all right?"

Agatha could not put into words the feelings which were invoked by going through her dead daughter's belongings. It brought back all the losses Agatha had endured in her life, and sadness welled up around her heart.

"I'm a little tired," Jane's grandmother revealed.

"Why don't you go downstairs and rest."

Agatha's resolute unwillingness to ask favours of any man, let alone the new owner of the Abbey, made her shake her head no, even though she would have liked nothing better than to rest. "I do not wish to lay my head down in this house. I shall be all right," said Agatha.

"You are not all right, and this is ridiculous. There is no reason for you to overtire yourself. I am not a child who has to be constantly watched. If you won't rest here at the Abbey, I shall have Pickering call for a carriage to take you to the gatehouse."

"And leave you here alone?"

"And leave me here alone," Jane said firmly. "What on earth do you think shall happen to me?"

Agatha thought about it. The Earl was gone for the day. She would prefer to leave all these reminders of the past behind. She thought about insisting Jane accompany her back to the gatehouse. They could begin this again tomorrow. Then Agatha remembered that the Earl might well be in all day tomorrow, might even take it upon himself to come up here with them.

"If I do as you suggest," Agatha said, "I want your promise you will be home before dark."

Jane agreed, telling her grandmother she would be back directly, long hours before dark. The older woman got to her feet, swiping at bits of dust on the hem of her grey woolen gown. Jane reached to help her down the attic stairs but Agatha protested.

"I'm just a little tired, that's all," the woman snapped feebly, but leaned on the strong young arm all the same.

They found Pickering in the upstairs hall, Agatha insisting to both of them she could and would walk without aid.

"Go back up and finish as quickly as possible," Agatha said to Jane.

Jane returned to the attic and watched from the small round window until she saw her grandmother handed into the carriage, looking very small and frail. Jane looked back to the trunks, sinking to her knees, the skirt of her patched blue gown spreading out in the dust around her.

In the next trunk she found a pile of letters bound with a faded red ribbon. Jane started to put them aside and then thought better of it. Perhaps they were her mother's letters. Curiosity about the reality of her mother's life prompted Jane to untie the packet and open the first letter, but it was not her mother's. The letter belonged to her grandmother and dated from more than forty years past. The first one was written to someone named Catherine. They seemed to be great friends. Agatha poured out her doubts and fears about a loved one.

Jane stopped reading, feeling as if she were intruding on her grandmother's privacy. Even if her grandfather was long dead, there was no reason to pry into their love life. An initial caught her eye as she started to fold the paper back inside the envelope. In the fastidious spidery handwriting her grandmother still used, the initial "A" was sprinkled liberally down across the page.

"Although A and I shall never be together I shall at least have this reminder always of our love," Jane read.

Jane stared at the page. Her grandfather's name did not begin with A. This person was some unknown part of her grandmother's life. Suddenly, the hair on the nape of Jane's neck felt as if it were standing up on end. She turned, frightened but unsure why. In that moment, the exceedingly levelheaded young woman very nearly fainted.

A man stood behind her, dressed in clothing from the last century. He was watching her and looked startled when her eyes widened. When she found her voice and started to speak, he took a step backwards, as if she might harm him.

"Who are you and how did you get up here?" she asked, her voice an uneven croak.

"What?" his voice sounded as if it were coming from a long distance away, and croaked as much as hers, either from fear or disuse. "You're talking to me," he said, nonplussed.

Jane forced herself to her feet, rewarded by his taking another backwards step. "I shall call Pickering and have you thrown out bodily unless you explain yourself this instant."

"You see me?" he said, astonishment in his eyes and his voice. "You've never seen me before." Then, before her very eyes, he faded from view.

Jane's eyes widened. She reached out, feeling the empty air where the man had been. "There *is* a ghost! Where did you go? What do you want?" she called out, but there was no answer. "Why haven't you let us know you were here?"

Jane waited for the apparition to reappear. When she finally gave up and went back to her work, she kept looking over her shoulder, hoping to see him again, but it was not until she had finally left that he returned. He waited until the door closed below and then drifted into visibility near the attic window, looking down towards the wide curving drive.

Jane emerged below, young Tim helping her with a basket. He put it in a farm cart as she climbed up inside. As they started away down the drive Jane turned quickly to stare up at the round attic window. She looked straight into the Ghost's eyes. He stared back for one brief moment and then faded from view.

Jane only half heard Timmy's talk of the new livestock the Earl was buying, her brain spinning. Her whole world was turning topsy-turvy as she sat beside the young footman, prosaically riding home in the farm cart. She could hear the farmhands in the fields herding the cattle towards the near pastures. The wind was freshening, whipping tendrils of her flaxen hair towards her flushed and excited face. Everything around her was perfectly normal, except that she had just come face-to-face with a real, honest-to-goodness ghost.

By dinnertime Jane was beside herself with barely repressed excitement. She wanted to shout that there really was an Abbey ghost—that the stories were all true—but she knew she would never be believed. She hardly believed it herself, and she had seen him with her own eyes.

Agatha had told Fannie she was fully recovered and felt perfectly well enough to come down to dinner, so all three were seated at the dining room table. Fannie and Agatha ate their steak and kidney pie and discussed household matters, until Agatha took a good look at her granddaughter.

"You have the worst case of the fidgets I've ever seen," Agatha told Jane.

"Aren't you hungry, Jane?" Fannie asked. "You've barely touched your food."

Jane looked down at the food she was pushing about with her fork. "No, I'm not very hungry tonight."

Agatha realised Jane too must have been deeply affected by the perusal of her mother's things. "We had a very tiring day," the old woman said.

Jane glanced at her grandmother through hooded eyes, remembering the packet of letters she'd discovered and put in the basket she had brought back to the gatehouse. They told of a secret part of her grandmother's life and presented Jane with a thousand questions she dared not ask.

Agatha felt the intensity of Jane's gaze. "Why are you looking at me like that?" she asked.

"I was just wondering how you are feeling, Gram."

Agatha studied Jane, then looked down at her own half-eaten dinner. "I'm still a little tired."

Jane glanced towards Fannie. "In all these years at the Abbey, neither of you have ever seen anything at all that might be a little like a ghost?"

"What?" Agatha looked up. "Where on earth did that question come from?"

"I just wondered. I mean, others seem to have seen him—or something."

"Child, what on earth are you prattling about?"

"Well, if there were an Abbey ghost, you would have had to have seen something over the years, wouldn't you?"

"You can't possibly be serious," Agatha protested.

"Of course she's not serious, she's just funning with us, Aggie." Fannie gave Jane a warning look, lapsing in her agitation into the familiarity the two older women used only when alone.

"I don't see where there is any humour in the subject. In fact, I have heard quite enough of that nonsense these past days to last me a lifetime."

A knock at the door interrupted her words.

Jane looked startled, but Fannie was glad of any change in the direction of the conversation. She feared Jane would end up saying something so corkbrained her grandmother would find out Jane really thought there might be a ghost.

Jane watched Fannie go to answer as the knock came again. "Who could that be?"

"Lord Warwick sent word he wanted to discuss something to do with the Abbey lands," Agatha informed Jane. "You may go upstairs, if you wish."

Jane met her grandmother's eyes. "Why?" she asked as Fannie showed the Earl into the small dining room.

"Lady Agatha, I'm sorry to interrupt your dinner. Miss Jane." Charles acknowledged them both.

"Would you care for coffee or brandy?" Agatha offered coolly.

"Thank you," he replied.

"Fannie, please show our guest to the living room. I shall be there directly."

Charles cast a glance towards Jane, then followed the servant into the next room. Agatha stood up. "You may finish your dinner, Jane, or retire if you wish."

"I'm neither hungry nor sleepy," Jane said, standing up and walking towards her grandmother and the doorway.

Agatha reluctantly allowed Jane to accompany her into the room which held the Earl of Warwick.

He stood up when they entered, and sat down again as they found chairs and Fannie handed him brandy. "I am grateful to you for taking the time to see me, Lady Agatha."

"It has been a very tiring day for us. I trust this interview will not take overlong," she replied.

"I won't trouble you for more than a few minutes." He glanced towards Jane. "I am thinking about the possibility of acquiring some additional land and I wanted your advice," he said and turned back towards Agatha.

"More land?" Agatha repeated. "One would have assumed you had more than enough to occupy you with the Abbey estate at this juncture."

"Yes. Well, of course, I may not go forwards. Still, I thought you might be aware of what was available in the vicinity and the worth."

"I'm afraid I can't help you. I have not been in the market for property."

Charles sipped at his brandy. "And you also know of none, I assume, Miss Steadford?"

"My granddaughter would hardly have any information on the subject," Agatha said crisply.

"Actually, that's not quite true, Gram." Jane smiled at her grandmother and then met the Earl's gaze. His eyes were staring deep into her own, something in his gaze affecting her composure. She could feel her cheeks beginning to burn, her heart already fluttering uncomfortably within her breast. "I have a great deal of information regarding the surrounding lands because of the surveys Great-Uncle Nigel requested. However," she told the Earl, "I am not aware of any land for sale in the near vicinity."

"I see," he replied.

"Have there been any more—strange happenings?" Jane asked him.

"It's been very quiet since—" Charles was very aware of Agatha's dark eye—"last week."

"If there is nothing else," Agatha stood up, abruptly ending the conversation.

Jane flinched at her grandmother's hasty dismissal of the nobleman. She was being quite definitely rude, and Jane told her so after the Earl had left.

"I am tired," Agatha said, dismissing the subject. "I am going up to bed."

"I shall help Fannie with the dishes, Grandma."

Once they were alone in the kitchen, Jane told Fannie she was going up to the Abbey.

"When?" Fannie asked, then she gasped. "You can't mean *now*?" Fannie was almost as aghast as Agatha would have been.

"Fannie, I actually saw something today," Jane explained, pleading with the woman.

"I don't understand."

"Neither do I, but I have to go back."

Fannie stared at the girl. "Miss Jane, I can't let you go to secret trysts with that man."

"I'm not. I swear it. I saw the ghost," Jane said dramatically.

Fannie opened, then closed her mouth, at a loss for words.

"Fannie, there's no way I can do this during the day. Gram won't let me! I have to do it now, while she's asleep."

"I will have nothing to do with your going up to the Abbey, and I will not stand here and watch you do it either. Your grandmother is still upset with me about your taking off for your Uncle Nigel's, and she will have both our heads if I let you do something that foolish again."

Fannie stood in front of the door, looking defiant. They stared at each other until Fannie's expression began to change—from defiance to concern and then to worry. Finally, unwillingly, she turned her back. Jane hesitated for one brief moment, then reached to hug the woman before she grabbed her cloak and ran towards the door.

Once Jane was gone Fannie's gaze rose skyward, praying she wasn't being an old fool. She heated milk while she finished drying their supper dishes, then took two mugs upstairs, where she tapped on Agatha's door.

"Are you awake?" Fannie asked, opening the door.

"Yes." Agatha was propped up in bed, her reading glasses on and a book in her hands.

"I brought you up some hot milk."

"Thank you. Is Jane still downstairs?" Agatha asked.

Fannie swallowed hard. "No."

"Good," Agatha said and asked no more. "I'm glad to have her safe in bed."

Fannie felt her conscience pricking her. She moved to a chair near the bed and fidgeted with her mug, but Agatha's thoughts were elsewhere and she didn't notice her servant's unease.

"I can't find my music box," Agatha said.

"What?" Fannie grabbed at the chance to change the subject.

"The big ivory jewel casket which has a music box inside."

"The one that jumped off the bureau," Fannie said, and then, thinking of Jane's words, she continued slowly, "You don't suppose there could be anything to the stories of a ghost, do you?"

"Good grief, don't tell me you're going to start nattering on about a ghost, too."

Fannie bristled a little. "Well, there have been stories over the years."

"From silly young maids. I'm more interested in finding my jewel box than chasing nonsense. I was sure I had packed it."

"I'll look for it in the morning. There are a lot of boxes left to unpack. Oh, I almost forgot. Mrs. Merriweather sent her man over this afternoon to say she'd like to have tea next week."

"That old hen just wants to ask questions about the Earl. Send our regrets and tell her we're busy next week with the move. I'm not going to have tea with that old gossip and sit around discussing Charles Graham all afternoon." Agatha finished her milk. "Did you see the way he kept staring at Jane? I don't like it above half, I'll tell you. In fact, I don't like it at all."

"I don't think there's anything to worry about. Our Jane is a good and sensible girl."

"How good and sensible was she when she let him kiss her?"

"She could hardly stop him," Fannie said practically. "He's as big as a tree."

"That's exactly what I'm afraid of—that she can't stop him."

Fannie watched her employer. "It brings back bad memories, all of this, doesn't it?"

Agatha's face closed over. "I won't have Jane suffer as I did. I simply won't allow her to be a fool."

Fannie stood up. Feeling very guilty she reached for Agatha's cup and bid her employer good night. On the way to the kitchen she prayed that Jane would come to no harm this night. If she did, Agatha would never forgive either of them.

- 14 -

WHILE FANNIE FRETTED over Jane's safety, Jane herself was sneaking into the Abbey through the kitchen. A night lamp was kindled near the doorway, its mellow light barely illuminating the stone-flagged floor. Jane closed the outside door very carefully and crept forward. She stumbled over something, startling the underfootman Tim out of three years' growth.

"Miss Jane," the boy cried out, "I feared you be the ghost they've all been talking of."

"Shhhh." Jane's own heart was racing. "Timmy, I need your help. You mustn't say a word about seeing me tonight. You must promise me it's a secret we'll share. You mustn't say a word."

"Oh, Miss Jane." He gazed at her with adoring eyes, glad to share anything with the pretty young woman. "I won't say nothing ever you don't want me to. Not if all the ghosts in the world tried to get it out of me."

She was more afraid of her grandmother and the Earl than she was of a ghost, but she gave him a tremulous smile. "Thank you, Timmy."

He watched her start for the back stairs. "Hadn't I best come with you? Just in case there really is a ghost?"

She hesitated. The night was dark and a little scary. It might be nice to have company. Then she remembered the ghost's shock when she had seen him. He might never appear if she brought someone else along.

"No, thank you, Timmy. But I think I'll take this."

She reached for a candle branch and lit it before starting up the servants' stairs. She peeked through the green baise door at the top, making sure no one was in the wide main hall before venturing out. The sounds of male conversation came from down the hall. The door to the Earl's sitting-room was open, the Earl and Pickering discussing additions to his wardrobe.

"I think the white-tops, Your Lordship. If you're planning on bringing the hunters down."

"Yes. And send to my father's tailor for country clothes, Pickering. I want the Duke to know I am becoming a model citizen."

Jane slipped across the hall and opened the attic door very carefully. It squeaked a little on its hinges. She halted, standing very still for a moment, hardly breathing. The voices did not stop. They hadn't heard.

Quietly, Jane eased the door open. She thought about closing it after her but, worried about the noise, left it ajar and started up the stairs.

A draft from above caused the candles to waver, then plunged the stairs into darkness. Jane's heart leapt. She could feel it pumping furiously as she took one tentative step and then another towards the attic floor above.

The room was bathed in soft moonlight, Jane moving as quietly as she could manage up the remaining steps. Something was across the room, near the pile of memorabilia she had been rooting out earlier. She stopped at the top of the stairs, hardly daring to breathe. The Ghost was sitting on one of her grandmother's trunks, drooping dejectedly and looking very sad in the pale light.

Lost in his own thoughts, he hadn't heard her yet. A floorboard creaked as she took another step, the Ghost's head jerking up. He swung around to confront her, looking startled and not a little frightened.

"Hasn't anyone ever taught you not to creep up on people? You could scare someone out of their wits."

"Well, my goodness, I didn't expect *you* to be scared of *me*," Jane defended herself. "It's supposed to be the other way around, isn't it?"

"Yes, it is," he agreed testily. "And you're not supposed to be able to hear me, either. You never have before."

"You mean you've been with me before?" Jane asked, her eyes round with surprise.

The Ghost looked annoyed. "You were such a pesky child. When you came along you chased me out of my favourite haunt, the old nurseries where nobody had been in decades. I found this little nook and now you've come traipsing up here as well. Disturbing my peace and quiet, and disturbing all the trunks."

"You were with me when I was a child playing up here?" Jane asked.

"No more than I could help," the Ghost said testily.

"And I never once saw you."

"No, you didn't. So why can you see me now?" he demanded.

"I have no idea," she replied. "Can everybody see you now?"

"No!"

"Whyever not?"

"It's one of the rules. No one's ever been able to hear me or see me," he said darkly, trying to look ferocious.

"Some of the maids said they'd seen you breaking things. That's what gave me the idea for—" she caught herself and stopped.

"Yes, I've heard my name being bandied about of late." He gave her a venomous stare, which she did not seem to notice, irritating him further. "But none see me. They see the results of my terrible temper, but not me. I have expended great energy scaring them, I can tell you. It takes me days sometimes to recover."

"Whyever do you do such silly things?" Jane asked.

"Silly?" He looked affronted.

"Yes. Why try to scare poor little housemaids?"

"Why?"

He tried to look murderous, lifting off the trunk, growing luminous and hovering in the air above her.

Jane merely sat down on the trunk he had vacated and watched him. "That light you get about you is very pretty," was her only response.

"Pretty!" he grumbled. Deflated, he floated to a sitting position on another trunk, losing his luminosity and looking very human. "Pretty!" he scoffed.

"Why do you try to scare people?"

"I don't *try* to scare people. I *do* scare people. How else would a ghost spend his time?"

Jane gave the question serious consideration. "It does seem there must be something more constructive you could be doing."

He started to protest and then just stared at her.

"What's wrong?" she asked him.

"I'm talking. I mean, I'm actually having a conversation with someone," he said. "It's been so long I forgot how pleasant it could be—even with a silly schoolgirl."

"Thank you, but I'm no longer a schoolgirl and I am definitely not silly."

"That's what you say. I can hear what others say."

She was entranced. "Really? What do they say about me?"

"None of your business. I also can see the silly things you do."

"For instance?" she demanded.

"For instance trying to impersonate me," he roared.

Her face fell. "That didn't turn out too well. I'm Jane, by the by."

"I know," he told her.

"What's your name?" she asked.

He stared at her. "Oh dear, I seem to have forgotten how to do this. Sorry. I'm called Harry."

"Harry?" She looked a little disappointed. "I was imagining a biblical name or some such."

"God's teeth, how old do you suppose I am?"

"I have no idea," she replied. "How old are you?"

He looked glum. "I've lost count."

Jane leaned forwards and as she did, he moved away, a little alarmed.

"Could I touch you or would my hand go right through?" Jane asked.

"I don't know, but I'm ticklish, I think. I used to be."

She straightened up. "Why do you haunt the Abbey?"

His expression turned wrathful. "I'm supposed to expiate past sins," he told her.

"You don't sound particularly contrite."

"Nor am I!" he thundered, pleased when she backed off a bit. "I was more sinned against than sinning if you ask me."

"Obviously someone differs with you on that, or you wouldn't be here, would you? How long do you have to stay, by the by?"

He looked gloomy. "I don't know. No one ever tells me anything, but I'm most devilishly afraid it may be until I am contrite and have done all that expiating."

Jane studied him. "You look as if you must have been quite handsome."

He preened a bit. "Some thought so." His expression darkened. "Not that it did me any good, I'll tell you. *Pride goeth before a fall*." He intoned the words as if he had just composed them himself.

"Why do you haunt the Abbey?" Jane asked once again.

He stared at her. "Because I can't leave. Why else?"

"I have no idea," Jane told him. "Having never met a ghost before I have very little inkling of anything about you, except that you seemed terribly sad when I came up here just now."

"If I am it's none of your business," Harry said.

"You can't very well spend eternity just moping about, now can you?" Jane asked.

"I bloody well can if I want."

"There's no need for bad language," she said primly.

"That's easy for you to say. What else have I got to do but mope and haunt and curse if I like? You only have to worry about a paltry hundred years, more or less. I've got thousands to worry about!"

"Why?" she asked.

"Why?" he demanded back.

"Why do you have to be a ghost? Why aren't you laid to rest like everyone else?"

"I *told* you," he said, obviously upset. "Because I was bad— because I *am* bad." He puffed himself up into a great cloud, trying to look ferocious and scare her. He came at her, his voice reverberating around her, "*Bad! Bad! Baaaaddddd!*"

He did not touch her. He approached as close as her breath, then soared away, hurtling towards the far wall.

"Stop! You'll hurt yourself!" Jane cried, but he was already disappearing through the wall.

"Come back," she cried out.

Jane turned and saw a figure in the darkness on the steps. "Harry?" she called out. "Is that you?"

"And who, exactly, is Harry?" the Earl of Warwick asked as he climbed the remaining attic steps and walked towards her, an oil lamp in his hand. "And what is all the shouting up here about?"

"Oh, it's you." She sounded disappointed.

"Who is this Harry?" Charles demanded. "Does your grandmother know you are sneaking about to tryst with men in the middle of the night?"

"How dare you?" she sputtered. "You don't know the first thing about it."

"Where is he?" Charles thrust the lamp towards the corners of the moonlit room, searching out the shadows. "And what is he doing in my house?" Charles demanded severely.

Before Jane could speak, Harry's voice rang out. "It is not your house, by Jupiter, and I can speak for myself."

Something shimmered just beyond the lamp light. "What the devil is that?" Charles asked, his eyes widening as he stared at what looked like the form of a man near the window. It reminded him of the trick of light in the hall a week ago. But when he moved towards it, the image faded.

Charles glared at Jane. "Just what tricks are you up to now?" he demanded.

"Can't you see him?" Jane asked.

"He saw me," Harry said from somewhere nearby, unseen by both and unheard by Charles. The Ghost sounded surprised. "He just won't admit it." Harry continued. "Good Lord, are you the one I am supposed to wait for? Damn and blast, this interloper can't be part of it."

"What are you talking about?" Jane asked Harry.

But Charles answered her. "I'm talking about why you are up here in the middle of the night!"

"You said he saw you," Jane told Harry.

"Miss Steadford, who the devil are you talking to?" Charles demanded.

"Can't you hear him?" she asked Charles.

"Hear whom?" The Earl looked as if he thought she might be demented.

Jane stared at the Earl. "But you saw him."

"I saw—something." Charles peered towards what was now a vague outline of a shimmering form.

"He sees very little and hears less. Typical human failing," Harry informed Jane. "I refuse to help this interloper. I don't care how many years I must serve. He stole the Steadfords' Abbey."

"He didn't exactly steal it. I mean, Great-Uncle Nigel did sell it to him," Jane told the Ghost.

"Who are you talking to about *stealing?*" Charles demanded.

"It is Steadford Abbey and there are no Steadfords in it now," Harry pointed out dramatically. "I must do my penance with *Steadfords*. Now, he has ruined everything."

"Why do you have to do penance with Steadfords?" Jane asked the unhappy Ghost.

"What the blue blazes are you talking about?" Charles shouted.

"Typical human attitude—ignore it and it will go away." So saying, Harry slowly evaporated.

"Don't go," Jane pleaded to the empty air.

"I haven't moved," Charles responded. He looked where she was looking but saw nothing now. The vague shimmering light was gone. "I will escort you down . . . now," he insisted.

"There's no need.," Jane said quickly. "He's gone."

"Now," Charles repeated, leaving her no choice.

He lit the way for both of them down the attic steps. On the next floor Pickering hovered near the door to the attic, looking extremely curious. Charles told his man he was not needed and, unwillingly, Pickering left, heading through the green baize door towards the back stairs and the kitchen below.

Charles turned his full attention on Jane. "I suggest you begin by explaining to me what was going on up there."

"You won't believe me no matter what I say," Jane told him.

"Try telling me the truth," Charles said in clipped tones.

"I was trying to find out why he was here when you scared him away."

"Scared whom away?" Charles demanded.

"The Ghost, of course. Who else?"

Charles stared at the girl. "I was told you were not quite right in the head."

"But you saw him," Jane protested.

Charles wanted to deny seeing anything at all, but his inbred sense of honour made him answer grudgingly, "I saw some sort of fluke of light, which you seem to have taken to be something sentient."

"You just won't admit you saw him. Good grief, you know he's been upset with you."

"Are you trying to tell me that your fictional ghost is not only real, but is haunting me?"

"And you were going to fire innocent people because of it," she accused.

"I cannot believe I am having this conversation."

"That's exactly what he said. He's ever so upset with you."

"Yes, it seems he is a ghost after your own heart; determined to rid the Abbey of my presence," Charles said dryly. "I just wish I could understand how you have accomplished this ghost business."

"I haven't accomplished it. I didn't know he truly existed." She gazed up at him in earnest. "Don't you want to know why he's so upset?"

They were on the grand stairwell, almost down to the entrance hall.

"By all means," Charles told her. "If I am to be haunted, I insist on knowing why."

"You may think this funny, but it's very serious to poor Harry."

"Harry?" he asked.

"Yes, that's his name—the Ghost. You should just see him moping about."

"I've heard him *pacing* about," Charles reminded her caustically. "All night long, for nights on end."

"He has to expiate his wrongs to the Steadford family. That's why he haunts the Abbey. He's upset with you because we're Steadfords and you sent us away."

"Then I suggest you give him your new address, and Nigel's to boot. That should keep him occupied."

Jane bit her lower lip in concentration, her brow furrowing. "I wonder why he didn't come with us, and I wonder why Gram has never seen him. If he is to help us in some way, in expiation of past sins, why hasn't he done so?"

Charles looked down at Jane's earnest expression. Her huge dove-grey eyes were deep in thought. Her hair, as pale as spun gold, haloed around the creamy skin of her oval face. She looked angelic—and completely sincere. Her lips were full and softly rounded, his gaze straying to study them as she spoke.

"I really do have to talk to him and find out more," Jane ended earnestly.

Charles looked incredulous. "Are you trying to tell me you talk to this brainchild of yours?"

"He is not my brainchild. He was very surprised I could hear him."

"So am I," Charles said dryly.

"Well, he can't just be left hanging about here, now can he?" Jane demanded of the Earl.

"I should hope not," Charles agreed. "Unless we can convince him to do his pacing and throwing in the daytime. And, speaking of throwing, that halberd nearly did me in. By Jove, he won't get away with that kind of thing around here!"

"How can you stop him?" Jane asked sensibly.

"I'll send him down to you and your grandmother."

"He is beside himself without us, it seems," Jane agreed.

"Yes, I am," Harry put in.

"Where are you?" Jane asked, looking beyond Charles.

"I beg your pardon?" Charles replied. "What do you mean, where am I? I haven't moved."

Harry shimmered white in the distance, near the front door. He was rewarded with a small gasp from Charles.

"At last, the blind see," Harry said sarcastically. "Even if he doesn't hear."

"In answer to your prior question," Harry intoned his words slowly, as if speaking to the very stupid, "I cannot leave the Abbey walls. I am doomed forever because of this human."

"What the blue blazes am I going to do about this nonsense?" Charles asked himself out loud.

"You'll just have to buck up and manage," Jane told Harry.

"Easy to say, hard to do," Harry replied glumly.

Charles answered her rather more acerbically. "Thank you for the advice."

"What?" Jane asked. "Oh, I didn't mean you. I was speaking to Harry." She looked back towards the Ghost. "The gatehouse is technically part of the Abbey, so you could come home with me."

"Who are you talking to now?" Charles demanded.

Jane glanced at the Earl. "Why, the Ghost of course. Who else?"

"Who else indeed . . ."

Charles stared at her and then squinted towards the door, trying to see the shimmering form more clearly, but all he could make out was light where none should be. He surveyed the windows and mirrors, looking for sensible explanations.

"You could," Jane repeated to Harry, "come home with me now. I'm sure the gatehouse counts as part of the Abbey, and you can't go on throwing things at the poor Earl."

"I did get a bit testy, but imagine how you'd feel, doomed to walk forever twixt heaven and earth."

"It could be worse," Jane said practically, "it could be between earth and—well—below. If you were as bad as you say. I mean—"

"I was. I am!" Harry sounded affronted and began to fade.

"Don't go yet," Jane called out.

"Miss Steadford—Jane—please, stop this nonsense," Charles implored her.

"But, Your Lordship, can't you hear what he's saying? He's leaving."

"I hear nothing but you, talking to yourself."

"Well, surely you can't deny you see him."

Charles would not look towards where the shimmering light had been. "I saw nothing but some trick of light."

"It was no such thing," she told him stoutly.

"All right. I don't understand it, but there has to be a logical explanation."

"There is," Jane told him. "Harry's real."

"Sighting a ghost is not a logical explanation," he thundered. "I will escort you home," he added in a somewhat more subdued tone.

"I shall walk back as I came," Jane told him.

"Fine. I shall walk you back. In any event I intend to have you far from the Abbey before I attempt to get some sleep this night."

On the walk to the gatehouse Jane tried to convince the Earl she was not crazed. That one had to believe in things one actually saw and heard with one's own eyes and ears. Other than muttering comments about Bedlam he did not deign to reply.

When they neared the gatehouse Jane stopped him, her voice lowering to a whisper. "Please don't come any farther. Gram might hear us."

Charles hesitated, looking down at her. "Your grandmother would be very upset about this night's happenings."

Jane touched his arm in supplication. "You mustn't tell her. Please. It would only upset her and it could mean disaster to Harry."

He covered her hand with his own. Jane was bundled into a dark cloak, her pale face beautiful in the moonlit night. He saw her expression change, seeing something of his own thoughts in her eyes. She did not pull away.

"I shall say nothing—at least for the present," he promised.

"Thank you." Her words were tremulous.

"But you must take more care in the future. You should not be wandering the estate alone at night. It isn't safe or seemly," Charles said, his gaze returning to her lips.

"I shall be more careful," she replied faintly. Her knees felt weak and something was drastically wrong with her heart. It fluttered wildly.

The hand on her arm slipped behind her elbow and drew her near.

"What are you doing?" she asked faintly.

His voice was husky. "I think I am going to kiss you."

Jane considered the mixture of emotions which tumbled within her breast. "No," she protested weakly.

Charles leaned to gently kiss her lips, drawing her into his embrace. Her breath left her, the night, her grandmother, and all else forgotten in his arms. He pulled away slowly, releasing her unwillingly. His eyes were solemn as he stared into hers.

"I've never met a more exasperating, more opinionated, more confusing, more fascinating, more lovely female in my life."

She smiled a little tremulously. "Not even in London?"

"Not even in London," he informed her seriously.

He drew her close again, crushing her near and kissing her soundly. When he released her he strode off towards the towering Abbey at the top of the drive, leaving a small smile on Jane's lips as she watched him go.

CHARLES ARRIVED BACK at the Abbey to find Pickering full of curiosity about his lordship's confrontation with Jane. He was, however, doomed to frustration as his employer was obviously preoccupied. The Earl barely spoke as Pickering helped ready him for bed.

"I was quite shocked to see that young person come down from the attic, Your Lordship."

"Hmmm?"

"I couldn't help wondering what Miss Steadford wanted so badly she was rummaging about in the attics in the middle of the night. Do you suppose they left some treasure here—or some dark secret?"

"Foolishness," Charles muttered to himself

"I beg your pardon, Your Lordship, I didn't mean to annoy," Pickering sniffed.

"What?" Charles looked up to see Pickering's aggrieved expression. "Oh, sorry, Pickering, just talking to myself. You may go now."

Crestfallen, the valet left the Earl's rooms, no further enlightened than when he entered them.

Charles sat by the fire in the master suite, a pipe in one hand, a decanter of brandy at his elbow. He stared into the leaping flames, lost in bemused thoughts of Jane.

Footsteps interrupted his reverie. The Earl's head snapped up at the sound, sudden anger quickly eclipsed by astonishment. Across the sitting-room a man dressed in tattered-looking antique clothes paced with his back to Charles. He turned and met the Earl's eyes.

"It seems you can see me too, blast the luck."

"My God," Charles replied, his eyes dilating with shock. "You *do* exist!"

The Ghost shimmered alarmingly, then collapsed back to a more regular shape, his tone sulky. "What is the modem world coming to, that's what I'd like to know. You people are so jaded, you don't blanch at anything."

"I am seeing a ghost," Charles said in wonderment.

"You're not seeing just any ghost," Harry told the Earl, "you're seeing me. My worse luck," Harry growled. "You could barely see me before. What happened to you in between?" Harry demanded. "At least you still can't hear me."

Charles rose from his chair, and the Ghost faded away from him. Charles sat back down. After a minute the Ghost came nearer.

"Won't you have a chair?" Charles offered politely.

"Thank you," Harry replied, sitting across from the Earl. "This is very civil of you, since I tried to kill you."

"I don't suppose you might talk a bit. Jane—Miss Steadford, that is—says you can talk."

Charles drifted off into confused silence. His mind told him his eyes had to be deceiving him. He was obviously dreaming. He thought he was awake, but he was dreaming. And, of course, after all the conversation about ghosts, he was seeing one in his dream—that was all.

"I'm dreaming," he said out loud. "That is the perfectly logical explanation for this impossible situation. I shall wake up soon," Charles comforted himself.

"Just hope you don't wake up like I did," Harry said sourly. "The failure of the human race to see what is as plain as the nose on its face is really quite appalling. If something doesn't fit into your narrow little scheme of things, you dismiss it as impossible. I ask you, was I that stupid when I was human?"

There was none to answer him, which was just as well.

"If you think it's odd for you," Harry continued, "let me just tell you it's odd for me, too. No one could see me, let alone hear me—not even Jane, until today. Now, you—tonight. I suppose the whole county will be coming to take peeks at me tomorrow! Something strange is going on around here and I think it has something to do with my release from this curse. But what the devil can you have to do with it?"

His visage turned even gloomier. "If this means I am to help you—you who took Aggie away from here—well, I want to assure you, I'll, I'll—" Harry considered what he would or could do. "I don't know what I'll do," he said as he began to fade. "But I'll think of something."

Charles watched the apparition evaporate before his very eyes, and assured himself that this proved he was dreaming.

*   *   *

The next morning, breakfast at the gatehouse was served in the alcove off the spacious kitchen, since Fannie was still putting the details of their new home together. Wintry morning sun streamed in through tiny panes of glass, warming the plain oak table across which Agatha was studying Jane's pallid complexion and heavy-lidded eyes.

"You look as if you hadn't slept at all, Jane," her grandmother told her.

Jane tried to smile. "I'm not used to the change yet, that's all. And—well—my mind's been on the stories of Har—of the Abbey Ghost."

"Stuff and nonsense, you see what that sort of thing brings? Sleepless nights and bad dreams and none of it worth a snap of the fingers. Jane, surely you know there is no Abbey ghost, or any other ghosts for that matter."

"But what if there were?" Jane leaned towards her grandmother, her face earnest. "What if ghosts really existed?"

"Jane, what is wrong with you?" Agatha watched her granddaughter closely. "These flights of fancy aren't like you at all. What if ghosts existed, indeed! What if goblins and fairies and Father Christmas existed? What if we could fly? What is the matter with you?"

"Nothing, Gram," Jane said quietly. She turned her attention to her meal, while her grandmother watched her with worried eyes.

"Are you sure you are feeling quite the thing, Jane?"

"I'm fine, truly." She hesitated, then went on in a rush of words. "The Earl sent word he needs me to come to the Abbey."

Fear settled around Agatha's heart. "When did he send word?"

"First thing this morning," Jane replied.

Agatha looked from Jane to Fannie. "And who received this word?"

Fannie looked unhappy. "He truly did, Aggie. You can ask young Tim. He's the one who came to the kitchen door at the crack of dawn."

Agatha looked grim. "I won't allow it. I won't allow you to go up there alone."

"But you must," Jane cried. "He's asked me to go over the estate books with him, and I've already sent word I will."

"You'll just have to send word back that he is to come here if he has any questions."

"But I can't, Gram. He'd have to cart all the estate books with him and . . . and . . . he's a titled nobleman. I can't ask him to upset his convenience and come here."

"He is a titled nobleman with a rakish reputation, and you would be alone with him. I will not have it."

"What do you think will happen to me?" Jane demanded, thoroughly upset.

"Exactly what happened in the hall that night," the old woman shot back. "He has ulterior motives. Mark my words!"

Jane pressed her hands together on her lap, her eyes downcast to her plate. Visions of last night—in the attic first, then Charles kissing her in the lane near the gatehouse—kept her silent. Perhaps he did have an ulterior motive as her grandmother said. And, just perhaps, Jane herself was not opposed to that motive.

"There's no need to pout, Jane. I simply won't have you branded an errant flirt."

"I'm not pouting," Jane said when she trusted her voice again. "Grandmama, I've done all the book work myself for the last five years and with you for the five before that. He needs my help verifying the rents and accounts and in case there is anything he doesn't understand. He has every right to insist upon it and can easily write to Great-Uncle Nigel and have him come down to insist."

Agatha's displeasure showed in her face. The thought of her brother Nigel coming anywhere near them was not one she relished and Jane knew it. "Then I shall go with you," Agatha pronounced finally.

"It is not necessary," Jane told her.

"It most certainly is necessary. Even if I were to give him the benefit of the doubt, which I don't, you are too young and too inexperienced and too easily swayed. If I had any doubt about that, your actions these past days would have convinced me all over again. You have changed, Jane, and there's none to blame for it but him."

"How can you say that?" Jane cried. "How can you blame him for anything to do with me?"

"I can say it because the change in you began the night he had the audacity to kiss you!"

"Gram, I am not a child of three."

"If you were, there would not be a problem," Agatha snapped back. "Even without that proof of his secret intentions, it would not be seemly for you to be in any man's house unchaperoned."

"The Abbey is full of servants who have been with us forever." She could see her grandmother's objections already rising in her eyes and gave in a little. "If you absolutely insist I cannot go alone, then Fannie can come, if you do not trust me. You can come with Fannie if you do not trust either of us. But I swear to you there is no need of your presence. Or Fannie's."

"What is happening to you, Jane?"

Jane met her grandmother's gaze. "I don't know what you mean."

"You have never been deceitful. You have never lied to me in your life. Even when you went to Nigel, you snuck out, but you did not lie to me."

"Nor shall I start now," Jane told her grandmother.

"You're not yourself," Agatha said sharply. "You've been wandering around in a daze, looking like you've gone soft in the head. And when you aren't off in some never-never land of your own making, you are argumentative and stubborn—and so flighty all you speak of is ghosts."

Jane reached for her grandmother's hand, answering only one of the old woman's complaints. "I've always been stubborn, Gram. I take after you."

Agatha wasn't about to be easily appeased, but Jane cajoled her into admitting that perhaps this once there was nothing to worry about. Unwilling to have her granddaughter think she wasn't trusted, Agatha relented enough to say that Fannie could walk her to the Abbey and come back if Jane made sure the doors to any rooms she worked in were open to the hall and the servants' eyes. Also, she must be back by noon or they would come after her.

Fannie used the walk up to the Abbey to impress upon Jane how very much she was worrying her grandmother. "And she doesn't even know the half of it," the abigail ended.

"Fannie, don't you hear me? I told you. I saw him! I saw the Ghost!"

"I heard you. And if I believed you, I would drag you back to the gatehouse right this minute. If there are such things as ghosts they are not the business of honest, God-fearing people. And if there aren't and you're seeing them anyway, you'll be locked up in Bedlam for sure."

Jane had tried to appease the abigail, but it was a distracted and concerned Fannie who arrived back to find Agatha in the parlour, going through the box of memorabilia Jane had brought from the Abbey. Agatha was fingering a faded red ribbon which banded together a packet of old letters.

"I put a word in Pickering's ear," Fannie said as she entered the parlour. She watched Agatha drop the letters back in the box.

"He is as concerned about appearances and propriety as you could wish and will keep an eye on them so that no tales can be told."

Agatha's gaze drifted towards the window which looked up the gently rising hillside to the Abbey's stone walls.

Fannie saw the direction of that gaze. "Let her be," was Fannie's advice.

Agatha turned to face the woman who had come to her a servant and ended by becoming a friend. "How do I do that? This is all my fault."

"What is all your fault?" Fannie asked.

"Jane is becoming enamoured of that man," Agatha replied.

"Our Jane? She can't stand him. She's done nothing but complain about his coming here."

"Don't be shatter-brained. She's not had one bad word to say about him since last week—since he kissed her," she added, fear making her words even sharper.

"Even if she were a little taken with him, wouldn't that be the very best thing for her, to form such an eligible connexion? She could make a splendid marriage."

"Or be cast off as used goods." Agatha's voice was shrill.

Fannie was startled by Agatha's vehemence. "Aggie, why do you insist that all this must end in tragedy?"

"Because he's a man," Agatha replied. "And because I have failed her. Jane is susceptible because I have sheltered her too much. If she had more experience, her head would not have been turned by the first man who kissed her. And trust me, it has been. I know the signs only too well."

"Aggie, it can be quite wonderful to have your head turned by the first man who kisses you."

Agatha stood up, too upset to sit still any longer. "You don't know what you're talking about," she challenged. "Her entire life will be ruined if she trusts this man."

"Or any man?" Fannie asked quietly.

"Or any man," Agatha agreed.

Fannie stood up too, smoothing her skirts. "You are dooming her to a life of solitude. Do you truly want your granddaughter to be as sad as you have been—as alone as I have been?"

Agatha searched the other woman's eyes. "No," she said slowly. "I do not want her unhappy, or hurt, or alone."

Fannie pressed her advantage. "Jane has a good head on her shoulders. She can handle the Earl perfectly well all by herself."

"I wish I had your confidence in that fact," Agatha said quietly. She gave Fannie a long, hard look. "And if you're wrong, Fannie, if you encourage her and you're wrong—then what?"

Fannie stared back at her employer, hearing the words and worry more than Agatha could know.

While Fannie and Agatha argued in the gatehouse, Jane was experiencing her own qualms in the Abbey study. Her grandmother's worries about ulterior motives weighed heavily on her conscience. If her grandmother knew she had let Charles kiss her again last night, she would be more than shocked. She would be very hurt.

Jane was even calling him Charles now, she chided herself. He was an Earl, the Earl of Warwick. He was his lordship, not merely Charles, and she must not let herself forget it.

Charles glanced up from the account book in front of him. "Is something wrong?" he asked. He looked as if he were about to say more and then didn't. The strange look in his eyes had been there since he first greeted her and escorted her into the study. The questions he asked did not seem to be so urgent he would send for her at the crack of dawn, but she answered them, one by one, nonetheless.

"Is something wrong?" he asked again.

"No, nothing," Jane replied.

"You looked worried."

"I was just thinking about my grandmother."

"Has something happened?" Charles asked.

"Not yet," Jane replied.

Charles gave her a questioning glance, then shoved the Abbey books away. "I think you've provided all the information I need at the moment," he said.

Jane stood up. "Then I should get back—"

"Wait," he said quickly, then looked down to the desk, searching for an excuse to hold her there a little longer. He seized a map and spread it out. "I want to show you something."

Jane came towards him slowly, standing beside the desk and gazing down at the parchment map he had unfolded.

"This is a map of the New World. My father's land is here, along what is called the Mississippi River."

"It looks so far away—so exotic," Jane said.

"Perhaps one day you'll see the New World yourself."

"I rather doubt it," Jane said quietly. "Well, if there's nothing else—"

Charles studied Jane's pensive face, still trying to find a way to keep her there with him. He looked back at the account books.

"I—I didn't see payments for the first four months of 1802 from the tenant farmers."

"They paid, but it was a very bad winter and they asked if the rents could be held until after the spring planting when they needed the ready cash for seed and equipment. They paid the past-due amounts out of their revenues in the next summer and fall. It's all there—" she added quickly, lest he think the farmers still in default.

"Show me where the payments were credited," Charles said.

Jane bent to the task, poring through the books until she found the notations which would prove their payments. As she worked, Charles watched the golden curls around her forehead fall forwards to frame her face with tendrils of silk, watched her absentmindedly worrying her lower lip in concentration.

She felt his gaze and looked up, self-conscious. "The payments are here."

"Jane," he called her name softly, looking into her eyes. There was something hypnotic about his gaze which she couldn't seem to resist. "I didn't send for you just because of the accounts."

Her heart stumbled. Her grandmother's warnings rang loud in her ears. She wrenched her gaze away from his and stood up.

"Don't go," the Earl said.

"I—I must." She appeared ready to flee the room and the house.

"I saw him," Charles told her and earned an astonished look as she turned back to stare full at him. "I saw Harry."

"Are you teasing me?" Jane asked.

"I am quite serious. I wasn't going to tell you. I tried to tell myself it was merely a dream. But I think—that is—did he wear very old-fashioned clothes, rather like tattered purple velvet?"

"Yes," she exclaimed, "and he looked as young as you!"

Charles stared at her. "I was afraid of that."

"I beg your pardon?"

"I was afraid it wasn't a dream," Charles replied.

"Why did you go back up to the attic?" she asked.

"I didn't. He was in my rooms."

Jane digested the Earl's words. "What happened? What did he say?"

"He said nothing," Charles replied.

"Nothing?"

"I saw him as plain as I'm seeing you, not the shadowy light pattern I had seen earlier. But he did not speak. Or, if he did, I could not hear him."

"I must talk to him again," Jane told the Earl. "I must find out why he can't leave this building and how we can help him. He is so lonely. I was hoping to see him this morning."

Charles watched her. "I rather hoped I might be part of the attraction."

"I—I do not understand."

She started to back away from the desk, but his hand came up slowly to touch the sleeve of her grey kerseymere gown. His fingers trailed down her arm, not holding her precisely, but moving, deliberately, towards her hand. She stood where she was, torn between her common sense and her heart.

"Please, Your Lordship, my grandmother is expecting me."

Still, Jane loved the touch of his hands. She could feel the now-familiar weakness begin to filter down through her limbs as she gazed up at him. For one brief moment all else was forgotten. Then she remembered her grandmother's words and moved away.

"Please, do not do this."

"What is wrong?" the Earl of Warwick asked.

Jane looked up at him with saddened eyes. "Everything."

"That's a rather tall order to fix," he told her gently.

"I owe my grandmother everything. Without her I would have been alone, cast adrift in the world—homeless, parentless, and penniless. She means the world to me."

"How does that affect us?" he asked.

Jane faced him, her voice tremulous but her resolve firm. "My grandmother does not trust men—any men. And, particularly, she does not trust—you."

He frowned. "Is she against me because I bought the Abbey?"

"I'm sure it broke her heart to leave her childhood home, the home her father had left to her. But I don't think that is the real reason."

"What else can she feel is to my discredit?"

Jane shook her head. "I'm not sure it is even that personal. I fear it may simply be that you are a man."

He looked down at his boots, then back up at her face, his expression very serious. "That reality would be rather hard for me to change."

Jane gave him a small smile. "And we didn't make her feel any safer the night we—"

"Kissed," he supplied and then continued. "She must have thought me a complete cad when she saw you in my arms that night." Jane did not disagree. "If she knew we had kissed—again—"

"She must not!" Jane's voice rose with her emotions. "It would cut her to the quick."

Charles clasped Jane's hands in his own. "You have nothing to fear from me. On that head or any other. I promise you that. No matter what you have heard of my reputation."

"Your reputation?"

Charles stared at her earnestly. "My father has told me for many long years that I must mend my ways. Until now, I have seen no reason to do so. I have been quite content with my life and my wayward habits. But you have made everything seem quite different somehow."

"I don't understand," Jane said shyly.

"Neither do I," Charles replied. "But I intend to ferret out the answer—ghosts or no."

Jane blushed, letting him hold her hands a moment longer, unwilling to sever the bond between them and trembling with emotions she did not want to acknowledge.

"I must leave," she told him finally, then fled from the room and the house before she had a chance to change her mind.

Charles Edward Graham, Ninth Earl of Warwick, stared after the retreating figure of the girl who had at first intrigued and then incensed and finally entranced him. He was, in fact, thoroughly entranced with this fey creature whose lips responded so willingly to his yet had so little experience, so little knowledge, of the opposite sex.

He intended to change that last circumstance. He had been indulged all his life, his slightest wishes being other people's commands. He was not accustomed to denial of any of his wishes— or appetites.

- *16* -

SPRING CAME EARLY. The Abbey grounds responded with green shoots of new foliage bursting from the winter-barren trees. The tenant farmers plowed and planted, the aroma of fresh-turned earth pungent in the still-crisp early spring air. At the gate-house Agatha attacked the gardens with a passion, planting new rosebushes amongst the already-flourishing ones. Jane worked with her grandmother in the loamy earth, trying to assuage her guilty conscience. Agatha was acutely aware of the changes in Jane, and her attitude towards her granddaughter was coloured by her own guilts.

They were pruning the older plants back on a fine spring morning with the dew still fresh on the damp earth when Agatha began, once again, to try to explain to Jane why she was so fearful.

"It is my fault entirely," Agatha was saying, Jane remonstrating with her, telling her to stop. "No, I cannot. I must take full responsibility. It is my fault you have led such a sheltered life. I have done you an unintentional disservice."

"You have ever done all that you could for me, Gram, and I will not listen to this," Jane said with some little asperity.

She unbent from her chores, wiping her hands on the apron she had donned over her plain grey gown. Worn by another, the grey flannel might have faded into nothingness, been drab and unappealing. But the gown matched the colour of Jane's eyes precisely, the small bit of white lace at collar and cuffs setting off her delicate features and long, tapered fingers.

The apron of snowy white cotton seemed to brighten her paleness, and the smudges of dirt from their rooting about in the gardens looked very like the work of a small pretty child, and equally sweet to the eye.

"You know nothing of men and that is entirely my fault. In attempting to shelter you, I have made you vulnerable to the first personable man who has paid attention to you."

"Please excuse me ladies," Charles's voice came across the gate which led from the small garden into the lane and thence to the wide drive beyond. "Am I interrupting you? I fear that I may be early—"

Jane was already on her feet, brushing at her skirts and looking a bit flustered. "I shall only be a moment." So saying she ran towards the gatehouse, untying her apron strings as she went.

She left two wary people behind her. Her grandmother cast a hard-eyed look at the Earl, then bent back to her work. He, meanwhile, sought a fruitful area of conversation, but was deterred by the impediment of Lady Agatha's back turned towards him. He was rescued a few moments later by Jane's reappearance, her plain chip bonnet tied beneath her chin by a wide pink ribbon.

Agatha straightened up slowly, one hand to the small of her back, as Jane and the Earl walked towards the waiting horses which Homer held for them. Fannie walked towards her employer.

"Are you all right, Aggie?"

"A little sciatica. Nothing important," Agatha replied, rubbing her back.

"I didn't mean your backside," Fannie said tartly. "I meant about Jane going off riding with his lordship."

Agatha gazed after their retreating figures as their steeds carried them away. "I have tried the alternatives, and I think it worse when I protest too much. She will only rebel and go to him behind our backs if I persist in those protests." Agatha's gaze turned inwards, remembering bygone days.

Fannie had the grace to look guilty. "I am sure she won't do anything foolish."

Agatha's reply was slow in coming. "I hope you are right, but I fear you are wrong. I fear Jane takes after me when I was young."

Far across the Abbey grounds, Jane and Charles were riding fast and furious, bating each other and enjoying the competition. Out of breath, they reined in at last, Jane's cheeks burning with excitement and the wind which raced past them. Charles looked windblown too, his dark unruly locks ruffled and appealing. He reminded her of a small boy caught in the act of having fun.

"Good Lord, that felt good," he exclaimed. "Even though you are the worst sort of female."

"I beg your pardon?" she objected.

He was smiling broadly. "You are competitive!"

"I am not!"

"Competitive and argumentative," he told her and laughed,

throwing his head back and letting his exhilaration rise towards the clear blue skies above them,

Jane smiled, then joined his infectious merriment, laughing herself at the exhilaration of freedom and fresh air and a good steed and—good company.

"This is wonderful," she exclaimed. "Perhaps you will not have to leave for your New World holdings after all. Perhaps you will be able to stay and—and ride the estates forever!"

He reached across the space between their steeds to grasp her hand. "Perhaps I would like to do more than ride."

Jane looked down, blushing, before meeting his eyes. "I had best get back to Gram."

He took a long breath and slowly released her hand. "I shall escort you," he told her.

That night Agatha heard Jane stirring in her room across the hall after the lamps were out. When the sounds of unrest continued, Agatha got up and put on her robe. She tapped on Jane's door and was greeted by a startled response.

"Yes?"

Agatha opened the door, hesitating on the threshold. "I thought I heard you still up."

"I'm sorry, Gram, I didn't mean to disturb you."

"You haven't disturbed me," Agatha said quickly. "I was just making sure you were all right."

"I'm fine," Jane replied.

Still Agatha delayed, choosing her words carefully. "I am worried about you, about your seeing that man. I feel it is my fault that he is turning your head."

"He isn't turning my head, Gram. It's not like that at all."

"Isn't it?" Agatha queried. "I was once young, Jane, and was very, very foolish. I let a man make a fool of me and had to live through the consequences."

Jane came near to hug her grandmother. "I swear to you on my honour, I shall never do anything to hurt you, Gram. I owe you everything."

Agatha shook her head, trying to control the tears which threatened to erupt. "You owe me nothing. I'm not worried for myself, child. I'm worried about you."

"I am fine, Gram. I am in no danger."

Agatha peered at her granddaughter. "I hope that's true, Jane. For your sake, I hope that's true."

Long after Agatha had left, her words rang in Jane's ears, making Jane more and more unhappy as she considered them.

At the Abbey the next morning Charles woke to find Harry perched on the edge of his bed. "Hell's bells, you're here again!"

"It's not quite hell's bells yet," Harry informed the Earl.

Charles stared at the Ghost. "My God, you said something! I heard you!"

"You couldn't have," Harry thundered. "You haven't heard me before!"

"Nevertheless, I seem to be hearing you now."

"How will I haunt this place if at every turn people say, 'Oh, so *you're* here again'?" Harry asked heatedly. "You've doomed me to haunt here forever, and you wondered why I was so upset I threw that halberd at you."

"How can you blame me for your predicament, let alone be willing to *kill* me? I didn't even know you existed," Charles defended himself as he reached for his robe. He swung his long legs out from under the covers and straight through Harry. "Oh," Charles sat up. "Sorry."

"Hmmm?" Harry was lost in gloomy thoughts of his bleak future.

"Didn't you feel anything?" Charles asked, astounded. "I'm afraid I managed to put my feet right through you."

"It tickled a bit. That's always been my problem," Harry told the human magnanimously, but he still looked dejected.

Charles rose from the bed, his mind still arguing against the existence of ghosts even as he stood there staring at one and talking to it. Charles eyed the demoralised Ghost.

"I am sorry if I've put you in a bit of a muddle, old man," Charles said, feeling foolish.

"You should be. I must warn you, I shall probably become fairly bellicose in the years ahead. I mean, it's all well and good to have someone to talk to, but you shall only be here for fifty or sixty years at best and I shall have to stay on through eternity—because of *you*. That could make for some hard feelings, and the Aldworths have always been known for their tempers rather than their patience."

"Aldworths?"

"Oh." The Ghost came to his feet, or something very near, and seemed to hover an inch or so off the floor. "My apologies. My manners seem to have disappeared with decades of disuse. I am

Sir Henry Daniel George Aldworth, Bart." He bowed his head slightly. "Or, at least, I was."

"Sir Henry," Charles acknowledged, "I am Charles Edward Graham, Earl of Warwick. But I rather thought you were called Harry."

"Ah, you've heard of me. Everyone used to call me Harry, and I prefer it. No point in being bloody formal when you haven't got a pot to your name—or even a proper body."

"If you'll forgive the impertinence, I really am most awfully curious as to why you are in this—condition."

"What's wrong with my condition?" Harry asked rather belligerently. He glanced down at himself. "I assure you I was always considered the picture of sartorial elegance."

"I meant the condition of being a—well—an apparition."

"I am not an apparition," Harry replied, obviously offended. "An apparition is a delusion, a figment of the imagination. I assure you I am definitely not a figment of your imagination."

"I sincerely hope not," Charles said. "I'm told insanity runs in the Steadford family, but it does not in mine. I should hate to be the first."

"What insanity in the Steadford family?" Harry demanded. "Who told you that?"

"Nigel Steadford."

Harry's face contorted into a pugnacious grimace. "Nigel Steadford is a pusillanimous, lily-livered puritan who wouldn't know the truth if it up and bit him."

Having delivered himself of this diatribe Harry seemed to feel a bit better and made himself comfortable by perching on top of the bedpost, which considerably disconcerted poor Charles.

"Doesn't that hurt?" Charles asked.

"What? Oh, the bedpost? No. One of the few benefits of being a ghost is that nothing can hurt you physically. The worst is a bit of a tickle, as I said earlier."

Charles went back to the matter at hand. "Are you saying Nigel Steadford isn't altogether honest?"

"Nigel Steadford is never altogether anything, let alone honest."

"He mentioned his sister, and some cousins marrying in Jane's case—"

"Balderdash! Jane name all right but cousins—Bah. They were so far removed, it don't signify. His grandfather's father was a cousin of Aggie's great-grandfather. What does that make them,

I ask you? And as for that nincompoop's mentioning Aggie—well, I'll tell you, if I still had my body I'd give him a proper melting just for his thoughts, let alone his deeds towards his sister."

"I gather there's no love lost between brother and sister," Charles put in.

"And why should there be when he was the first to cast blame at poor Aggie, the first to throw stones?"

Charles looked totally perplexed. "Cast blame? Throw stones? About what?"

Harry quieted. "Nothing. It was a long time ago." His tone hardened as he continued. "But it was he who forced her to marry his idiot friend Smyth, and it was Nigel who encouraged Smyth's gambling and had him sign over Aggie's Abbey as collateral for gambling debts—most of which were owed to that scoundrel Nigel Steadford himself."

"You seem remarkably well informed," Charles said quietly.

"And why not? Wasn't I in the room when he did the dastardly deed?"

"But you did not appear—in the flesh, so to speak—to them?"

"I couldn't," Harry said, looking very dejected indeed.

He drifted down from his perch and ended up on the chair farthest from the fireplace. It was a lovely cherry-wood piece with the cabriole, curved legs which identified it as a Chippendale, but neither Harry nor Charles were taking note of their surroundings.

"I was just getting started, you see," Harry said. "Feeling my way, as it were. I hadn't gained any control over my new powers and none of my old ones worked at all."

Charles digested this information. "So you have not been a ghost for very long."

Harry looked grumpy. "If you were me, you'd think it plenty long enough. How would you like to spend the next three decades hovering about with no one to talk to?"

"You've been a ghost for three decades?" Charles asked.

"Didn't I just say that?" Harry complained impatiently.

"I'm sorry, but you must give me a moment. All this is quite new to me. I'm not in the habit of conversing with ghosts."

"Well, I'm not in the habit of conversing at all, so that makes us rather even, wouldn't you say?"

A tap at the outer sitting-room door startled them both. "Yes?" Charles called out as Harry began to fade.

Pickering came in, crossing the sitting-room in a stately, stiff-backed pace. "I thought I heard you, Your Lordship."

"Heard me?" Charles queried.

"Actually, I thought I heard you speaking to someone."

Charles glanced towards where the Ghost had been sitting. "Nonsense. Who would I be speaking to?"

"I wouldn't know, Your Lordship," Pickering replied.

Harry spoke from beside Charles's right ear. "You'd best watch out. If Nigel hears you're wandering about talking to yourself, he'll call you crazed too."

"Damn Nigel Steadford and his meddling," Charles replied.

"I beg your pardon?" Pickering said as Harry laughed and clapped Charles on the shoulder.

"By Jove, at least we agree on that," Harry said.

"Nothing," Charles replied to Pickering.

There followed a brief pause during which Pickering attempted to gauge his employer's visage. Pickering had very acute hearing, and he could have sworn he had heard the Earl's voice raised in quite lengthy conversation before he tapped on the door.

Curious as to who had invaded the Earl's chambers at such an early hour, Pickering spoke noncommittally. "Are you quite all right, Your Lordship?"

"Quite all right," Charles told his man. "What the devil is the matter with you this morning, Pickering?"

"Me, sir?"

"Do you see anyone else here?" Charles demanded.

"No, Your Lordship. I am sorry, Your Lordship. I, ah, I didn't sleep very well last night."

Charles turned away, untying his robe, and allowed his valet to help him dress for the day.

JANE HELPED FANNIE with the cleaning chores at the gatehouse and then took off in the early afternoon for a solitary walk. Early crocuses and hyacinth mingled with bleeding hearts and the woodland mosses which massed beneath the great oaks and chestnuts. Yellows and lavenders and reds blended with the deep green foliage, carpeting the world in spring finery.

Jane wandered through the Abbey woods, an ancient gnarled oak rising before her as she went deeper into the forested gloom. The oak grew upwards from a curved fork, as if the tree trunk had been split in two. Heavy branches new-laden with young spring leaves reached out in all directions above the wide fork from whence two thick trunks stretched upwards toward the sky.

Jane drew near and then lingered beside the huge old oak, fingering its rough bark. Her thoughts were a million miles away. She reached down to pluck a wild violet from the clump of stray plants which flourished in the shelter of the tree.

Holding the tiny blossom Jane stepped up onto one of the oak's thick, exposed roots, smoothing the skirt of her plain blue dress. A bird called out to its mate whose trilling notes answered as Jane leaned back in the juncture made by the branching of the thick tree trunk.

Sounds of movement made her look up to see the Earl's grey picking his way across the leaf-strewn meadow, walking sedately as he neared the stand of oaks. Charles looked regal aboard the handsome grey—his dark, unruly locks wind-blown, his riding clothes of the very finest cut, his face as chiseled as a Greek god's. Jane watched him dismount. He tethered the horse to a thick branch and left him to nose through the nearby mosses and violets. Coming closer, Charles stopped a few feet away.

"I hope I'm not interrupting your reverie."

Jane's smile was a little tremulous, her voice shy. "I was merely resting for a moment."

Charles came still closer to where she sat cradled in the tree's branching trunk. "You looked very sad."

She gazed past him, towards the horse foraging in the violets. "Have you seen Harry again?"

"Harry is becoming quite accustomed to showing up for chats and earning me a reputation for rather strange behaviour."

"Truly?" Jane's eyes widened.

"Truly. Pickering thinks I'm acting very strangely. I answer questions he hasn't asked and talk to the walls and generally seem off my stride."

Jane was smiling. "That's famous!"

"You may think so, but I assure you Pickering is ready to commit me for observation." Charles was smiling back, strangely happy at the sight of her dancing eyes. "I haven't seen you for days on end."

Jane faltered. "I've been busy helping Grandmama."

"You've been avoiding me," he told her, seeing the truth in her eyes. "Tell me why," he persisted.

"I've not—"

Charles took possession of her hands. "Tell me why," he repeated.

Jane looked down at the long, blunt, well-formed fingers holding her own slender ones. His touch warmed her heart, her love shining from her eyes when she met his gaze. "Gram is terribly worried and wants me with her constantly."

"Because?"

"Because she thinks you are turning my head."

Charles watched Jane. "Am I?" he asked softly. She didn't answer. He brought her fingers to his lips.

"Charles, please—"

"There is something I must tell you. I have received word from my father that I must journey to the New World to protect our lands. The new American government is having trouble keeping control over their holdings, and the French have land very near ours. It is a beautiful place I'm told, but still brutal. There are even wild Indians, Jane."

"It sounds dangerous and fascinating." She spoke in a low tone. "Does this mean you are leaving the Abbey?"

"I will have to leave soon." He saw quick tears form in her eyes.

"I shall miss you greatly," Jane told him in broken tones.

"You don't have to miss me," Charles said.

She looked confused. "I don't understand."

"Jane, I want to marry you." The words came tumbling out in a passionate rush. "I want you to come with me to America."

Jane stared up into his eyes. "If only I could."

His heart leapt in his breast. "Truly? Do you truly feel the same? Tell me you want me, too."

"No, please, Charles, don't even say it. We can't even think about it, or about ourselves."

"Why do you say that?"

"Because I could never leave Gram." She spoke simply, her words dropping like stones in his heart.

"Everyone leaves home sooner or later, Jane. She cannot expect you to live your whole life for her."

"She has lived hers for me," Jane told him.

"But that's different."

Jane found the tears welling up in her eyes and had to look away, blinking them back. "I must get back to her."

Charles helped her from her perch and then, slowly, released her hands. "Will you at least think about it, or allow me to ask her for your hand in marriage?"

"No!" Jane implored him with her eyes. "You must not worry her with it. I shall never leave her, Charles. Never. Not even to go to the next county, let alone the New World."

The Earl of Warwick watched helplessly as Jane walked away from him. When she was near the edge of the stand of oaks she looked back, her face forlorn but resolute. The Earl untethered the grey and swung himself up into the saddle, his face set in harsh lines as he rode in the opposite direction, back to the Abbey.

When he arrived he was abrupt with the stableman who helped him dismount, striding past him and up the stairs with a barely civil nod in answer to Homer's questions about his ride. Inside the huge entry hall Charles's boots slapped the floor hard, the sounds echoing up the stairwell.

"Pickering!"

The valet appeared from the back of the house, one of Charles's boots in his hands. "Your Lordship called?"

"I want to send a letter to my father immediately."

"Yes, Your Lordship, I'll just finish—"

"Put the blasted boot down and get me my writing paper," Charles thundered.

Pickering wisely kept silent. The Earl's foul mood descended like a dark cloud over the entire staff as the day wore on.

Jane arrived back at the gatehouse to find her grandmother watching out the window. Agatha let the curtain drop as Jane came inside.

"Have you been out with the Earl again?" Agatha asked without preamble.

"He happened to be out riding, Gram, that's all. We spoke a bit."

"About what?" Agatha demanded. "What does a Peer of the Realm have to discuss with my granddaughter? More estate business, I suppose?"

"Gram, please—you need have no fears on that head. I shall never do anything which would upset you."

Agatha's hands twitched at her sides. She stared into Jane's unhappy face. "I know you think me unreasonable, but I am worried for you."

"I know you mean the best for me," Jane said, then turned away. "I shall wash my hands and help Fannie with dinner."

"Jane, please wait," Agatha said. She sat down on a narrow Queen Anne chair and picked up the packet of old letters she had kept close at hand ever since Jane brought them from the Abbey. "I must make you understand my concern."

"It's all right, Grandmother."

"No, it's not. You think me hopelessly old-fashioned and him an honourable man from whom you have nothing to fear. Believe me, nothing could be further from the truth."

"Gram, you don't even know him." Jane looked reproachful.

"Hear me out, Jane. I've had a long talk with Mrs. Summerville. Charlotte had a Season in London last year. Mrs. Summerville knows all about the Earl of Warwick, as does the rest of London. He is a rake and a roué and consorts with the lowest types. His father ordered him away from London for his gambling debts and, I'm told, was very near disinheriting him."

"This is preposterous gossip."

"It is the sad truth. He had every young girl dangling after him and went from one to another with abandon, as he has done for some years past, according to the London set. They warned Margaret to keep Charlotte safe so that her reputation would not be ruined."

"He isn't like that."

"Leopards don't change their spots, Jane. I tell you this because I want to save you from harm. I want to save your virtue."

"He loves me," Jane burst out.

It took Agatha a moment to digest the words. When she did her own came slowly. "You're not the first he's told that, nor shall you be the last. If you do not believe me, ask Charlotte or Margaret Summerville."

"He wouldn't say the things he does. He couldn't. I'd know if he were not in earnest," Jane defended.

"You have no experience of men. They will say anything and make it seem the truth—until they have their way with you."

"No!"

"Yes! I know, Jane. I know." Agatha faltered a little and then went resolutely on. "I made the mistake I am trying to protect you from."

Jane had no words to answer her grandmother's admission. She looked down at the older woman who sat ramrod straight on the edge of the narrow chair, her fingers grasping each other as if to give her strength to continue her confession.

"I loved not wisely but too well. I was young and in love and believed everything he told me. He wanted to hold my hand, and I saw no harm in it. He wanted to kiss me, and I said no but he kissed me anyway. I—I thought us both in love." Agatha's eyes pleaded for Jane's understanding. "He left me, Jane, and took my reputation and my good name with him. He deserted me and his desertion forced me into a marriage of convenience with a man I could never love. I've sheltered you so that none could tar you with the same black brush."

"Gram, I'm sorry." Jane knelt down in front of her grandmother, reaching for her hands. "I am truly sorry, but that was another time, another person. It's not all men."

"It is all men. Sooner or later they show their true colours, from Nigel to all others. They use us for their own purposes, Jane. You can never, never trust a man."

"Gram, don't." Jane sounded anguished.

"I have to make you understand that men are not to be trusted. I won't have happen to you what happened to me."

Jane sprang to her feet, tears filling her eyes. "Please, stop."

"He will say anything, promise anything, to get you to trust him, and once your virtue is lost he will tire of you and throw you aside," Agatha continued relentlessly. "He will go on to his next conquest with nary another thought for you."

"No!" Jane ran out of the room. Wrenching the front door open, she ran outside and up the lane, blinded by tears.

"What do you think you are doing?" Fannie asked from the doorway behind Agatha.

"Saving her the worst grief of all—being ostracized from polite society, whispered about behind her back. Jane has no inheritance such as I did to tempt a bounder like Smyth to accept damaged goods."

"Have you considered the possibility that the Earl really does feel some affection for our Jane? She is a lovely child, with her own charms."

"More than enough charms to get her in trouble," Agatha replied darkly.

"How can you be so sure he is a bad one?"

"They are all bad ones, given the chance," Agatha said.

Fannie looked out the window at Jane's retreating figure as she ran across the meadow, her shoulders hunched forwards. "She looks to be crying, the poor thing."

"Better crying for a lost dream than over a ruined life."

Fannie studied her employer's unhappy face. "Is life worth living if we have no dreams?" Fannie asked the words quietly, not waiting for a reply as she turned towards the kitchen.

Alone once again, Agatha stared at the beribboned packet of old letters. It had been so very long ago. He had been tall and dark and handsome and very much like Charles Graham. He had left her to face the consequences of their love alone. He had given her a son who left home at the earliest opportunity because of the man who was her husband and whom he had thought to be his father. Her son Daniel had been lost fighting the French. She felt hot tears forming behind her eyes and fought them back. She had never seen him after his fourteenth birthday and never would see him again.

Her resolution became even more firm. Jane would be spared knowing any of those agonies—no matter what the cost.

- *18* -

JANE SLOWED HER headlong flight, her breath coming in jagged spurts, a painful stitch in her side doubling her over. She was near the south side of the Abbey. The windows and doors of the long-closed public rooms were heavily draped and silent just beyond where she stood, gathering her breath.

The tears dried on her cheeks as the wind whipped through her dishevelled hair. She glanced at the Abbey, her attention drawn to an undraped doorway. She peered into the darkness of the empty ballroom, wondering why this lone door had been left open. Then she caught a glimpse of movement.

Taking a few steps closer she saw Harry and stopped. He seemed to be motioning to her. He was dressed in dark colours which blended with the darkness of the room's interior. He motioned again, but she still hesitated. A fleeting thought of the fearfulness of such an unnatural being stopped her.

She told herself she could just possibly be crazed even to believe Harry existed, let alone that she was seeing him again. But Charles had seen him, too, and had spoken to him, so it could not just be a trick of her mind.

Harry was much too real for that.

He came to the doorway, staring out at her. "How is she?" he asked. "How is Aggie?" Jane walked forwards answering, "Gram is a little put out with me and my talk of ghosts, but she's fine otherwise."

Jane walked through the terrace doors into a fifty-foot-long ballroom which had once upon a time, in Agatha's youth, been filled with music and laughter. All the countryside had come from miles around to attend the Steadfords' balls and dinners and levees. Now it was an empty dark chamber, with rather more dust than it would have if the maids bothered to do their work thoroughly.

Harry had retreated back into the room. "Are you afraid of me?" he asked.

"No," Jane replied, "but it's so dark—"

"If you're not afraid of me, you have nothing to fear from the dark," Harry told her. "There's nothing else here but me. I'd know."

He was rewarded with a small smile. "I suppose you'd be sure to," Jane said.

"I've been hoping to see you for weeks," he told her. "I thought you'd at least come by to see how I was faring."

"I wanted to," Jane told him.

"Well, then, why didn't you?" he asked.

"Gram does not want me up here," she said quietly.

"Did you tell her about me?" he asked.

"I tried to. But she insists that ghosts do not exist and won't listen to a word of it."

"She always was a stubborn female. You come by the trait honestly enough," he said with more accuracy than courtesy. "She wants you to stay away so that you'll stop talking of ghosts?"

"Not exactly," Jane said slowly. "She says I'm not to see Char—I'm not to see the Earl."

"Damn and blast!"

"Harry!" Jane remonstrated, shocked. "That is not proper language to be using in polite company."

He looked grumpy. "Well, she's fast on to making this a proper Cheltenham tragedy the way she's mixing in where she doesn't belong."

"I don't understand," Jane said.

Harry retreated farther into the room. Jane watched him and then followed him towards a red velvet window seat which filled one of the bay window embrasures.

"I am doomed to this miserable half-existence unless I can help the course of true love run smooth," Harry said as he sat himself on one side of the wide seat. "I thought I told you."

"You told me no such thing." Jane sat down across from Harry, reaching to pull the heavy red velvet drapes back a bit. A stream of sunlight fell upon the seat between them and the floor beyond, cutting a bright swath across the dark room and meeting the sunlight which streamed in through the undraped and open terrace door.

"You told me you had to expiate sins against the Steadfords. What can the course of true love have to do with that?" Jane asked the ghost.

"You are an intelligent girl. I don't know why you can't see what's as plain as the nose on your face. Think about it, girl. After all these years of ghostly solitude, two humans can see and hear me. Two people who love each other. Don't try to protest and blush it away. I can see right through you, too, you know."

"Can you?" Jane looked startled and quite intrigued with the idea.

"Both of you," he averred. "Now—since you're the only two lovers I know and the only two who can talk to me, and I have to help true love—doesn't that suggest something to you?"

"What?" she asked.

He looked disgusted with her. "Why, that I am to help you, of course."

Jane stared at him. "Do you think you could?" she asked earnestly. "I mean, I really don't see exactly how you can."

Harry looked a little discouraged. "That's the part I haven't quite figured out yet either, but I'm working on it."

Jane was quiet for a few long moments. Then, "Charles says he may be leaving the Abbey soon to go to the New World."

Harry swelled with indignation. "He can't do that to me."

"You didn't want him to be here in the first place," Jane reminded him.

Harry eyed her. "A perfectly reasonable mistake." He dismissed her words. "After all, I had no way of knowing he was to be the one I had to help."

"Perhaps he isn't. Perhaps we aren't," Jane said slowly. "After all, I've lived here for years and years and never saw you before."

"It doesn't signify. You were never in love before." He saw her look down. "What is it?"

Her large grey eyes were filled with sadness when she again looked at him. "I can never go against Gram's wishes. She has spent her life taking care of me. Now that she is older I can't simply walk away from her."

"Then she shall have to go with you," Harry said, a strange expression crossing his face.

"What's wrong?" Jane asked.

Harry looked glum. "It seems no matter what, I'm to be foxed." Then he spoke more bracingly. "There's nothing for it but to do the best we can."

Jane stood up. She didn't want to cast him into despair, but she could see that he was engaged in a hopeless task. "I'd best get back to my grandmother. I left rather awkwardly and she'll be worried for me."

"Are you sure she is all right?" Harry asked, his concern showing.

"She's well, but she's worried for me out of all proportion. I think she's afraid I'll leave her. She said she had experienced the perfidy of men firsthand and wants to save me from it."

Harry looked disquieted. "Who was she speaking of?"

"I'm not sure I should discuss it. It's rather personal."

"You know I can't gossip about it," Harry said practically. "No one can hear me. And even if I could, I wouldn't."

Jane watched the changing expressions on Harry's pale face. "You truly care about my grandmother, don't you?"

Harry looked disconcerted. "We've lived here together for quite a long while. I'm—used—to her."

"You haven't exactly lived here together. I mean, she doesn't even know you exist," Jane put in.

Harry looked almost wistful. "I know she doesn't."

Jane reached out to touch him but stopped with her hand in midair. "I'd best get back to her."

Harry didn't argue. He floated upwards and stayed near her as she walked towards the terrace door. "It's a dead bore around here without Aggie."

"When I get the chance, I'll tell her you said so," Jane answered, smiling.

She slipped out and across the grounds as Harry stood near the door and watched her leave, looking rather mournful as her figure grew smaller in the distance.

Jane walked through the early spring day, hearing the birds calling out from the trees and the distant lowing of cattle, her thoughts all wrapped around Charles and her grandmother. The tender feelings Charles invoked warred with her loyalty to Agatha. Jane didn't know how to reconcile the two. She was still trying to find answers when she arrived back to find a sober-faced Fannie waiting for her.

"Now you've gone and done it."

Jane's face fell. "What's happened?"

"Your grandmother took to her bed."

Fannie's plain words cast fear in Jane's heart. They both knew Agatha never rested during the day and was never in bed except when asleep or ill.

"I'll go right up," Jane said.

"Take this with you," Fannie said, handing over a covered mug she was holding. "It's a bit of chicken broth. See if she'll drink it."

Jane did as Fannie bid, tapping on her grandmother's door before opening it. Across the room Agatha lay against her pillows, an afghan covering her.

"Gram?" Jane came slowly forwards. "Are you awake?"

There was no answer. Jane walked to her bedside, placing the mug of broth on the nightstand beside the bed.

Agatha's eyes opened. They looked dull with pain. Jane's brow furrowed. "Gram, what is it?"

Agatha's voice was weak. Jane had to lean forwards to make sure she heard the words. "I don't know . . . just felt weak. Perhaps my . . . heart."

"But you're never ill." Jane's anxiety grew as she looked down at the old woman who suddenly seemed very fragile. She touched her palm to her grandmother's forehead. "I think you might have a bit of fever."

"I'll . . . be . . . all right."

"Of course you will," Jane said bracingly. "You must drink this broth Fannie has made you."

"I'm not hungry," Agatha said with a little more strength, then closed her eyes. "I think I just need a rest."

Jane tried to protest, but thought better of it, not wanting her grandmother to use up what little strength she had arguing.

"Please drink some of the broth, Gram."

"I'll be fine," Agatha said, her eyes still closed. "I just need a little rest." Her eyes opened. "Were you at the Abbey?"

"There is no reason to worry, Gram. I promise you, you have nothing to fear. I'll not leave you."

Agatha's eyes closed. "He will convince you."

"Never," Jane said with conviction. She sat down across the room to watch her grandmother sleep.

"Go, please," Agatha said after a while. "I want to sleep for a bit."

Jane left unwillingly, heading down to ask Fannie what she thought was wrong. Fannie shrugged slightly, looking up from the basket of mending she was going through. "She kept talking about the Earl. She is terribly worried about you, Jane."

Jane sighed. "I know. She is afraid I shall leave her."

"She is afraid you shall harm yourself," Fannie corrected. "She is afraid you will be hurt."

Jane looked glum. "What has happened to me, Fannie? I shouldn't even like the man. I didn't like him until—until—" She tried to remember when her feelings changed.

"Until the night he kissed you," Fannie said bluntly, "and you began to see him as the hero in a story."

"I do not," Jane defended herself. But deep inside she had to admit that he was as handsome as the heroes she had read about in Fannie's books.

"I take full responsibility for your head being swayed by those stories. Your grandmother was right, I should never have let you read them."

"My head isn't turned." Jane stamped her foot in frustration.

"You've been mooning about like a love-sick calf," Fannie said stoutly. "It's no wonder your poor grandmother's beside herself." Fannie thought about her own encouragement of the Earl's advances in days past, her guilt making her defence of Agatha more spirited as she warmed to her subject. "She's an old woman and she's much more frail than we imagined. We must not give her more cause for alarm."

"I agree," Jane said quietly.

Fannie lapsed into silence, going back to her sewing as Jane sat down across from her, gnawing at her bottom lip. Fannie noticed the little gesture of worry and handed Jane a skirt which needed hemming. "Here. Make yourself useful," Fannie said.

Jane took the cashmere material from Fannie and reached for needle and thread from the lap box Fannie had beside her on the table. "She'll be all right, won't she, Fannie?"

"She'll be right as rain in the morning," Fannie promised.

"I don't know what I'd do without her," Jane said softly. She bent towards the oil lamp, threading the needle.

"Never fear, we won't lose her for a long time to come," Fannie told her.

"I hope you're right," Jane replied quietly.

"Of course I'm right. I'm always right," Fannie fibbed.

But in the morning Agatha was no better, and Jane's worry grew. For the next few days she sat by her grandmother's bedside, reading to her from ancient volumes of poetry. When she seemed to drop off to sleep, Jane would get up and tiptoe out, her grandmother's voice calling to her from the bed, suddenly wakeful. "Are you going out?"

"No, Gram. Do you want me to read you more?"

"Not right now. But you'll be here, if I need you?"

"I'll be right downstairs."

"You're not going out?" Agatha would ask again.

"I'm not going out, Gram," Jane promised.

She kept that promise. She helped Fannie make wild-strawberry jam and preserves. She polished the furniture and helped with the mending and ran up and down the stairs at her grandmother's bidding. A silver bell sat by Agatha's bedside, ready for her to ring for whatever she needed. After bedtime, Fannie slept on a straw pallet in Agatha's room in case she was needed. The third night Fannie was wakeful, sitting in a chair by the window and staring out at the stars far above.

"Fannie," Agatha said from the bed, "have you checked on Jane?"

"Yes," Fannie replied to the nightly question. Two or three times in the night Agatha or Fannie would open Jane's bedroom door and check the sleeping girl. "She isn't about to run away, Aggie."

"Then why are you sitting up?"

"Because my back is killing me from that pallet. I still don't see the need to break my back convincing Jane you are on your last legs."

"She was going to sleep in here herself," Agatha reminded her servant.

"Well, let her," Fannie said. "Better her than me. She's younger."

"You know very well the only time I can get up and move about is at night. If she were here I'd be bedridden all day and night and I soon would be bedridden in earnest."

"I told you this wouldn't work," Fannie said.

"It is working," Agatha replied with some spirit.

"For how long?" Fannie demanded. "How long can you keep on with this farce? And what will you do then?"

"I've been thinking about that," Agatha told Fannie. "And I have a plan. First thing tomorrow I want to send a note to Mrs. Merriweather."

"You can't stand that old gossip. You've said so a million times."

"Yes, but this time I can use that mouth of hers to good advantage. The answer to our dilemma is not to keep Jane away from the Earl. It is to make her see his true nature so she shan't *want* to be near him."

"How are you going to manage that?" Fannie asked.

"One step at a time," Agatha replied. "The first step is that old biddy Merriweather."

Fannie made a face. "All I've got to say is you'd best make a swift recovery before my back gives out entirely."

"I shall be up and about tomorrow."

- *19* -

THE NEXT MORNING was greeted by a wonderfully recovered Agatha. Jane was happy to see her up and about, but very concerned when Mrs. Merriweather's footman arrived to say his employer would be coming to tea.

"Gram, you should not exert yourself on your first day up. You don't want to become ill again."

"It will be good for me to have some company, and I need you to do me a service, Jane. I need you to go up to the Abbey and ask the Earl to let you go through the old accounts and find for me the date we sold the silver service to Mrs. Merriweather."

Jane looked perplexed. "When did we ever sell Mrs. Merriweather silver?"

"Oh, quite a while ago. I'm not sure exactly, but could you look into it this afternoon—if it's all right with his lordship, of course." Agatha looked very innocent.

"I thought you didn't want me to see him."

"I was wrong," Agatha said placidly. "I realised that while lying abed. I trust your own good judgement and common sense." And so saying, she smiled at her granddaughter. "Come kiss me and then run along."

Jane was afraid her heart would burst on her way up to the Abbey. She had seen nothing of Charles in this last week except glimpses from a distance as he went about the Abbey business with the bailiff or took off for solitary rides.

He had ridden past the gatehouse and she had seen the grey take off across the meadow for the stand of oaks where they had met by chance, but she had resolutely kept her promise to her grandmother and stayed within calling distance, inside the house and garden.

Now Jane was being sent to the Abbey to talk to him. Her steps were light, her elation barely contained as she ran upstairs to change her old blue gown for her best sunny yellow one. Her fingers worked unsteadily as she hurriedly did up her hair, her anxiousness making her clumsy. A few minutes later she flew down the stairs and sang out that she was on her way.

Fannie turned to her employer, her brow furrowed in question. "What sale of silver?"

Agatha allowed herself a small smile. "None. But she will have to go back through years' worth of entries before she finds that out. It should keep her occupied until I'm through with that old biddy Merriweather."

"I hope so. What if she comes back early and brings it up to Mrs. Merriweather, or asks the next time she sees her?"

"Fannie, you are becoming tiresome. I shall handle all of that," Agatha told her serving woman complacently. "Are the tea cakes ready?"

"Tea cakes." Fannie made them sound like an unforgivable mistake. Muttering to herself about harebrained schemes, she went back to the kitchen as Agatha watched Jane skip up the long drive to the Abbey.

Leticia Merriweather was a little surprised to be invited to Agatha Steadford-Smyth's in the first place, since they had never exchanged courtesy calls and her one attempt to do so after the Earl arrived had met with failure. Nevertheless, Mrs. Merriweather was also very curious about the Earl and the Steadfords' new life, and even about where Jane was hiding herself.

"Jane's up at the Abbey," Agatha told the woman, "helping the Earl with the Abbey books, I believe."

"Does she spend much time there?" the woman asked, trying to sound innocent.

"Oh, Fannie and Jane have had to do quite a bit up there," Agatha said airily.

"The entire village is wondering what he is really like," Mrs. Merriweather said. "We've seen nothing of him except at church services occasionally." She waited with obvious anticipation, hoping to take home some wonderful gossip.

"He has been busy organising the Abbey to his liking," Agatha replied pleasantly. "Actually, I've been thinking about the very same subject myself. He doesn't really know any of the local gentry. I've been thinking of hostessing a welcoming party at the Abbey. Quite a do, you know? A ball or some such. And just for the best people, you understand. He seems to be terribly lonely. And he is most eligible, you know, so young and handsome and rich. It's a pity he can't meet a personable young lady and settle down. He often talks of it."

Mrs. Merriweather's expression lit up, but she was cautious. "I can't imagine why you haven't thought of him for your Jane."

"Oh, my dear Letty, don't think I didn't have high hopes. But, alas, they seem to have no kindred sympathy. Such a pity. It would have been wonderful to make such a match. Can you imagine? His wife will be a countess, and someday a duchess. He is the Warwick heir after all."

Mrs. Merriweather's pale blue eyes were alive with possibilities as she accepted more tea and cakes from Fannie. "There are some people who simply must be invited of course—to your party, that is."

"Yes," Agatha agreed. "And I will have to rely upon someone to help in that area, since I have been a recluse for ever so long."

"You know, of course, you can count on me," Leticia Merriweather told Agatha.

"Truly?" Agatha looked terribly relieved. "As you get around so very much more than I, you would be doing me a great favour if you could help," said Agatha, smiling benignly.

To say Mrs. Merriweather got around was to say she was one of those small-town people who thrived on everyone else's business. She would use her position as Agatha's helper to make social capital with the gentry of the surrounding county and would pass herself off as a dear friend of the Earl's, one in whom he placed total trust. She would probably pass off the entire party as her own idea. This thought made Agatha smile even more benignly. The old gossip would help ensure the success of her little plan.

"I was wondering, Letty dear," Agatha said as if the idea had just come to mind, "what you think about the Summervilles?"

"Emmm," Mrs. Merriweather pretended to consider the question. "Of course it would be hard to slight them."

"I was thinking about Charlotte," Agatha said.

"Yes, I do catch your meaning. She does have a wee bit of a reputation for being fast, doesn't she? But again, she is by far the most beautiful of our younger set, excepting your Jane, of course."

"Oh, I think the truth must always be told. Charlotte can quite overset Jane for looks and for address. After all, Charlotte is much more experienced in handling the young bucks."

"Yes. I was tremendously surprised she didn't make an eligible match in her London Season." Mrs. Merriweather leaned towards Agatha. "Speaking confidentially, just between the two of us, I rather think she was disappointed her dear mother did not allow the Earl to pay a call on her in London. But we both know how old-fashioned Margaret can be."

"Yes," Agatha murmured, biting back any retort. Margaret Summerville had let Charlotte run wild, and everyone in the county knew it.

"Actually," Mrs. Merriweather continued, "dear Margaret can hardly complain if Charlotte and the Earl have the chance of seeing a bit of each other now. After all, it seems fate itself has thrust them together all the way out here in our quiet little backwater."

Agatha found her smile freezing on her face. She looked towards Fannie for help, but the serving woman seemed deliberately to avoid meeting Agatha's eye. It was all well and good for her not to approve of these schemes but she did not have to be so unhelpful, Agatha complained inwardly.

"And Margaret all alone in the world—you did say he was the heir, did you not? Imagine. The mother of a duchess and all her financial fears forever over."

"Yes, indeed," Agatha said, closing the noose around Mrs. Merriweather's stout neck. "If Charlotte and the Earl do take a fancy to each other, Margaret should pay you a matchmaker's fee, dear Letty." Agatha looked the soul of innocence. She did not appear to notice the avaricious light which now lit the other woman's face as she bid a rather hasty farewell. "I'm so eager to begin to spread the word and help you make arrangements," she said, standing up. She popped another tea cake into her mouth before allowing Fannie to escort her out.

Agatha came with them to the door and walked outside to the woman's waiting carriage. "I am so glad you find the idea to have merit."

"Agatha, my dear, you are always most modest. I think it a wonderful idea and so necessary for the Earl to meet his nearest neighbours. I shall handle just everything, I assure you. Never fear. When will it be?"

Agatha saw Fannie staring at her pointedly. "I'll send word to you in the morning about that."

Agatha waved her good-byes, shading her eyes against the spring sunlight and waiting for Fannie. The serving woman looked after the departing chaise and then turned to face her employer. "You realise that woman will be taking all the credit for getting people invited."

"That is the plan, Fannie."

"You also realise you have no permission whatsoever from the Earl to give the party or to invite people to meet him." Fannie's hands were on her hips as she stared frankly at the woman who was her employer and her friend. And at the moment in danger of making an utter fool of herself.

"Don't worry so," Agatha said.

"Just how do you think you are going to get him to agree?" Fannie demanded.

"You'd be surprised," Agatha replied.

While Mrs. Merriweather had shared tea and cakes with her grandmother, Jane was poring over old account books in the Abbey study.

Charles arrived back from riding out to check the new farm buildings he had commissioned to be told that Miss Jane was in his study. He took the steps two at a time, striding rapidly down the hall and throwing open the study door. She was there, her eyes lighting up at the sight of him.

"They said you were here," he told her. "I didn't dare believe them until I saw you with my own eyes."

She smiled. "My grandmother needed some information from the old books. You weren't here, but I didn't think you'd mind my starting to look through them."

"Why should I mind?" He came farther into the room. "I feel better just seeing you." He saw her blush and smiled at her. "You have the most becoming pink to your cheeks."

"Do not tease me, sir."

"And why not? It is a pleasant occupation," Charles said. "You will have tea with me."

"I really—"

"Can," he interjected. "I'll call for it immediately." As he walked to the bellpull he continued to speak. "Harry has told me about your conversation. I think he fancies himself quite a matchmaker."

"This is not seemly. I shall have to insist you stop this outrageous flirting," Jane said primly.

"Nonsense," he replied. "I shall flirt as excessively as I please. And you shall enjoy it."

"Is that an order?" she questioned, her eyes alight with mischief.

"Absolutely."

They were laughing when a footman came to the doorway, saying they were to hurry to the gatehouse. Jane stared at the boy in horror as she rose to her feet. "What's happened?"

"I don't know, Miss Jane. But something's wrong with Lady Agatha according to the story I got from Homer. Fannie sent him riding to get you."

Jane started towards the front door, Charles falling in step beside her. "I shall drive you down myself."

"No, it will take too long to harness the carriage and I don't think your coming is a good idea."

"Oh, no, Miss Jane," the footman interrupted, "Fannie was most particular as how you both were to come."

"Both?" Jane was surprised. Charles led her to his grey and was already handing her up onto the horse, following himself so that he sat behind her.

"Hurry," she told him. "She's not been well. I knew she was overdoing, but I couldn't convince her of it this morning. Oh, please, do hurry."

At the gatehouse a grim-faced Fannie was waiting by the door. Charles thought it odd that she should be down below instead of up with her grievously ill employer, but Jane's thoughts were only on her grandmother's condition as she fled up the narrow stairwell. Fannie accompanied the Earl after her.

"Perhaps I should wait here," the Earl said.

"She particularly wants to see you," Fannie told the nobleman.

A little perplexed, the Earl followed the servant to Lady Agatha's room. They found Jane already leaning over her grandmother, placing a fresh cool cloth on her forehead. There was a pile of cloths and a basin of cool water on the night table. Jane glanced up, surprised to see Charles walking into her grandmother's bedroom.

Before she could protest, Agatha saw and greeted him. "Please, sit, Your Lordship. Forgive my weakness. I've not been well lately."

"Your granddaughter informed me. She is terribly concerned about your health, Lady Agatha." So saying, the Earl came forwards to a chair between the bed and the window, opposite where Jane stood fussing over her grandmother.

Fannie was pouring sherry from a cut-glass decanter into tiny crystal glasses which already sat on a table near the hall door.

"My only excuse for being so remiss is my aging body," Agatha said when they had their sherry in hand. "I hope you can forgive me, Your Lordship."

"I know of nothing amiss or remiss, Lady Agatha. And I assure you, I hold you in the highest esteem."

"I must come to the point. Something has been bothering me so very much I must ask you a favour," Agatha told the Earl.

"Anything I can possibly grant, you have only to ask," Charles answered, earning a loving glance from Jane.

Agatha, seeing his glance flicker towards Jane, looked up to see Jane's expression and the change in his eyes as he met her gaze.

"Thank you," Agatha said, bringing his attention back to herself. "I want very much to give a welcoming party for you. I should have done it earlier but it was all such a shock."

"That is not necessary," Charles assured her, but she was adamant.

"Yes, it is," she replied. "Thanks to Jane's early impression and village gossip, you are still considered by many as an usurper." Agatha saw Jane's abashed look and continued, "I want to correct this impression and to introduce you as I should have long since."

Charles studied the woman. "It would, of course, make life a bit easier. I should be glad to meet the county, but now is not the time to discuss it. Perhaps when you are feeling better—"

"I could manage easily with the Abbey staff. Of course it would mean that we would have to stay at the Abbey for a week or two. I couldn't manage the walks and rides back and forth. But if you would not mind our staying for a short period of time—"

Agatha let the sentence dangle, watching the reactions around her. Jane's eyes lit up. Charles appeared surprised at first and then very, very pleased. Only Fannie looked sour. She shook her head when Agatha caught her eye, and her gaze moved heavenwards, as if seeking help from a higher power.

"I would be pleased to have you stay for as long as you like," Charles was saying. "Particularly now, when you are not feeling quite up to the mark, it would be better for you to have the staff available to you."

"Yes, there is that," Agatha said. "I *am* a little tired. Perhaps we could discuss the details later?"

"Of course." Charles stood up.

"I'll just see his lordship out," Jane told her grandmother, who nodded and waited for the sound of their steps to recede down the stairs.

Agatha smiled at Fannie when they were alone. "I told you I could manage it."

"Manage what? This is bound to end badly."

"Nonsense, as the Earl would say." Agatha spoke bracingly. "We shall soon have this problem settled for once and all."

"That's what I'm afraid of," Fannie said darkly.

Outside, Jane was bidding Charles farewell, her anxious look prompting him to reassure her that all would be well. She wasn't so sure. "She feels so strongly about appearances, about not living under the same roof with a bachelor. She must be feeling much worse than she's letting on. I don't like this at all."

"Well, I for one think it's a capital idea. I shall have you at breakfast with me and dinner and supper. We can play chess, and I can watch your lovely face by the firelight."

"Charles, please, don't continue. We can't think about ourselves."

"I cannot help it," he told her. "The Abbey has been dismal and bleak without you in it. Imagine how happy Harry will be."

Jane's expression cleared a bit. "Yes, there is that."

"I can't wait to tell him."

"Jane," Fannie called from an upstairs window. "Your grandmother needs you."

Jane said quick good-byes to Charles, their gazes holding fast to each other for a long moment before she pulled herself away and hurried back inside the gatehouse.

- 20 -

THE MOVE TO the Abbey happened the next day, Agatha taking to her old bed as she directed the household from its soft recesses. The housekeeper, the cook, and the staff ran up and down at her bidding. Even Pickering's aid was enlisted. Agatha found him very forthcoming about his many and varied experiences in just this sort of large gathering.

A week later plans were well under way when Agatha woke just after dawn from an uneasy night's sleep. She had awakened many times in the night since she arrived back to the Abbey, sometimes feeling as if someone were in her room, watching her. She ignored the vague disquiet, telling herself she was becoming as imaginative as Fannie and Jane.

This particular morning she woke as the first fingers of dawn crept into her room. She turned in the bed, her eyes opening sleepily, to find that someone *was* in her room. She came awake, staring at the vague figure which looked like an almost-transparent man. He was standing in the sunlight, his face in the shadows above the shaft of light. She half rose on the bed, blinking, but when she opened her eyes the apparition was gone. She closed her eyes again and opened them, seeing the sunlight streaming in but no strange shadowy figure now.

She reached for the bellpull, summoning Fannie. Fannie arrived, a little sleepy-eyed, and was told Agatha must be truly getting old and soft in the head. Now she was even seeing things that weren't there. Yawning, Fannie was of the opinion that they were fools on a fools' errand up here, and the sooner they were out and gone the better.

"But you are the one who wanted to make a match between them, I remember," Agatha said primly.

"I was wrong. You've told me what his true colours are and I now think he's much too sophisticated for our Jane. I say that throwing them together is not going to end up in the way you imagine."

* *. *

Downstairs, Charles and Jane sat to breakfast an hour later, Agatha eating in her room as she had since they arrived.

"Have you seen Harry at all?" Jane was asking.

"Not in days. Why?"

"I rather thought I'd have seen him by now, and I rather thought he might show himself to Gram," Jane said.

Charles grinned, teasing her. "Don't you remember? He only appears to lovers."

"We are not lovers," she reminded him.

"We should be," he told her, earning a blush and a downcast look. "Come now, you must not mind my teasing you. I shall do a very great deal of it over the years."

"Years?" She looked up at him. "You said you would be leaving for the New World."

"I've written my father telling him I cannot go. I know why he was sending me, and it is no longer necessary," the Earl said.

"Things are working out over there?" she asked.

He smiled. "On the contrary, things are working out over here."

"I don't understand."

"You will," he promised.

"You speak as if we have a future, and you know we do not," Jane told him, her face set into sombre lines.

"I know no such thing. We can and we will. We must," Charles decreed. "I insist upon it. In fact, I shall speak to your grandmother at the first opportunity."

"No, you mustn't!" Jane spoke urgently, beseeching him not to worry her grandmother. "It will only upset her and she might have another relapse. If anything should happen to her because of me, I would never forgive myself. I couldn't live with it."

"Jane, it's quite all right. I shan't say anything until the time is right. I promise you," he told her. "But there will be a right time, and I have just the solution so that you need never worry about her being alone. I have given it a great deal of thought and I am sure I can convince her she shall live with us, here or abroad in the New World."

Jane rather thought this solution to be impossible, but she said nothing. How could she tell him Agatha's antipathy was not to him in particular but to men in general?

"You look distressed," Charles said, undaunted by her troubled expression. "I assure you I can be most persuasive when I set out to be."

"I know," Jane told him shyly, her affection for him growing no matter what she tried to tell herself about its impossibility.

"So you must have faith in me."

"Grandmama is just so very dead set against the male of the species, I don't think she will listen."

Charles considered Jane's words. "She cannot in good conscience insist you stay with her if she will not consider our offer. That is too selfish by half, Jane."

"She doesn't mean to be selfish." Jane began to defend Agatha as Fannie appeared in the doorway. Charles looked towards her, Jane seeing the movement and turning, concerned. "Fannie?" she questioned.

"She wanted me to send you up," Fannie said without preamble.

Charles questioned Agatha's servant with a quizzical expression. She had seemed strangely reticent since their temporary move back to the Abbey. Her old teasing ways and sharp tongue were gone.

Fannie saw the Earl's intent interest and looked away. "I'll get her hot chocolate."

Jane accompanied Fannie into the hall, asking how Agatha seemed this morning.

"Your grandmother seems the same to me," was Fannie's noncommittal reply. "Except—"

Jane's anxiety grew. "Except what, Fannie?"

"She was talking about getting older, about seeing things. Didn't sound like herself at all."

"Seeing things?" Jane queried. "What things?"

"Lord, how would I know? You'd best get up there or she'll be ringing that bell and have the whole staff running after you." Fannie left Jane to her own devices and headed towards the kitchen.

Jane looked back at Charles and then walked forward, up the stairs towards her grandmother.

Provisions for the party—extra linens for guests who might have to stay over, thorough cleaning of the long-unused guest rooms and public rooms, waxing of the ballroom floor with beeswax and elbow grease, handwritten invitations being finished and posted— kept the household busy from dawn to long after dusk as the week lengthened towards its end.

Jane carried instructions back and forth from one end of the huge establishment to the other, seeing Charles in passing during the day but eating her supper in Agatha's sitting-room, where each evening Agatha made the seemingly valiant attempt to sit up instead of being served in bed.

Agatha was very pleased with herself and her plan. In point of fact Jane was so busy running errands and helping with the party preparations that she was seeing even less of Charles than she had before the move. Living at the gatehouse and keeping them apart had made Jane bend every effort to see him whenever she could. Living in the same house, running into each other in prosaic pursuits, was much less romantic.

After supper on Friday night Jane wandered through the long gallery, stopping at each of the ancient portraits in turn and staring up into her ancestors' faces.

"A motley bunch of brigands, wouldn't you say?"

Startled, Jane whirled around, peering towards the shadowy recesses of the long gallery which extended across the front of the house and around the length of the front stairwell.

"Where are you?" Jane asked the empty air around her. "Harry? Where have you been?"

Something stirred the drapes at the front windows. She looked towards the movement and then heard his voice behind her, speaking almost into her ear, "I'm not deaf, you know."

"Oohh!" Jane gasped. "You startled me!"

He looked satisfied. "Now you know how I felt that night in the attic."

"I certainly didn't mean to startle you," Jane contended, "and you did this on purpose."

Harry drew himself up several feet, glaring convincingly down at her from near the ceiling. "I am a ghost," he declaimed. "I am supposed to startle people."

"Well I for one think it is a pretty silly occupation for an obviously grown man—ghost—whatever."

"You would," Harry grumbled. "Just like a Steadford. The best of them are stubborn and hard to please."

"I am not," Jane put in. "And they probably weren't either."

"Ah ha, you see this sober-faced cutthroat in front of you? That is the unfeeling scoundrel who forced Agg—who forced your grandmother into a loveless marriage!"

Jane looked up at the face which was vaguely familiar from the idle glances of a lifetime. She had never really studied any of the portraits before. "He looks like Great-Uncle Nigel," Jane realised as she stared upwards at the dour face.

"The only thing I ever felt sorry for Nigel Steadford about," Harry agreed. "You see the woman next to him? That's his second wife and the original wicked stepmother all the stories must have been fashioned after."

Jane was regarding him curiously. "Harry, have you haunted the Steadford family for a very long time?"

"It seems eons," he responded.

"Were you great friends with my ancestors in life?"

"Friends?" He stared at her, incredulous. "We were mortal enemies!"

Jane blanched, taken completely aback by his vehement reply. "But you said you had to help us."

"One of death's little ironies," Harry replied.

"Why is your future dependent upon us?"

Harry shrank to a pittance of his former size, despondent. "I must atone to a Steadford or I shall never be free."

"Don't leave yet," Jane implored him. "You're always leaving in midconversation or disappearing for days and days on end."

"I can't help it. It takes a great deal of energy to become visible, and even more to speak. After I spend the nights in—that is— I haven't got the strength to keep up an appearance for very long these days." Harry complained and became even more transparent as he spoke.

"What is it you have to atone for?" Jane asked.

"It's a long story," he replied morosely.

"What exactly are you to do to atone?"

"That's the problem. No one's given me any instructions. I was in France when I went to sleep and I woke up here, just like that." He tried to snap his fingers but no sound was heard. He tried again.

"Don't waste your strength," Jane told him.

"I suppose you're right. But you can see it's damnably awkward. How would you like to wake up tomorrow a ghost? I ask you."

Jane tried to imagine this occurrence. "I can see where I would be terribly disconcerted, to say the least. Not to mention inconvenienced."

"To say the least," Harry agreed. "I knew when I woke that I was to atone to the Steadfords, and it had something to do with love but no one could see me. I gave all kinds of advice—and all of it good—but no one ever paid the least attention. No one could even hear me. Now, I ask you, what was I to do? I was so frustrated I began trying to learn how to become visible, but all I accomplished was scaring the wits out of a maid or two. No Steadford ever saw or heard me until you, and then he did too.

So you see, I must be meant to help you."

"Help me do what?" Jane wanted to know.

"I don't know. What is it you wish to do?" Harry asked, trying to be helpful.

Jane suddenly looked forlorn. "There's no way to help."

Harry came nearer, looking very serious. "You have to let me try. You're the only chance I've got."

Agatha's sitting-room door opened behind them. "Jane?" her grandmother called out. "Are you out there? Who's there with you?"

Jane hesitated and then, seeing Harry disappear, spoke softly, "No one, Gram."

"Who are you talking to?" Agatha demanded.

"I was just—talking to myself."

"I'll see what I can do," Harry whispered in Jane's ear.

"To yourself?" Agatha was asking at the same time, her tone full of disbelief. She stared at the closed door to Charles's suite. "What in the name of common sense would you be doing that for?"

Pickering came up the stairs, pausing a moment to nod briefly in their direction. "Pardon the intrusion. The Earl sent me to collect his favourite pipe."

Agatha gave him a piercing look. "Sent you? Where is his lordship?"

"In the library, Lady Agatha. Do you wish a message sent to him?"

"No," she said, a little subdued.

"May I say it is encouraging to see you up and around?" Pickering said politely.

Agatha realised her mistake and leaned against the doorjamb. "I felt I might gain strength by walking a bit," she told them both. "But I find I am now in need of help."

Jane went to her grandmother's side as Pickering asked if she needed any assistance.

"No, we can manage by ourselves," Agatha said quickly.

Pickering took her at her word and went in search of the missing pipe, leaving the women to their own devices.

Jane let Agatha lean against her as they walked slowly down the upper hallway. Behind them in the shadowy portrait gallery Harry stood near the stairwell, watching Jane help her grandmother walk away from him. At the far end of the long hallway near the green baize door which led to the back stairs, they made a turn, then walked slowly back the way they'd come.

Agatha was murmuring about feeling a bit better as Jane glanced ahead. She saw Harry shimmering faintly. He came nearer the end of the gallery, watching them with sad eyes. Pickering stepped out of the master suite and unknowingly walked right through Harry's shimmering figure. Jane gave a little gasp.

Agatha glanced at her helper. "Jane?"

"I'm fine, Gram," the young woman managed to say as she watched Harry fade from view.

Her grandmother squinted at her. "You are acting most peculiar these days, Jane."

"I suppose I am, Grandmama," Jane replied meekly.

"I can't imagine why," Agatha fibbed. "You're not feeling ill, are you?"

"Just a little tired, Gram," Jane said, steering her grandmother into her suite.

"You need a good dose of salts," Agatha decreed as she let herself be guided towards her waiting bed. Jane did not respond to the unpleasant suggestion, sinking Agatha into deeper thought about her granddaughter's current circumstances.

21

A WEEK LATER, on the afternoon of the Abbey ball, Jane and Fannie were finishing the lace on Jane's ball gown when Agatha joined them to see how they were doing. Jane was none too sure Agatha should be up and about so much but Agatha told her she felt fine.

"Absolutely fine," Agatha informed them both. "In fact I feel quite my old self."

She surveyed their work on the ivory-coloured satin gown shot through with pink silk moiré ribbons and edged with lace at the demure neckline and at the cuffs of the puffed sleeves. Jane tried it on as Agatha watched and pronounced it perfect.

A knock at the sitting-room door brought in a new young maid Pickering had hired for the occasion. She carried a tray of hot chocolate and sticky buns.

"I sent for a little treat for just us three before the party begins," Agatha told Fannie and her granddaughter.

Jane looked doubtfully at the rich food. "Gram, this is perfectly lovely of you, but I don't think I can venture a sip."

Fannie reached for a cup of the thick, sweet chocolate, keeping an eye on her employer all the while. Sensing something was afoot, Fannie told herself it was none of her never-mind and she would stay well and thoroughly out of it.

Agatha picked up a delicate white china cup trimmed with tiny pink and green flowers. She filled it from the pot of chocolate and reached to hand it to Jane, who demurred.

"Gram, I really can't—"

Agatha thrust the cup again towards her granddaughter. "Jane, I know much more than you about parties such as this and you really should—"

The cup tilted a bit in its saucer, then tipped over and spilled dark, staining chocolate down the bodice of the ivory satin.

"Oh!" Agatha exclaimed.

"Oh, no!" Jane cried, staring at the devastation wrought on the pristine satin.

"My dear girl." Agatha looked distraught. "I am so sorry. What have I done?"

Jane's teeth bit into the inside of her mouth, the pain stopping her first angry reactions. She held back the crushing disappointment, catching Fannie's eye and then deliberately ignoring her.

"Don't worry yourself, Gram. It's not important."

Agatha looked terribly upset. "I wouldn't hurt you for all the fortunes in the world and just look what I've done."

Fannie stood up, her face set into severe lines. "I think it's time for your medicine, Aggie."

Agatha's eyes flew to Fannie. She started to protest and then saw a determination in her serving woman's eyes which would not brook objections.

"Medicine," Fannie repeated. "Strong medicine," Fannie said. "You need it *now*."

Agatha thought about protesting, but one look at her granddaughter's despairing countenance changed her mind. She followed Fannie into the bedroom. Fannie closed the door to the sitting-room where Jane stood staring down at the ruin Agatha had made of her ball gown.

The two old friends, servant and employer, faced each other.

"I feel a little faint—" Agatha began.

"You should feel faint or worse," Fannie said sharply.

"I don't want to discuss this."

"And well you shouldn't. But unless you want me to walk out this door and off this property this very moment, you will stop what you are doing."

Agatha stared at Fannie. "You wouldn't do that."

Fannie met Agatha's gaze squarely. "I have nowhere to go. You would give me no references, but I will leave if you push me to it."

Agatha knew Fannie too well to deny her words. Agatha tried another approach. "I don't know why you're so upset."

"You know precisely why," Fannie replied. "Jane is a good girl, and she doesn't deserve what you're doing to her."

"I'm protecting her," Agatha protested.

"You are denying her a life of her own and, what is worse, you know it," Fannie replied harshly.

"Get out of here," Agatha demanded.

"Gladly," Fannie shot back.

She opened the door to the sitting-room, and closing it softly behind herself, tried to find the words to comfort Jane. But Jane was not in the sitting-room. Fannie picked up the discarded ivory

gown, her heart hardening against Agatha anew at the sight of
the ugly brown stains which ruined the bodice, discolouring ivory
satin, blue silk ribbons, and creamy lace alike.

Gathering the dress in her arms, Fannie decided to try to clean
it. Perhaps a miracle would happen. She went in search of Jane
to tell her not to give up hope, but could find her nowhere.

The sounds of the first arrivals were already wafting up from
below. The clip-clop of horses in the courtyard heralded their
approach long before the carriage stopped in front of the wide
stone steps. Fannie went quickly through the family rooms looking for Jane and then hesitated at the Earl's sitting-room door.

Within she could hear Pickering's town-bred voice prosing
on about the slapdash way the Abbey had been run, about the
disgraceful disuse of the public rooms, and something more she
could not hear as he walked farther away beyond the closed door.
Fannie did not knock. There was no reason for Jane to be in the
Earl's rooms and, if she were, Pickering had more decorum than to
be denigrating her grandmother's household management in front
of her.

Fannie caught a glimpse of the elegantly clad strangers who
were being led across the wide entry hall below by a nervous
young footman. Her heart began to break for Jane. They had
lived such a quiet, frugal life that this was to be her first real
ball, and now she would be reduced to wearing her best Sunday
dress instead of the gown they had worked on for days.

Jane was a sensitive girl. She had considered hiding upstairs
and feigning illness rather than watch the Earl of Warwick made
much over by all the beauties in the county. Fannie had convinced
her that she could hold her own with the best of them and spent
many late nights teaching her dance steps after her grandmother
was safe asleep.

Fannie went down the back stairs into the kitchens and asked
the first footman she saw to go in search of Jane through the
public rooms.

While Fannie looked for her below, high above in the attic
room just off the uppermost stairs Jane was slumped disconso-
lately on the floor, her oldest navy day dress picking up feathers
of dust from the untended floor. Her head was in her arms
on the top of one of her mother's trunks when Harry found
her.

"You've certainly got the house in an uproar," he said in a
despairing tone. "People hopping about all over the place. All
my favourite haunts have the worst sorts of noisy conversations

rattling on. They are already stuffing their faces and the party not even half-begun."

Jane looked hopelessly unhappy. "I can hear the orchestra. The party has begun and I shall not be there."

"Nothing's begun until the master and mistress of the house make their appearance—or, in this case, until your grandmother is led in by the Earl." Harry eyed her. "You look excessively miserable. What did you say about not going?"

"I cannot."

"Well, you must. This is the only tiny corner of this whole establishment where I can get the least bit of peace and quiet tonight and you'll quite cut it all up if you remain. You'll want to talk or sniffle or something. Everyone needs a bit of privacy sometimes, even a ghost—especially a ghost. The more I see of humans, the more I realise I've gotten quite used to being alone. So, you will have to leave for my sake."

Tears sparkled on her long eyelashes, but she was determined she would not give in to them. "There's been an accident," Jane said, "and Gram—"

"Has something happened to Aggie?" Harry interrupted.

"No," Jane answered quickly, seeing his agitation. "She ruined my ball gown, that's all."

Jane's crestfallen countenance brought Harry closer. "Ruined your gown?"

"You see?" she said, the tears sparkling in her eyes. "As I said, it is not so very much of a tragedy."

A tangle of silken curls obscured her face and hid the tears which splashed down onto the skirt of her old navy-blue dress.

"I can't quite see the dilemma here," Harry told her. "Just wear another gown," he said practically.

Her voice was muffled and forlorn, her face still deliberately hidden. "I have no other gown."

Harry considered her words. In his experience women had boxes and closets and trunks full of gowns. But then again, the women he had known would never have worn the plain navy-blue dress which was now becoming so very tear-splashed.

He faded, leaving her some privacy and wandering rather irritably through the newly readied guest rooms, trying to find one which did not show signs of pending occupancy. The sounds of the party below made him glower as he passed through one wall and then another.

The most quiet rooms he found were the Earl's, where Pickering was putting the finishing touches on his master's elegant attire.

From the tip of his dark curly head to the soles of his black
dancing slippers, Charles looked magnificent. His fitted black coat
had been superbly cut by Weston to the exact measurements of his
broad shoulders and narrow waist. His black pantaloons fitted as
smoothly as his skin. His white shirt was topped by a perfectly
folded snowy cravat and fronted by rows of falling ruffles which
were partially obscured by a black velvet vest and coat. His only
ornaments were the heavy gold signet ring bearing the Warwick
crest and the row of pearls which fastened his cravat and the
ruffled shirtfront.

Charles was watching Pickering's ministrations through the
pier-glass when he seemed to sense Harry's presence. He peered
behind him through the glass but saw nothing.

Harry considered becoming visible, then thought of Agatha
and slipped away, passing through the walls and peeking at her
struggling with her own buttons. He watched her frustration and
sensed her unhappiness, another thought encroaching which sent
him hurrying back to the attics and Jane.

"I have the solution to your problem," Harry told her even
before he materialised.

"There is no solution," Jane said hopelessly.

"There is always a solution," Harry said bracingly. "Some you
must simply search for harder. Come look."

Rather listlessly, Jane got to her feet and moved towards the
trunk Harry was indicating. The top seemed to open by itself,
which made Jane's eyes widen and Harry very proud of himself.

"So far so good. This is the first time I've tried this. Now, stand
back a bit."

He raised his arms and an old blanket floated upwards. "Whoops,
sorry."

It fell to the floor and Harry tried again. This time folds of
red material rose out of the tissue-thin paper which surrounded
it. The paper fell away, and the lines of the dress began to fill
out as it rose upwards in the air at Harry's command. Jane gave
a little gasp of surprise as the ball gown seemed to come to life
in front of her.

It was made of richest, softest red velvet with a daringly low
neckline. The bodice was crisscrossed with gold braid as were the
tight-fitting long sleeves which ended in gold satin points at the
wrists. The skirts were wide and full, the overskirt of red velvet
gathered up in scallops by more gold braid, to reveal the gold
satin underskirt.

"It's beautiful," Jane said, breathing the words. "It looks as if it belonged to a princess in a fairy tale."

"I just remembered it," Harry told her, pleased with her reaction. "You'd best take it down and try it on."

"Whom does it belong to?" she asked.

"It's a long story," she was told. "Take it now. I can't keep this up forever."

Jane reached for the dress, doubtfully surveying the low-cut bodice. "I don't think Gram will approve of this gown."

"Then don't show it to her. Good Jasper, girl, you must exert yourself a little if you are going to help me help you," Harry lectured.

While Harry preached to Jane in the attic, the Earl of Warwick emerged from his rooms, followed closely by Pickering, who hastened to Agatha's sitting-room door. Fannie answered his knock, looking grim.

"His lordship awaits Lady Agatha and Miss Jane," Pickering announced formally.

Agatha appeared from within the room, a tight smile on her face. "Jane has had a problem dressing and will be down later," she told the Earl.

Charles glanced from Agatha to Fannie. Something was definitely amiss between them. "We can wait for her, if you prefer," he said.

"That won't be necessary," Agatha replied.

"It might be a long wait," Fannie said darkly, earning a warning look from Agatha.

Charles offered his arm to the elderly woman and walked beside her to the top of the stairwell. After a backward glance towards Fannie's troubled face, he escorted Agatha down the stairs and into the public rooms to greet the guests who were now steadily arriving, with carriages pulled up and waiting all along the drive.

"Agatha, dear—" Mrs. Merriweather cried out, sailing towards them as soon as they entered the main parlour. Beyond her the sliding doors to the ballroom stood open, with musicians visible across the length of the two rooms. "This was such a lovely idea," Mrs. Merriweather almost simpered as she cast a coy glance upwards at the handsome Earl.

Agatha's smile was forced. "You remember Leticia Merriweather."

"Of course," he said, smiling and bowing slightly.

"You must call me Letty," Leticia Merriweather told him. "I simply insist. All my friends do."

"Thank you," Charles said, but his thoughts were upstairs with Jane. He kept looking towards the door, waiting for her to enter.

"We arrived ever so early," Leticia told both Agatha and Charles. "Have you seen Charlotte Summerville and her mother? We were your very first guests this evening. Charlotte is so sweet and tonight she looks absolutely lovely, don't you think?"

"I've not seen her yet," Agatha said.

She couldn't help feeling a twinge of guilt when she thought of how Jane would feel arriving in her bronze-green Sunday dress instead of the lovely gown she had fashioned. Agatha assured herself that firm resolve had been needed for Jane's best interests to be served and there was no reason to be feeling guilty.

"I think you've already met Charlotte, Your Lordship—in her London Season last year." Leticia Merriweather was smiling up at the tall man, trying to keep his attention which kept wandering, along with his eyes, towards the door.

"I beg your pardon?" he said. She repeated the remark, and he agreed that Charlotte was indeed a lovely girl and her mother a pure jewel. In truth, he had only the vaguest of ideas whom they were talking about. Fortunately, Agatha extricated them from Mrs. Merriweather's clutches and introduced Charles to the others, moving slowly across the room towards the buffet tables which were laid out with food and drink, a footman standing beside each table ready to assist the guests.

Meanwhile, Leticia Merriweather searched through the throngs of people, her short height causing her difficulty in surveying the crowd and finding her prey. At last she spied Margaret and Charlotte and made her way through the crush to where they stood near the ballroom doors.

"My Lord, what an absolutely frightful squeeze," Margaret was saying to Squire Lyme's wife, Eleanor.

"Frightful," Eleanor agreed, enjoying every minute of it. "Hello, Letty, we thought we'd lost you for good."

"Nothing of the sort," Leticia said. "I want to take Charlotte to say hello to the Earl."

Charlotte Summerville smiled at her mother's friend. Charlotte's gown was of sapphire satin, with a fitted Russian bodice. Margaret surveyed her daughter with a proprietary look. When Letty first suggested the matchmaking and told of engineering a party at the Abbey, Margaret had felt she was exaggerating, even for Letty. But she had done all she promised, all for Charlotte.

With that in mind, Margaret turned an affectionate smile upon her old friend and agreed, "Yes, of course."

As they crossed the room Leticia Merriweather moved with the pride of a woman who had worked miracles. After all, everyone knew Lady Agatha did not give parties. Therefore, the credit for this night must descend upon Leticia Merriweather's more-than-willing shoulders, especially since she had dropped hints, upon any who would listen over these past weeks, about how often she was called upon for help by the aging former owner of Steadford Abbey. The fact that Leticia was only five months younger than Agatha was a well-kept secret.

"Your Lordship, here is the lovely young person we were just discussing." So saying, Leticia interrupted Charles's conversation with the squire and gave Charlotte a small push forwards.

Charlotte executed a pretty curtsey, her eyes lowering and then rising to meet his in a very direct gaze. Charles was a bit taken aback by her forwardness. She was obviously quite the accomplished flirt. He regarded her with frank appraisal and could not but like what he saw. She had dark hair burnished with red highlights in smooth curls which framed dark eyes and an almost Spanish complexion. She looked the exotic amongst the country redheads and plain, fresh-faced young women of the county, many of whom were totally lacking in town polish.

Agatha greeted Charlotte as if she were a long-lost daughter, insisting the Earl must begin the dancing with the lovely Charlotte on his arm. Margaret was pleasantly surprised by Agatha's attitude and more than ever disposed to think kindly of Mrs. Merriweather's attempts at matchmaking between Charlotte and the Earl. If Leticia Merriweather could convince Agatha to support the match when she had little Jane to consider, Charlotte just might end up a countess after all.

Charles, surrounded by feminine persuasion, accepted the rather obvious strategising with good grace and gave Charlotte a full bow. "Would you consent to a turn on the floor, Miss Summerville?"

"Thank you, Your Lordship."

They walked towards the dance floor, with others following suit as the Earl took the floor with Charlotte to join in a quadrille. When the dance had ended, he escorted her to the refreshment table, helping her to a lemonade and accepting a claret cup himself. Squire Lyme approached and asked Charlotte for a dance.

Meanwhile, Charles was glancing towards the doorway yet again and paying scant attention to the conversation around him.

Thus, he was the first to see Jane when she appeared. He stared transfixed for a moment, then walked straight towards her, all others lost from view. Others watched his progress and then saw Jane. The stir in the room was audible.

She was a vision in crimson and gold, her hair a fall of golden curls woven with red velvet ribbons which matched her crimson and gold gown. Her lips and cheeks were flushed with vivid red. Her creamy skin shone to perfection against the velvet which outlined the breasts they barely covered. If there was something antique about the cut of the gown, that only made it more extraordinary and Jane, the most original of beauties.

Her wide grey eyes saw only Charles, watching his expression as he came towards her and captured her hand.

"By God, you're the most beautiful creature in the world," he told her.

Across the room, Charlotte turned in her dance with the squire to behold the meeting. She lost her concentration, missed a step, and tried to recover gracefully. The squire awkwardly attempted to right them and apologised, making a comment about his *faux pas*.

"Are you quite all right, Miss Charlotte?"

"Yes," she answered quickly.

"You seem preoccupied. Are you sure you're feeling quite well?"

"I'm fine, I assure you. I'm simply—minding my steps—that's all."

Charlotte caught her mother's eye and indicated the doorway with a nod. Margaret Summerville noted her daughter's signal and answered Agatha while glancing towards the door, where she saw Jane Steadford walking forwards with Charles, her hand upon his arm. They crossed to the dance floor behind Agatha, who was at the moment answering Eleanor Lyme's query about Jane's late arrival.

"Actually it was my fault," Agatha told the squire's wife. "Poor Jane had worked so hard on her gown, and I ruined it."

Margaret turned her full attention on Agatha. "She made that herself?" Margaret was incredulous.

Agatha was surprised by Margaret's tone. "Yes, with Fannie's help. She's very good with a needle."

"Good Lord, yes," Margaret exclaimed, earning yet another surprised look from Agatha.

Margaret's gaze drifted to the dance floor. Agatha glanced up and saw Charlotte coming towards them.

"Charlotte has grown up to become a real credit to you, Margaret. She is a lovely girl."

"Thank you," Margaret replied. "But I must say I had no idea Jane had become so—so sophisticated."

"I can't imagine anyone thinking of Jane as sophisticated," her grandmother said and then greeted Charlotte as she reached them. "I was just saying how lovely you look, my dear."

"I feel a complete dowd next to Jane. She looks ravishing."

"Really?" Agatha appeared almost startled. She was positive not even Fannie could have removed the dark chocolate stain from the ivory satin, and the rest of Jane's wardrobe was of the plainest variety. "Has she come down then?"

Agatha looked about, first at the crowds around the refreshment tables, which were loaded with plates. An enormous epergne filled with fruit was the centerpiece of the largest table.

While Agatha surveyed the moving throngs, Harry watched from the musicians' balcony, leaning comfortably against the columned wall and congratulating himself on a job well done. The Earl and Jane made a very pretty couple. Harry's gaze wandered until he found Agatha, who was also gazing about as if searching for someone. Harry waited for her to see Jane—and the dress Jane wore.

Agatha, however, did not see her granddaughter until she turned towards the dancers. Even then Agatha could not at first discern among the press any but the couples closest to her. Then the pattern of the dance shifted. The couples closest moved away as others came forwards.

Agatha saw Charles dancing with a shimmering vision of a young woman clad in red velvet and cloth of gold. As they moved through the intricate steps the girl was laughing, a gentle peal of laughter which rose above the sounds around them. The Earl echoed her laughter, obviously happy. Then Agatha realised the girl was Jane. Agatha stared, stunned by the realisation. And by the red and gold gown.

The music ended. Jane saw her grandmother's astonished expression and came towards her with Charles. Jane was all smiles.

"Gram, look what we found."

Agatha was horrified. "Where did you get that dress?"

"It was in an attic trunk—"

"No! It was burned. How could you do this?"

Agatha seemed to be making no sense at all as Charles, Jane, and the others watched the older woman's outburst. Only Harry understood her words, his expression saddening.

Charles still held Jane's hand. "Lady Agatha, surely no harm has been done."

Agatha stared at Jane. She felt the room begin to spin as she heard someone call out that she was falling. Charles caught her as she slumped forwards, raising her in his arms as others cleared a path towards the door amid the startled, murmuring guests.

"Please tell them to go on with the music," Jane said to Leticia Merriweather as she picked up her skirts and ran out of the room.

Leticia rose to the occasion, calming people, motioning the musicians to play, and urging all those nearby to continue with the party and enjoy themselves.

22

UPSTAIRS HARRY WAS already hovering about Agatha's room when Jane opened the door for Charles. Fannie stood up abruptly at the sight of Agatha in Charles's arms.

"My God, what's happened to her?"

"She fainted," Charles said.

"I knew this was all too much for her," Jane cried, leading the way into the bedroom and taking her grandmother's hand, chafing it between her own as Charles laid Agatha in the bed. "We should have insisted she wait before giving the party."

Fannie brought hartshorn and water, the smelling salts reviving Agatha. She looked up at Jane, then closed her eyes, not wanting to face Jane's concern or Charles' curiosity. Harry waited by the head of the bed, invisible and worried.

"Gram, are you all right?"

"I don't want to see that dress," Agatha said faintly.

Jane bit her lip. "I'm sorry, Gram, I'll take it off." She looked up at Charles. "You had best see to the guests."

"Are you sure you'll be all right alone? Should I send for the doctor? After all, in your grandmother's weakened state—"

"She'll be fine," Fannie interjected firmly, surprising Charles by her lack of worry over the obviously agitated condition of her employer.

"I'll go downstairs then, if I'm not needed." Charles gave Jane an encouraging smile. "If you need me, you have only to ask."

"Thank you," Jane responded quietly. Standing up, she moved towards Fannie. "If you'll help me with the back buttons, I'll take this off."

"I don't see why you should," Fannie answered Jane but really spoke to Agatha. "It is a lovely gown, and you look perfectly beautiful in it. Unless that's the problem," Fannie finished with asperity.

Agatha opened her eyes to see Fannie's accusing gaze staring back at her. Jane left the room and the two older women behind, moving with dejected step as the sounds of the party swelled from below.

Downstairs Charles answered queries about Agatha's health and said good-nights as guests departed, unwilling to impose on Agatha's obviously weakened condition. Charlotte Summerville stood beside Charles, sharing the farewell duties and introducing him to people he had not yet met. She laughed a little impishly when they were alone for an instant.

"This is altogether tragic," she said lightly.

He misunderstood. "Oh, no, she was quite all right when I left her."

"I don't mean that," Charlotte said, tapping his shoulder with her fan. "I meant the party is breaking up so early that none of us will have to stay overnight as we planned."

Charles looked perplexed. "I don't think I quite understand."

"Why, My Lordship," she smiled coquettishly. "I won't have any excuse to spend the night under your roof."

Charles realised she was flirting with him. Before he could reply, other guests had approached, expressing their concern and their appreciation of his invitation.

He promised the squire there would be more Abbey parties in the future, said goodnight to the squire's wife, and turned to see Margaret Summerville walking towards her daughter, with Leticia Merriweather in tow.

"I trust Agatha will be all right," Charlotte's mother said.

Charlotte smiled at her mother. "I was just telling his lordship how much we had looked forward to having time to chat in the morning."

Margaret was taken aback at her daughter's direction and amazed when Charles seemed not even to notice. "Charlotte, it's time we left and allowed his lordship to get back to Lady Agatha and more pressing business."

Charlotte took her mother's suggestion in bad grace, sulking as Charles talked to Leticia, who agreed it had been a wonderful evening, and they must do it again soon, and Agatha was sure to be better in the morning. In his distraction the Earl could manage only monosyllables as response until he had them out the door.

Then, taking the steps two at a time, he ran upstairs to Agatha's rooms, tapped on the sitting-room door, and waited impatiently until Fannie opened it.

"How is she?" he asked.

Fannie smiled a little. "Better than poor Jane." The serving woman saw the look in his eyes and stood back. "She's in with Aggie now."

Charles started past the woman, then looked back at her. "You call her Aggie?"

Fannie shrugged. "Only in private. We don't believe in being all that formal out here in the country."

"I wasn't questioning that," Charles told her. "It's just I heard someone else call her that."

"Oh?" Fannie looked surprised. "Who?"

Charles looked her straight in the eye. "Jane's ghost."

"What?" Fannie laughed. "You're funning with me. I didn't realise Aggie—Agatha—was all that friendly with any of the villagers, to be using a nickname, I mean. She's been a recluse ever since I came here."

"It wasn't a villager," Charles said, then let it go. "Why has she not been friendly with the village? Do you know?" Charles asked the woman.

"It had something to do with her marriage, I think, and a lot of talk at the time. She doesn't like—company."

"You mean she doesn't like men," Charles replied.

Fannie smiled a little. "There's no reason that should ruin our Jane's life, is there?" she asked him plainly.

"None at all," Charles replied.

Fannie smiled as she nodded towards the open bedroom door.

Charles entered to find Jane looking up from beside her grandmother's bed. Putting her finger to her lips, she left her sleeping grandmother and came out into the sitting-room. Fannie went into Agatha's bedroom, closing the door gently and winking at Jane as she did so.

"How is she?" Charles asked Jane as the door closed.

"She's sleeping. I thought she might be upset at the dress—its decolletage—but I never thought it would affect her like this," Jane said.

"She certainly seemed upset by that dress," Charles agreed.

Harry appeared, sitting by the fireside and looking depressed. "It wasn't your fault, it was mine," he said, startling them both. "I thought she'd remember—"

"Remember what?" Charles asked.

"Why did she think it burned?" Jane asked.

"One at a time," Harry replied testily, answering Jane first. "She thought it burned because she told her maid to set fire to it. I saved it and hid it away."

"Why?" Charles asked.

"Why is a long story," Harry replied.

"We have the time," Jane told the ghost.

Harry shook his head. "There's never enough time in life. It is always too short, no matter how long it lasts."

"You died quite young, I take it."

Harry looked over at Charles. "Why do you say that?"

"You look to be in your thirties or thereabouts," Charles replied.

Harry looked glum. "It was in the American campaign."

"So you've only been a ghost for thirty years or so," Charles said.

"Only?" Harry answered. "I'd like to see you shut up in a house with no one to talk to and nothing to do for three decades."

"I meant no affront, Sir Henry," Charles said formally.

"Sir Henry?" Jane questioned.

"Sir Henry Aldworth," the ghost said rather grumpily. "But everyone called me Harry."

"Aldworth—I've heard that name." Jane's brow furrowed into a picture of pretty contemplation.

"Family's in Kent," he said. "What's left of it."

Jane was watching him carefully. "Why did she want to burn the dress?"

"She wore it the night she met her husband," Harry said slowly. "She was a beauty—a real rare one—still is."

"She is a lovely woman," Charles agreed.

The door to Agatha's bedroom opened, Fannie peering out at them strangely.

Jane spoke first. "Is something wrong?"

"I don't know. I thought I heard you talking to someone," Fannie said.

"Just amongst ourselves," Charles said truthfully.

Fannie looked from him to Jane and straight through Harry, seeing nothing.

"We'll be more quiet," Jane promised.

Charles stood up. "We can walk a bit if you like."

She glowed, warmed by the light in his eyes as he looked down at her. She was dressed in her old navy dress, only the golden ribbons and ringlets reminding of her appearance earlier.

His voice was low and thick with emotion when he spoke, as if he had read her thoughts. "You would make all heads turn just as you are. You have no need of fancy dress."

She blushed, letting him capture her hand and lead her forwards. Behind them Harry was morose, talking to himself as they left. "Don't say good-night. Don't ask me along, I'm just a fifth wheel around here, forgotten the minute something else comes along. Lovers, bah! They never really have eyes for anyone but each other."

He thought about creating a fuss, maybe scaring one of the new maids for a bit of amusement and then decided it wasn't worth the effort. Instead, he drifted back into Agatha's room, sitting on the window seat and watching her sleep as Fannie nodded off in a chair by the bed. Soon only the sound of Agatha's breathing and Fannie's soft snoring were to be heard in the darkened room.

Outside Agatha's rooms, Jane walked alongside Charles, pacing the upper hall to the stairwell and then down to the lower floors where the maids and footmen were removing the food and the signs of the party, supervised by Pickering. The musicians were finishing the supper they'd been promised, their instruments waiting to be packed up.

Pickering came towards the Earl, asking if there was anything needed upstairs.

"No, all is well," Charles told his man. He looked towards the musicians, and Pickering remarked the direction of his gaze.

"If you remember, Your Lordship, they are to stay the night as they came such a distance."

"Yes, of course." Charles looked down at Jane and then back at the musicians. "Pickering, ask them if they would favour us with some music."

Pickering blinked and then left to do as he was bid.

Charles smiled down at Jane. "May I have this dance?" he asked.

"Yes," she replied softly. "Please."

The musicians wiped their mouths, glancing towards the Earl as Pickering spoke to them. They finished their food and went in search of their instruments, tuning up a moment. Then the leader cleared his throat. "Ah, excuse me, Your Lordship. What would you like played?"

"The best dance music you know," Charles replied.

The conductor hesitated, then turned towards his men, speaking to them a moment before they began to play.

Charles favoured Jane with a deep bow, then took her by the hand. The music welled up around them as they began to dance, alone in the huge ballroom. Pickering motioned to the other servants to cease their work here, then walked out into the large main parlour himself. Slowly the others followed, one by one, each casting quick shy glances at the elegantly clad Earl and Miss Jane—her hair coiffed beautifully, her plain gown old and worn—

as they swirled around the room, lost in each other's eyes.

Up above, the soft sounds of music accompanied Agatha's sleep. Fannie woke, thinking she had dreamt the music, then realising she was still hearing it. Tiptoeing out of the room, she followed the sound down the stairs to the door of the ballroom, where she could see the musicians playing as Jane danced with the handsome Earl. Pleased, Fannie stepped back into the dark hallway, watching Jane's flushed and happy face as she moved through intricate steps around the room, guided by Charles.

Charles was at a late breakfast alone the next day when the morning post was delivered to him by Pickering. One letter in particular caught his eyes, his father's crest in the wax wafer that sealed it. He broke the seal, scanned the contents quickly and then, frowning, reread it more carefully.

Pickering came back into the dining room a quarter of an hour later to inform his employer he had guests.

"Guests?" Charles asked, frowning. "Who on earth is it?"

"Mrs. and Miss Summerville, Your Lordship, come to pay a call on Lady Agatha, and they would like to pay their respects to you as well."

"Oh, Lord." Charles grimaced. "You'd best see if she's up to it. Tell them I shall be with them directly after my meal."

"Very good, Your Lordship."

Pickering removed himself from the room. He knew the Earl well enough to deduce that something in the morning mail had bothered him, for he had been happy, even jovial, upon awakening this morning.

Lady Agatha was sitting up in bed, sharing a breakfast tray with Jane when Fannie ushered Pickering in to announce the arrival of the Summervilles. Agatha was no more pleased with the news than Charles had been.

"I suppose you'd best bring them up, Pickering. I don't see how in good conscience I can dismiss them without seeing them."

"His lordship sends word he will join you when he is through with his meal," Pickering told her.

"I would wager the Summervilles made that request," Agatha said shrewdly.

"Actually, they asked to pay their respects to his lordship separately, but he sent word he would be up directly he is through." Pickering left after he had delivered this information.

"Jane," her grandmother began, "would you go to Cook and ask her for tea and cakes and then get the accounts on what foodstuffs are on hand? We shall send whatever is too much for the household to the parsonage for distribution."

"Yes, Grandmama."

When Jane left Fannie confronted Agatha. "Why did you send her out?"

Agatha tried to look innocent. "There's no need for her to have to suffer through a dull visit." She saw Fannie's disbelieving expression and spoke more sharply. "I'm sick and tired of explaining things. I know what I'm doing."

"Do you?"

"Yes," Agatha replied with spirit.

She would have said more, but the sound of footsteps heralded Margaret and Charlotte Summerville's arrival. Greetings were effusive, the three women settling down for a polite chat as Fannie went to get the tea tray.

"You look wonderfully refreshed, Agatha," Margaret told her.

"Thank you. I am dreadfully sorry the evening had to end so early. I was looking forward to having you both stay overnight."

"Yes, well, it was early enough to leave and the Earl seemed quite distracted by your falling ill," Margaret explained.

"Did he truly? I assured him I was fine and that the party should continue," Agatha said. "I was quite specific about it."

"In any event, it was wonderful to be at an Abbey party again, after all these years," Margaret said.

"His lordship said he fully intends to have many more," Charlotte put in.

Agatha smiled at her. "One glance at you, and I'm sure he could see the value of having excuses to see you again, dear."

"Do you really think he might?" Charlotte asked and then looked unconvinced. "I don't think he noticed anyone last night but Jane."

Agatha's expression clouded a little. "I'm sure he was simply startled to see her in such a shocking outfit."

"But Jane's gown was lovely," Margaret offered.

"A total mistake. And I'm sure his lordship was aware of that," Agatha said flatly.

As Agatha spoke Fannie showed the man in question into the room. He bowed to the ladies and accepted a chair from Fannie, setting it to one side of Agatha's bed.

"Where is Jane?" he asked.

"I'm not sure," Agatha responded. "She has many chores to do for me."

Charlotte smiled at the Earl. "She was just leaving when we

entered, Your Lordship. She said she had to look into some kitchen items, I believe." Charlotte smiled at Agatha. "You must be wonderfully pleased to have such a dutiful granddaughter, Lady Agatha."

"Yes," Agatha said, wanting to get off the subject of Jane as soon as possible.

"I think she is to be commended for her frugality as well. Although I think it might behoove her to do a little something with her appearance," Charlotte said sweetly.

"Her appearance?" Charles put in.

Charlotte preened, sitting straighter to show off the lines of her morning gown of jonquil crape. "I believe that part of a woman's mission in life is to make a man's world prettier and more comfortable. A husband, for example, should be greeted in the morning by a wife who takes great care of her appearance. I don't think it enough merely to be frugal, do you?"

"I've never considered the subject," Charles answered frankly.

Charlotte flashed him a brilliant smile. "Perhaps I shall have a little talk with Jane about taking care of her appearance."

"I guarantee you, there is absolutely no need," Charles said. "Jane is always the most pleasing thing the eye could hope to behold, no matter what she wears."

"Well, really—" Margaret Summerville was quite put out by Charles's obvious championing of Agatha's granddaughter.

Agatha was even more so. "I would appreciate, Lord Charles, your not referring in such intimate terms to my granddaughter. Her appearance is none of your concern, I assure you."

Charles looked Agatha in the eye. "And I assure you, it is most definitely my concern. As a matter of actual fact, I do not appreciate my future wife's habits being discussed in her absence."

Stunned silence greeted his words. Three pairs of eyes were staring at him—Charlotte gaping open-mouthed—when Fannie walked in with the tea tray.

"Well!" Margaret Summerville stood up, nearly bumping into Fannie. "I have never seen such ill manners in my life. Come along, Charlotte."

Charlotte had blushed beet-red, her eyes turning angry as she rose from her chair.

"The tea—" Fannie said, only to be cut off by Charles, who stood up as the women did.

"I am sorry if my abruptness startled you, Mrs. Summerville," the Earl said.

Margaret glared at Agatha. "And you encouraged Charlotte!"

"Margaret, I am as appalled as you are," Agatha said quickly. "Not quite as appalled."

Fannie watched, wide-eyed, as mother and daughter swept out of the apartments. Charles turned back towards Agatha. "I am sorry I blurted the news out like that, but I think it's for the best that we be honest. I intend to marry Jane, and we both want you to accompany us to my properties in the New World."

Fannie nearly dropped the tray. She moved carefully to place it on the table and then sat down.

"New World?" Agatha stared at him in horror. "I don't know what you're talking about. What has been going on behind my back?"

"Nothing, I assure you. We have been most frightfully proper. I would hardly be less with my future wife."

"No," Agatha said.

Fannie spoke up then. "You can't say no, Agatha. You can't deny Jane a future and a family of her own. You said he was a rake and a roué, but he is not trying to steal her virtue. He is offering her his name, his title, his fortune. You cannot deny Jane her own life."

"Jane hasn't wanted me to ask for her hand while you were not feeling well. But I have received word I must leave within the fortnight for my father's properties in America and I want to take Jane with me—and you, of course, as well. She does not want to go without you. You will have a home with us forever," Charles assured her. "Besides, you don't want to stay here with no company but a ghost."

"Don't start that ghost nonsense again," Agatha said.

"But it's true," Charles told her.

"Have you lost your senses?"

"You've truly never seen him?" Charles asked.

"I don't make a habit of seeing ghosts, and how have you decided it's a him and not a her?" Agatha demanded.

"I've seen him," Charles said. "We both have."

"Both?"

"Yes, actually," Charles told her. "He even found the ball gown for Jane to wear after you'd spilled chocolate on the other one."

A strange look came into Agatha's eyes as she listened to his words. "Found that dress?"

"Yes. Isn't it odd that you've never caught a glimpse of him yourself?"

Agatha lay back on her pillows, closing her eyes. "I need to be alone," was all she said.

Charles thought about pressing his case and then decided to wait. He caught Fannie's eye, then went in search of Jane to tell her of what had transpired.

When he had left, Agatha opened her eyes and stared at Fannie. "You can go, too," Agatha said.

"I'll go, but you'd best give them your blessing," Fannie said.

"My blessing?" Agatha looked at Fannie as if she were demented.

"Your blessing," Fannie repeated. "Unless you want Jane to be the next Steadford girl who ends up unhappy for life—like you did."

"Go away," Agatha said. "Just go away."

Fannie complied, leaving her employer to toss and turn on the big bed.

A faint sound of tinkling music came from the next room. Agatha felt chills when she heard the ghostly sound. She pulled the covers close, pressing her hands to her ears. The sound became fainter. She took her hands away and the sound was stronger again.

It was real and not in her imagination. In the moment she realised this, she sat up, throwing the covers off as she got out of bed. She walked towards the door, staring across the sitting-room at her ivory music box. It sat, open, on the table near the fireplace. A sudden rush of anger filled her as she moved to the bellpull and yanked it for Fannie.

Fannie walked in a few moments later, Agatha's wrath turned on her in full force. "What is the meaning of this?"

Fannie looked towards the box. "I don't understand."

"Why did you bring this up from the gatehouse?" Agatha demanded.

"I never did," Fannie replied.

"I know where it was. I packed it myself and then it went missing and now you have brought it here and opened it so that it would play and I want to know why."

"It's not open," Fannie pointed out. "Nor is it playing."

"Of course it is!" Agatha said. But it was not open. She stared at it, still hearing the music. "This is impossible."

As she said the words the music stopped.

Jane came rushing into the room. "Gram, Charles was wrong to worry you so. He had no right to tell you like that."

"I'd like to be alone," Agatha said.

Jane fell quiet, worried for her grandmother. "I thought you might want me to tell you how all this has happened."

"Not now," Agatha said.

Jane hesitated and then left, sad-faced. "Whatever you want, Gram," she said as she left her grandmother's room.

"Aggie, you'll lose that girl's love and trust forever," said Fannie.

Agatha heard the words but did not acknowledge them. She was looking at the music box when Fannie left. Finally alone, Agatha walked to the music box and opened it, letting it play. As the tinkling music filled the room, Harry appeared near the fireplace, watching her lovingly.

23

AGATHA KEPT TO her bed throughout the day, while Jane worried beyond measure for her grandmother's health. Fannie told her not to take it so to heart. Her grandmother would be just fine after a little rest. The next morning Charles asked Jane to go riding with him after breakfast. She began to say no but he cajoled her.

"There's nothing you can do or say until she's willing to talk about it. Come along, please. We need to talk ourselves."

Pickering had horses brought up from the stables and waiting when Jane and Charles walked outside into the warm spring sunlight. They let the horses have their heads as they raced across the Abbey lands, chestnuts and elms and oaks shading their paths. They reined in under the shelter of the tall oaks of the Abbey spinney, dismounting and walking hand in hand, leading their horses behind.

"It's just that I owe her everything. I can't do anything which would harm her, Charles."

"We shan't hurt her, sweetheart. We shall make her feel welcome with us wherever we go, always. I promise you," Charles reassured Jane.

They walked on and on through the spring day, content just to be in each other's company. They had walked for almost an hour, the horses pacing slowly behind, when Charles drew Jane to him and enfolded her in a passionate embrace. She leaned into his arms, letting the sweet feeling of total surrender soften her heart and weaken her limbs.

"We must get back," she told him breathlessly at last, but he captured her lips again before releasing her.

"All right, but we must face her when we do," Charles said.

"I know," Jane replied, her face collapsing into a worried frown as they remounted and headed back towards the Abbey.

On the way across the fields they could see a cart coming up to the Abbey from the gatehouse. It began unloading, and Charles and Jane arrived to find packing cases open on the steps and in the wide entrance hall.

"Those are my clothes," Jane cried out. "What is happening here? Fannie!"

Fannie appeared up above, then Agatha looked down at them from the top of the steps. "I see you're finally back," Agatha said.

"What is happening?" Jane asked.

"Young lady, you can't travel all the way to the New World with just what's on your back, now, can you?" Agatha replied, earning a dumbstruck look from Jane and a wondrous smile from Charles.

"But you mustn't do this. Gram, you're too weak."

Fannie interrupted Jane's words, her eyes fastened on her employer. "Aggie, either you tell this girl the truth or I shall." Fannie turned to face Jane. "Your grandmother is no more sickly than I am. It's all been a plot against you."

"Against the two of you, actually," Agatha herself said. "I shall tell them all about it, Fannie, but not here, shouting up and down the staircase."

Agatha told them to change and meet her in the blue parlour after she had a chance to freshen up. Charles saw no reason to waste time changing out of his riding habit and so busied himself with papers and coffee until the two women came down a half hour later.

In the blue parlour Agatha shook her head. "It seems an eternity since Nigel came to tea and brought you with him, Charles. I assume I shall be calling you Charles at this point, since you are soon to be my grandson."

"I would like nothing better," he told her.

"I have tried to keep you two apart. I have feigned illness and made an unsuccessful attempt to throw Charlotte Summerville at Charles's head, because I know much more of the world and of men than does Jane. You must admit, you have a reputation which is not of the best."

Charles smiled a little. "My only excuse is that I had not yet met Jane."

"In any event, you were too much like someone I once knew. I was sure I could show you up, and in revealing your true colours to Jane, protect her from making a fool of herself." Agatha searched Jane's eyes. "I must tell you that marriages are not always made in heaven and that I am still not sure that Charles will be the husband you imagine. He has not had a reputation for faithfulness or frugality, and you have no knowledge of the heartache a gambling husband can bring to one. However, despite all my efforts, the two of you have decided to fall in love anyway. And so, a little reluctantly, I am leaving the decision entirely to Jane. She may do as she pleases."

"Oh, Gram!" Jane was overjoyed. She hugged her grandmother and then sat down on the footstool by her chair. "You will love it. This will be an adventure for you."

"I beg your pardon?" Agatha looked down at her.

"She means you will enjoy America," Charles put in.

"I am not going to America," Agatha told them.

"But, Gram, you just said it was all right for us to be married."

"And it is—if that is what you want."

"But you have to go with us," Jane cried. "I can't leave you here alone."

"You are not responsible for me, child. And, I shan't be alone. I have Fannie and my whole life here." She smiled a rueful little smile. "I even have your ghost." She became more serious. "I would never be happy in some far-off land. This is where I was born, and it is where I want to live and die."

"If the Abbey is what you want, I will make provisions with my London solicitors," Charles told her. "They will turn the Abbey over to you legally."

"No."

The room was silent for a moment. "I don't understand," Charles finally said.

Agatha spoke quietly. "I have the gatehouse you were kind enough to deed to us. That is quite enough."

"But Gram, you don't want the Abbey to go to someone else," Jane told her.

"It already has, child. This place is much too big and cold for me. The gatehouse will do just fine for Fannie and me." She patted Jane's hand. "Let's just say there are too many memories in this house, and it's much too big. I should have realised it a long time ago. You must keep it or sell it or whatever. It is yours to do with as you please. As for me, I shall be quite content in the gatehouse. Did I mention that I called the reverend?"

Jane looked from her grandmother to Charles. "I don't understand."

"You can't very well leave for America with this man without being well and truly married to him."

Charles smiled. "Lady Agatha, I don't think you quite trust me yet." He looked towards Jane. "However, I think your grandmother is right. We shall be married as soon as possible."

But in order to do so, Agatha had to insist on special dispensation from the church in order to have the ceremony performed before they left for the long journey across the Atlantic Ocean.

On her wedding day Jane spent some time alone in the long gallery, whispering good-byes to Harry which went unanswered. "Are you here?" Jane asked quietly and then paced along the almost unending rows of Steadford family portraits.

From the fifteen hundreds to the present, three centuries of Steadfords looked down from the walls of the long gallery each of them had traversed in their lifetimes. Sober and rakish-looking fathers and sons, sour and sweet-looking wives and daughters, dressed in the court dress of the Tudors, of the Stuarts, and of the Hanovers, told of unnumbered lifetimes lived within the Abbey walls.

Only the owners of the Abbey and their wives had their portraits placed here in individual glory. Some few of the portraits displayed mothers with their children, thus immortalising some of the other lives begun under the Abbey's huge roof, but most were imposing studies of individuals.

Jane stopped beneath the portrait of her great-grandfather Steadford, staring up at the man who looked so much like his son Nigel. Next to the portrait of Ambrose Steadford, Nigel's and Agatha's father, hung the latest portrait. It was of a young Agatha, the heir to hundreds of years of tradition. It occurred to Jane that it was unusual for a daughter to inherit over a son, even if the daughter were the elder of the two. Old Ambrose must have seen what his son Nigel was even then.

Jane stared up at the sombre features of the man, at his side-whiskers and dark, intense eyes. In Nigel these eyes were weakened in colour as well as intensity. His father's eyes showed strength and some of the same purpose his daughter's did. He was a realist, his eyes seemed to say, and he knew where the strength in the family lay.

Unfortunately, he had not protected the inheritance from Agatha's future husband, nor had he lived to see that husband gamble away the result of nine generations of Steadford industry and common sense. Gamble it away to the very son old Ambrose had distrusted.

Jane studied the faces, ending up in front of Agatha's portrait. As with many familiar things, she had seen it so often it was a part of her life, something she looked at without really seeing— until this night when her world was changing around her and everything seemed rather unreal.

She gazed with fresh interest at the picture of a young, vibrant Agatha, trying to see behind the eyes to the girl who gazed back, forever captured in the dark oil colours. Suddenly, Jane found herself staring at the dress her grandmother wore in the painting. It was crimson and gold, with a low neckline. It was the same dress she had worn to the ball—the dress that had caused Agatha to faint.

A thousand questions pressed into Jane's mind. "It's the same dress," she said the words out loud.

Harry shimmered, half-visible near the painting. Jane saw him and repeated the words.

"Yes," he said finally. "It is."

Jane tried to read the truth in the features which wavered before her—almost real, almost substantial. "Did you know it would upset her?"

"No! I didn't mean to hurt her. I never would hurt her."

"Why?"

"Because she's the only Steadford worth caring about, except you."

"You said you were here in bondage to your mortal enemies. Why should you care about my grandmother or any of us? Why?"

"I can't tell you," Harry said unhappily.

"Can't or won't?" Jane asked him, a determination to understand in her eyes.

"Can't," came the reply.

Jane hesitated and then spoke quietly. "I came to say goodbye."

"I know," he said.

"You look terribly unhappy," Jane said. "Haven't you accomplished your purpose now? Aren't you to be allowed to leave?"

"Yes," Harry said unhappily, "I suppose I might be able to go now."

"Then why are you so glum?"

Harry hesitated and then answered slowly. "I can leave, or I can stay here, whichever I choose. But if I go, I shall not be able to be near her. If I stay I must abide by the rules and stay within the Abbey walls, but she won't be here. Whatever I do, I won't be near her."

Jane took in his meaning. "You're still talking about my grandmother, aren't you?" When Harry didn't respond, Jane continued. "She is only, after all, living in the gatehouse." He shimmered in front of her and became almost substantial as he drifted to a tall narrow chair and sat down, dejected.

"She might as well go to the moon, or America," he said. "I'll never see her again whether I stay or whether I go."

Jane came nearer. "But the gatehouse is part of the Abbey. I'm sure you can go there without breaking any rules."

He looked up, a little hopeful, a lot doubtful. "Why are you sure?" When she had no answer he lapsed back into glumness. "You can't be sure," he answered. "You didn't even know ghosts existed. How would you know the rules of conduct?"

Jane was a little exasperated with him. "Harry, what is the worst thing which could happen to you if you disobeyed?"

"I'd have to leave here—leave her."

"But you've already said you'll not be with her in any event. So what have you to lose by trying my theory?"

He thought about it, looking quite forlorn. "If I stay on here, she might come near, upon occasion."

"Jane?" Fannie's voice came up the stairwell towards the long gallery. "Are you there?"

"I'm here, Fannie." Jane moved to the railing which walled one side of the long gallery, looking down towards the entrance hall where the serving woman stood.

"They're waiting for you."

"I shall be down directly," Jane replied, then looked back towards Harry. "You should come with me," she said. "You should give me away, Sir Henry. Without you, this night would not be happening."

"Jane?" Fannie called from below, waiting for her.

"I have to go," Jane told the ghost.

He stared at her and said nothing.

In the blue parlour Agatha, Charles, and the priest were waiting for Jane and Fannie to appear. Pickering came to open the parlour door for them, bowing, and then nodded to the waiting household staff who had been standing in the hall. They followed Jane and Fannie into the room.

"Well, well, our little Jane," the reverend said, smiling at the girl in her plain bronze-green gown. "Are we ready then?"

"Yes," she said softly, looking up at Charles. He took her hands in his, pressing them gently and then looking towards the minister.

"Yes, we are ready," Charles said again in a very definite tone.

"Dearly beloved, we are gathered here to witness the joining in holy matrimony of this man and this woman—" The man of

God began intoning the words that would bind them together.

Harry stood near Agatha, his gaze never leaving her face. He seemed to be trying to commit her well-beloved features to memory. A sadness surrounded him which was palpable.

Agatha felt something, her shoulders moving with the feeling, but her eyes remained fixed on Jane. As the young couple spoke the ancient words which would make Jane a wife and take her halfway around the world, Agatha did not feel the sense of loss she had feared. She had no desire to leave the Abbey grounds. A curious comfort seemed to surround her as she stood there, hearing Jane pledge to love, honour, and obey.

Agatha prayed for her granddaughter to a God she respected and obeyed but wasn't quite sure she believed in. Agatha prayed for Jane's happiness with this man, and felt a sudden warmth within her breast, almost an answer that all would be well.

"I now pronounce you man and wife," the reverend told them, the cook sniffling at the back of the room, her handkerchief to her eyes.

"I've known her since she was born," Cook whispered to Pickering and one of the new maids. She sighed and wiped another tear away. "Our Jane, a countess—who would have thought it?"

The Earl of Warwick kissed his bride soundly, clasping her in his arms as if he would never let her go. Then he looked up to see Agatha and Harry. Charles gasped, his eyes widening and drawing Jane to look towards what he saw. Agatha gazed back, perplexed, thinking herself the object of their scrutiny.

Jane realised the others could not see Harry and uttered a little peal of laughter, then reached up to bring her new husband's lips back to hers, earning clapped hands from the servants and Fannie.

Agatha gave Fannie a quelling look, which she ignored as Jane and Charles walked towards the two women. Charles reached for Jane's grandmother as Jane hugged Fannie, and Agatha found herself being embraced by the handsome Earl. She stiffened, very embarrassed and a little pleased, all at once. He released her, and Agatha folded Jane close. "You look so happy, child."

"I am, Grandmama. I truly am." Jane's eyes shone with the truth of her words. Agatha acknowledged that truth with a wry little smile.

"Love triumphs after all—sometimes."

A shadow clouded Jane's face. She glanced at Harry, then quickly brought her gaze back to her grandmother's dark eyes.

"I shall miss you ferociously," Jane said.

"I expect a long stream of letters until I see you again, Jane."

Jane smiled tremulously. "You shall have them."

Charles caught sight of Sir Henry, standing near Agatha, mute and miserable. "Lady Agatha, are you quite sure you won't reconsider and stay on in the main house?"

Harry perked up a little, but his hopes were immediately dashed by her reply. "I shall be much more comfortable in the gatehouse, and there's an end to that discussion, please."

Fannie smiled up at the Earl. "We shall get on famously in the little house. Truth to tell, this giant old place is a bit much for my weary bones."

"Fannie!" Jane looked at her reproachfully. "You sound as if you're ancient."

Fannie smiled a little. "Some days I feel it, too."

"Never," Charles said gallantly, making Fannie blush. He could see she was unused to compliments and just as unused to blushing. She looked rattled.

"Good grief, Fannie, you are blushing," Agatha pointed out, discomforting her serving woman further.

"I am not," Fannie defended herself stoutly. "It's merely the warmth in here."

"Act your age," Agatha said. "We're long past that kind of thing."

"Speak for yourself," Fannie replied tartly, her rounded chin up in the air a bit pugnaciously. She looked back at Charles and Jane. "I knew this would work out from the beginning."

Agatha gave a very delicate but most decided snort of derision. "You and your romance novels," she said darkly, but a wry humour shone in her eyes as she spoke.

Jane kissed her grandmother's cheek as Fannie continued. "You must be good to one another and you must follow your own hearts. We shall be fine here, and we shall want to hear every last thing about your adventures in the New World."

"You shall," Jane promised.

"Sweetheart, Pickering says the coach is ready."

Jane looked from her grandmother to Fannie, tears welling up. "I only wish we had more time."

"You shall come back and visit," Agatha told her. "You are the Countess of Warwick now and must act accordingly." Her words were said firmly. "You must be a credit to your husband and your position, my girl. You must not allow yourself emotional displays in front of the servants."

Jane swallowed her tears and nodded bravely, attempting a small smile. "I must say good-bye to them."

Jane went to the cook and the others, saying her good-byes as Pickering came forwards and bowed to Agatha. He walked right through Harry, who muttered an epithet no one heard and then disappeared from view.

"Lady Agatha, his lordship has left instructions you are to stay on here as long as you wish and that, in the event of the sale of the property, you will be the first informed and given ample time to withdraw anything you choose from the Abbey."

Agatha acknowledged Pickering's words but did not agree. "Fannie and I are returning to the gatehouse in the carriage when it leaves. I've had our personal things sent down already."

Pickering bowed formally. "As you wish."

"We could wait a bit, if you like," Fannie said to Agatha.

"I want to get settled, Fannie. We have our own lives to go on with."

The coach was ready, their final leavetakings put off until the coach stopped at the gatehouse, delivering Fannie and Agatha to their new abode. Jane hugged her grandmother fiercely, releasing her to see tears which matched her own sparkling in her grandmother's eyes.

"You must promise me you will try to visit with Harry."

Agatha shook her head, "Jane Steadford Graham—Lady Jane," she said in an admonishing tone. "You had best rid your head of ghosts once and for all."

Charles poked his head out of the large black coach, "But truly—"

"Nonsense I said," Agatha interrupted sharply. "And nonsense I mean. Now get along, the two of you. You have a long ride to the coast and your ship. Off with you!"

Unwilling to endure any more emotional displays, she sent them on their way. Fannie walked out into the drive to wave at the coach long after it had passed under the gate clock and wended its way down the long drive to the country lane beyond. Her eyes were moist as she returned and passed by Agatha in the rose garden.

"I think I'll see to some tea for us, then."

"I shall look to the roses. They've been sadly neglected these past weeks," Agatha said as if nothing in the world had changed in her life, but when she was alone she allowed a lonely expression to steal across her face.

At the top of the hill, Harry stood in the doorway of the Abbey—the fact that the door was closed posed no problem— and looked longingly down the drive.

"She said I could do it," Harry told himself. He sounded unconvinced.

He stuck one foot outside, trying to assess what would happen. Nothing did. He hesitated and stepped out onto the porch.

"The porch is definitely part of the Abbey," he informed who- ever might be interested. Only the late spring winds answered.

One step, then another, brought him close to and then down the wide, shallow, stone steps. Feeling awkward and worried, he stepped off the final step and onto the drive. His eyes closed, waiting for a bolt of lightning or some such to lay waste to him. Again, nothing happened. He opened his eyes. He didn't feel any differently.

"There's nothing to be afraid of. This is Abbey property. The walls of my instruction are merely a metaphor . . . or maybe the walls referred to are the gate walls," he said to himself hopefully, before he took the final plunge and wined himself forwards.

In the gatehouse rose garden, Agatha stood alone and rather forlorn, her hand shading her eyes. As she watched the distant carriage recede from view, Harry came up beside her, looking off in the same direction.

"All will be well, Aggie. I'm still here with you."

She gave no indication of seeing him or hearing his words, but when he bent to kiss her lightly on the cheek, her hand flew to it. She looked startled and turned in his direction, vainly searching for something.

Fannie came to the kitchen door. "Tea's ready. What's wrong? Why are you holding your head?"

"I'm not holding my head," Agatha said with a wee bit of temper. "I'm brushing something off my cheek."

Fannie looked knowingly at her friend and employer. "Tears are good for the soul," she said prosaically.

"I'm not crying," Agatha answered with asperity.

"Of course you aren't," Fannie told her. "Tea's ready," she said again.

As Fannie spoke, Harry took the opportunity to kiss Agatha's other cheek. Her hand flew to the spot of the strange sensa- tion.

"What in the name of fiddlesticks are you doing?" Fannie asked.

"Nothing. The wind must be coming up."

"Well, you'd best come inside before you catch your death," Fannie told her from the doorway.

"I'll be there in a moment," Agatha said, pulling her shawl closer about her shoulders.

Fannie went back inside the gatehouse as Agatha walked slowly amongst the roses, trying to understand the peculiar sensation and feeling strangely unwilling to leave the garden.

Harry paced beside her, concerned for her. When Fannie called out again, Agatha turned reluctantly towards the kitchen door. Harry stayed where he was, perplexed and unsure whether he should follow.

Across the yard Agatha was about to close the door and looked back outside, staring straight at Harry. He stared back, surprised. She was smiling, and his heart leapt at the sight. As Agatha closed the door, Harry rubbed his ghostly hands together, his face alight with a smile all its own.

"Ah, Aggie, we're going to get along famously. Just famously, we are!"